A PENGUIN MYSTERY

SHADOWS ON THE LAKE

Giovanni Cocco was born in Como in 1976. **Amneris Magella** was born in Milan in 1958. They are married and live in Como, Italy.

Stephen Sartarelli is an award-winning translator and the author of three books of poetry.

SHADOWS ON THE LAKE

GIOVANNI COCCO
AND AMNERIS MAGELLA

TRANSLATED BY STEPHEN SARTARELLI

PENGUIN BOOKS

PENGUIN BOOKS

An imprint of Penguin Random House LLC
375 Hudson Street
New York, New York 10014
penguin.com

Published in Penguin Books 2017

Originally published in Italian as *Ombre sul lago* by Ugo Guanda Editore.

LIBRARY OF CONGRESS CATALOGING-IN-PUBLICATION DATA
Names: Cocco, Giovanni, 1976– author. | Magella, Amneris, 1958– author. |
Sartarelli, Stephen translator.
Title: Shadows on the lake / Giovanni Cocco and Amneris Magella; translated
by Stephen Sartarelli.
Other titles: Ombre sul lago. English
Description: New York: Penguin Books, 2016.
Identifiers: LCCN 2016012231 | ISBN 9780143127253
Subjects: LCSH: Police—Italy—Fiction. | Detective and mystery stories. |
GSAFD: Mystery fiction
Classification: LCC PQ4903.O34 O4313 2016 | DDC 853/.92—dc23

Printed in the United States of America
1   3   5   7   9   10   8   6   4   2

Set in Scala   •   *Designed by Elke Sigal*

SHADOWS ON THE LAKE

**Ministry of Finances Report
on the Seizure of Jewish Properties***

MEMO FOR THE DUCE

Re: Seizure of Jewish properties—
Situation on 31 December 1944—XXIII

At the end of the first year of the enforcement of the legislative decree of 4 January 1944, XXII, no. 4, which provides for the seizure of properties belonging to citizens of the Jewish race, I hereby submit to you, DUCE, the statistical data relating to the work thus far accomplished.

In all of December of 1944—XXIII, 5768 confiscation orders have been filed with the EGELI, and they break down as follows:

Moveable and immoveable properties 2590 orders
Possessions deposited with third parties 996 orders
Businesses 182 orders
[. . .]

Limiting calculations to the seizures reported above, the bank deposits in cash amount to the overall figure of 75,089,047.90 lire; Government bonds to 36,396,831 lire (nominal value); industrial and other securities, valued according to end-of-December listings, to 731,442,219 lire. There are also many other securities concerning

*R. De Felice, *Storia degli ebrei italiani sotto il fascismo*, new expanded edition (Turin: Giulio Einaudi Editore, 1993), 610–11.

the value of which it was not possible to obtain any quotes.

All securities, deposits, and stocks are in the process of being transferred to preestablished entities that provide greater guarantees of safety.

[. . .] *National Post, 316/1, 3/12/1945—XXIII*

1

A light *breva* was blowing across the lake.

Stefania Valenti crossed the long boulevard that led from the Hotel Regina Olga to the wharf. Not many people about at that hour: a boy with a dog, an old man bundled up in an overcoat, and a slight, bony young woman struggling to carry two plastic shopping bags.

At that time of year, between the end of winter and the start of the warm season, Cernobbio might seem a town like so many others. In a short while the hotels would be back in business, and once they were open, the whole western shore of Lake Como would witness the annual ritual of German, Russian, and American tourists pouring in, the conventions of the rich and powerful, the summer events sponsored by the municipal government, and the appearances of a few Hollywood stars.

She cast a glance at the lake, eyes lingering on the silhouette of the Villa d'Este on the left, and then headed for the Caffè Onda. She ordered a cappuccino and then left in a hurry, lighting her first cigarette of the day.

For once she had managed to get Camilla to school on time, secretly thumbing her nose at the school officials in military pose outside the gate.

Sitting in the backseat of her mother's Opel Corsa, Camilla had muttered only a few words that morning, engrossed as she was in her Game Boy. They'd said good-bye in a hurry like every morning. Camilla's last words had been lost in the noise of the slamming car door, and her pink parka had vanished into the already closing entrance door to the school.

Arriving punctually at school was the least of her problems. In the end, even if Camilla had arrived late, the teacher would not have demanded an explanation. Responsibility, blame, merit—and the car keys forgotten in the other purse—were part of their daily morning ritual.

"But doesn't your dad drive you to school sometimes, Camilla?"

"No, because Dad doesn't live with us."

"Ah, right, of course."

What did she mean by that "of course"? thought Stefania, irritated by the mere thought of the time that Camilla told her about the convoy of blond mothers in SUVs double-parked outside the main entrance of the Foscolo Middle School.

She went back to the car, put on her glasses, and started up the engine, checking the clock display out of the corner of her eye.

Ten minutes to eight.

She ducked into a driveway to turn around.

It was too late to get bread and focaccia at Vago's, which was just outside the city walls of Como. She would just postpone everything, shopping included, until the afternoon, after she went to pick up Camilla. The supermarket focaccia wasn't exactly the same thing as the baker's, but it would have to do.

Her job, her daughter, and the separation from her husband had made Stefania—or at least part of her—extremely practical. Going to the shopping center (a big prefab building made of little red bricks and cement as far as the eye could see at the far end of the northern suburbs of Como, easily accessible from the road to the lake) was not only, deep down, a pleasant task because she would find everything she needed there. It was also part of the everyday ritual she shared with Camilla. Where else could she find bread hot out of the oven at eight P.M. or batteries for her television remote early on Sunday morning?

That morning was going to be very tight. As usual, she would have to skip lunch.

Her calculations as to her work hours were interrupted by an electronic version of the melody of *The Blue Danube*.

Where the hell had that come from? Stefania wondered. Then she remembered that Camilla had been playing with her cell phone the previous evening. It wasn't the first time she'd changed the ring, Stefania thought with a smile.

The voice of Lucchesi, as usual three octaves higher than necessary, boomed in her ears.

"Inspector, when you come in, you should know that the assistant prosecutor was looking for you. As was Chief Inspector Carboni."

"Got it, Lucchesi, don't worry. I'll be there in five minutes."

She was lying shamelessly and knew it. With the insane rush-hour traffic and the queue of vehicles that had formed between Cernobbio and Villa Olmo, it would take her at least twenty minutes to get to police headquarters. She turned the button of the car radio, tuning to Radio 105, which at that moment was presenting the news.

After an exchange of hostilities with a Swiss-plated BMW—the typical border dweller having descended into Italy to go shopping, thanks to the favorable exchange rate—she stepped out onto Viale Innocenzo, leaving the police parking lot behind her, where she'd parked her car in the middle of the courtyard. Seeing Marino in the guard's booth, she tossed him the keys with a wink.

"Inspector!" the guard shouted.

"Give me just one minute, Marino, then I'll move it. And I'll buy you a coffee."

Dashing up three flights of stairs, she arrived at the vending machine just in time to find Chief Inspector Carboni right in front her, coming out of his office, necktie loosened and shirtsleeves rolled up in a slightly overweight version of an American sheriff from a TV series.

"Come into my office for a minute, Valenti," said Carboni.

Stefania was thinking of the hot cappuccino and croissant with jam she would eat in the bar behind headquarters. That morning, once again, she hadn't come in early enough to treat her colleagues to breakfast.

"We just got a call from the Lanzo station. Some workers demolishing a cottage above San Primo have found some human bones. The worksite has been shut down for the time being, since the cottage is right along the new road they're building. They've all been left hanging. Assistant Prosecutor Arisi will also be going there. I want you to go up there with Piras and Lucchesi in the four-by-four."

Carboni, normally a rather measured, phlegmatic sort, seemed to have an electrical current running through him that morning. Arisi, on the other hand, was known as one of the most feared prosecutors, a straight-shooting Friulian who was serious, trustworthy, and determined. Stefania wondered what could have driven a prosecutor as elderly as he to venture all the way up to San Primo and get mud all over his fancy loafers.

A pile of bones in a tumbledown cottage, she thought. What's the big deal?

Usually she settled such trifles, as well as ordinary administrative matters, over the telephone. She would get the opinion of the local Carabinieri station and then, at the most, authorize the confiscation of the evidence. Normally, in these situations, it ended there.

Then something else occurred to her.

Maybe Valentini Roadworks, the road-building firm, had a few saints in heaven and wanted to be sure that the whole thing would blow over quickly. Who knew how much it cost them, she wondered, to shut down a project like that?

Searching her memory, Stefania saw a fleeting image of a nearly uninhabited village perched on the mountainside: a few stone houses, some wooden Alpine huts, a few scattered stables, a handful of cows grazing, an old road climbing up in endless curves to the top, to the mountain pass that crossed over to Switzerland. She must have gone there with her father as a little girl one summer many years ago.

The perfect background for a chocolate advertisement, she thought.

Too bad the tunnel of the new road had to run through that very spot on its way to the customs barrier. Five minutes later, there was Switzerland and a bridge to send shudders down your spine, with the environmentalists all having conniptions.

And now we have to go up there, naturally, and negotiate all those curves ourselves, she thought. If Piras drives, I swear I'll throw up.

By eleven-thirty Arisi still hadn't shown up. Unexpected engagements at the courthouse.

Screw the hurry, thought Stefania.

Meanwhile she'd managed to drink a cappuccino from the machine and scarf down a brioche from another automated vendor.

As she quickly dealt with her outstanding correspondence, Stefania realized that she would have time to go to the supermarket that afternoon. She would have the afternoon free after four-thirty. She would pick up Camilla, and together they would see the latest Harry Potter episode at the Cinema Astra, the only one left in town, followed by pizza and maybe a few cuddles on the sofa.

But everything seemed to be going wrong these days.

When they got to the scene it was almost one o'clock. They all seemed in a bad mood. Arisi had been silent the whole way there, beside her in the backseat. Lucchesi and Piras had traded quips about a brawl among drunken immigrants along the lakeshore drive that they'd had to break up the day before. None of the four had had lunch yet. Stefania was hoping that this might be the key to her getting out of there early, since the prosecutor and the other two were not, unlike her, in the habit of skipping lunch. They pulled up the four-by-four in the middle of the worksite, right in front of a group of laborers sitting and smoking and another bunch just setting their shovels down.

The site foreman, a man of about fifty, all muscles and beard, pointed at a steep slope marked with crawler tracks.

"We were told not to move from here," he said. "The marshal is up there with a doctor. They've already been waiting a while. Five minutes, straight up in that direction," he added.

It was a beautiful day.

And a good thing, too, thought Stefania; otherwise they would have had to trudge through the mud.

They climbed the stripped hillside, following the furrows left by the excavators. Panting heavily, they came to a grassy open field, at the far end of which began the woods, which in that area were not very dense. Through shrubs of hazel and leafless chestnuts you could see patches of meadow and small cottages built in the gray stone typical of those mountains.

If not for the stakes planted here and there amid the felled trees and the ribbons of white-and-red plastic tape extended between the stakes, the spot would have looked like a normal, deserted Alpine pasture getting ready for spring. Cows and goats would arrive before summer, followed by farmers, children's voices, milk, cheeses.

"There they are," said Lucchesi, the first to notice the small group of people above them waving their arms, trying to get their attention.

"This is Sergeant Corona, and this is Dr. Sacchi of the medical administration," Marshal Bordoli said solemnly. "We've been waiting for you. We've already done our initial searches of the place, with photos and all the rest. And we've spoken with the workers at the site. They'll be coming into headquarters tomorrow to sign their depositions," he added. "We can go to the cottage now, if you like."

The marshal apparently wanted to appear professional in front of his counterparts from the city and the assistant prosecutor, who limited himself to nodding affirmatively.

A few minutes later, after stepping over tree trunks, piles of sawn branches, stacks of planks and round iron bands, they reached the spot where the human remains had been found.

More than the scene of a crime, it looked like a place that had just been hit by a hurricane, and even the big yellow excavator, sitting still with boom and stick resting on the ground, looked as if it had fallen straight out of the sky.

"This is the cottage. Be careful, there's a big hole. You, too, signora, be careful."

Signora.

As if she were just passing through, Stefania thought bitterly. What bloody cottage was he talking about, anyway?

All they could see in front of them was a pile of rocks with freshly moved earth, and another pile of rocks covered with ivy, moss, and wild fig roots. At best, and with a bit of imagination, you could call it a ruin of a wall.

"Nobody's been through here for years," Bordoli added. "Snow and bad weather probably brought the house down, like so many others—or it may even have been burnt down during the war. We really have no way of knowing."

Arisi and Stefania examined the site carefully.

"This morning one of the Valentini workers started the demolition," the marshal continued. "At a certain point a big chasm opened up. A lot of these cottages have a *nevera* under them, which is what we call a cold storage cellar. But here you can't see anything. Who knows how long it was all buried there? When the worker realized there was a collapsed *nevera* underneath, he kept digging until he found that," he concluded, pointing at one point in the pit.

"Be careful, Inspector," said Arisi, "it's slippery."

They found themselves peering down into a sort of underground well. Its vaulted lid was almost completely collapsed, revealing a cubicle not more than two by two meters in size, with walls of blackened rough-hewn stone and rocks.

"It looks like a sheepfold," said Piras, who was from somewhere near Nuoro, in Sardinia, "the kind where they keep kidnapping victims or where bandits hide."

Stefania shrugged. She'd spent her childhood summers in mountains just like this and knew perfectly well what a *nevera* was. She'd seen many of them. Often when playing hide-and-seek she would go into one and shiver, partly from the cold and partly because it was scary. At the time, however, the worst she might have encountered in there were the smells of milk and mildew. Whereas outside she would find the comfort of her father, a silhouette in sunlight smoking a cigarette.

"The door, Piras," Stefania said to her colleague, who had gone down into the pit. "See if there's a door with a padlock or bolt. A small, wooden door," she added, handing him the flashlight.

"Why would there be a door, Inspector, if it's underground?"

Piras directed the beam of light along the mildewy walls.

"There's nothing here. It's all rocks, earth, and roots."

"Where did you find the remains?" the sharp voice of Prosecutor Arisi cut in.

"Over there," said the marshal.

Piras pointed the light towards the ground. "You're right. You can see some bones. But not very many." A moment of silence. "Now I can see the head," he continued. "Oh my God! He's still got his hair, poor guy."

"It's all been photographed, and the doctor has already been in there," Arisi said impatiently. "Let's get going and take that stuff out of there. What are you waiting for?" he continued, addressing those standing around him.

"Two workers from the site are already here with a box," said the marshal.

What's with him? thought Stefania. Has he got a plane to catch in Milan or something?

She felt a pang in her stomach, and only then remembered that she hadn't had lunch. She looked at her watch. Three thirty. Camilla.

Her daughter would be getting out of school in an hour. And she wouldn't manage to pick her up in time.

"Piras, you keep an eye on what they're doing. This shouldn't take long."

She stepped aside and started making phone calls. First to her sister-in-law, then the babysitter, then the woman next door.

In the end she had to take a different tack, the very one she would rather have avoided.

"Sorry to ask a favor of you, but I don't know what else to do. Signora Albonico doesn't feel up to it, and Martina is in Milan for an exam. I'm still here in Lanzo. I realize I'm calling at the last minute, but . . . Yes, okay, I can wait. Thanks."

She distractedly watched her colleagues in action.

"Okay, I've managed to get free," said her ex-husband, returning to the phone. "I'll pick up Camilla myself. I had some other appointments, but I've postponed them. And since I don't have the keys to your place, I'm going to take her to the office. She can do her homework there, and then we'll go to the movies. I phoned the school to tell them I'll be picking her up ten minutes late. They put her on and she said she wanted to see Harry Potter. Just let me know if you'll be back by dinnertime—let's say eight o'clock. Okay?"

"Okay. Thanks."

Stefania stood there staring at the display of her cell phone, feeling uneasy. It was always like this when she asked a favor of Guido, Camilla's father. He always managed to resolve a problem in less than fifteen minutes; he thought of everything, and it was a sure bet that if he'd had ten more minutes he would have managed to pick up Camilla right on time. The whole faculty would surely honor him with their usual smiles. He was always so authoritative.

She hoped with all her might that Camilla's clothes, parka, and stockings were spotless that day, and that her blouse was buttoned correctly. Then she heaved a big sigh.

Recovering the human remains took longer than expected, despite the fact that the two workers placed at their disposal had worked hard, collecting the bones one by one along with the stones and the soil that had covered them after the vault had collapsed.

Stefania, Lucchesi, and Piras stayed behind to oversee the operation after Arisi had left in a hurry with the marshal. The assistant prosecutor had, in the meantime, granted the site foreman the authorization to resume operations.

Sacchi, the doctor from medical administration, also stayed behind, more than anything to make sure that the bones recovered constituted an entire skeleton. He didn't say much, limiting himself to pointing out, every so often, what was needed: "We're missing another of these." Or: "There should be another three of this length."

Stefania asked the workers to collect everything else they found around the bones. The two young Maghrebians only looked at each other and said nothing.

But there was indeed something there: it might be some fabric or perhaps some bits of rusted metal. Or maybe it was only dirt. By the time they were finished, the wooden crate with the remains had become very heavy.

The curses were flying—made all the more comical as they were uttered in the *laghèe* dialect by the two foreign laborers—when they had to carry the crate all the way back to the worksite. Then it wouldn't fit in the four-by-four, and so Valentini Roadworks made one of its own vehicles available.

"Tell us where you want us to take it," the director of human resources said over the phone. "It's always a pleasure to work with law enforcement," he concluded.

Right, as long as it's not the customs police, thought Stefania.

At five o'clock the crate with the evidence was in the van made available by Valentini Roadworks and ready to go. The driver was in a hurry. The other workers, in the meantime, had peeled off one at a time. What was left of the cottage would be gone by the following morning, and the construction company's infernal machine would resume inexorably chewing up other trees, other walls, and other grass.

The sun had set. The wind was blowing.

Stefania stood there contemplating the open pit at her feet and the boulders around it. She couldn't tear herself away. Perhaps because she felt as if she couldn't grasp what she saw. She went back down into the *nevera*. She shone the beam of the flashlight again on the walls, then focused her attention on one point right above the floor of beaten earth. The stones that made up the rest of the wall were not the same as the others. Even with the naked eye one could see that they'd been at least a little squared. Then there were some remains of chiseled solid rock, some smaller stones, and then dirt, together with some darker fragments that were almost black. They looked like coal, or wood. It was anybody's guess what it was. Earlier she'd had a sample collected and put in a bag.

She remembered how as a child she often liked to collect "special" stones that were different from the rest. She would set them aside and catalog them, always in the hopes of finding something extraordinary, maybe a treasure, a vestige of an ancient civilization, something that nobody had ever discovered before. She liked to think that her specimens were rare things, precious or unknown substances. After cleaning them carefully she would arrange them in a corner of the garden, making sure that nobody saw her.

Who knew what had become of her stones? she wondered as she climbed down the steep slope to rejoin the rest of the group.

"We'll take it to the Lanzo cemetery," Stefania said to the last two workers remaining, referring to the crate. "We'll leave it in a locked room next to the mortuary chamber. I've already informed the parish, and the sexton will be waiting for you. Dr. Sacchi, I'll expect your report by tomorrow afternoon," she added.

The doctor came up to her and took her aside.

"Inspector," he said, "if you think it would be useful, I'll come back up here tomorrow morning to look things over calmly, and of course I'll prepare the report you want. But if you really want to open an investigation, as you seem to be indicating, then perhaps it's better to have everything examined by someone professional, a coroner or specialized institute."

Stefania gave him a questioning look.

"It's true," the doctor continued, "in my opinion that man was shot. In fact, there's no doubt about it. There's a hole in his skull. And he looks to me like a young man, a lad, tall and healthy but for his right leg."

"His right leg?" Stefania asked.

"Yes. He probably broke it. I think he must have limped a little."

⌣

Camilla was very excited. She hadn't stopped talking since her father dropped her off outside the front door.

"So we went into Papa's office to do homework. But I did it fast and then we played a little on his computer and then we had a snack of chocolate and pastries. And then we went to see Harry Potter and Papa bought me popcorn and then—"

"And then you need to take a breather, Cami. If you keep on talking like that you'll die. Now go and start your bath, and I'll come and help dry your hair. Meanwhile I'll start making something for dinner."

"I'm not very hungry, Mama. Can't we just have fish sticks and ketchup?"

Fine, Cami. After a box of popcorn at six thirty, how are you going to be hungry at eight?

Stefania was starting to get in a bad mood. Not for any precise reason. On the other hand, yes: she felt upset. Over a box of popcorn.

Later, after Camilla had fallen asleep in the big bed, Stefania lay there watching her. It always ended up this way. The little girl would come in, "but only to say good night for just a second, then I'll go back in my room." A second under the duvet would become ten and more minutes, until she fell asleep. Finally Stefania would take her in her arms and carry her back to her little bed. And so it was that night, too. Ron, their ginger cat, slept at the foot of the bed in a comfortable quilted basket.

Stefania woke up a little past four in the morning. It was pouring outside. The worksite was going to be a bog. But she had to go back there just the same.

That morning there was a brawl between three drug dealers in the area around the stadium; some illegal squats of apartments reported in the former industrial quarter of Ticosa; and a break-in of a tobacco shop in the center of town, behind the

Broletto. But all in all, Como was a quiet town asleep on the lakeshore.

"So, what else is there this morning?" asked Stefania.

"Marshal Bordoli of the Lanzo station called, Inspector. He wanted to let you know that he's already received the report from the doctor, that guy who was at the site. They're asking what they should do with it."

"Have them fax it here, Lucchesi, and tell them I'll get back to them. As soon as the report comes in, bring it to me upstairs in my office."

When the report arrived, Stefania shut herself in her office after dismissing Lucchesi and Piras with the usual "Okay, guys, everybody out of here for the next half hour." Then she lit her first Muratti Light of the day.

She quickly read the seven-page report and then started ruminating over the details.

Catalog of bones found. Skeleton almost entirely reconstituted and well preserved: a tall man, six feet, maybe more. Young, perfect teeth, fair hair, blond or reddish.

Two holes in the skull, one at the nape, the other in the forehead. Two vertebrae and several ribs damaged, probably by falling stones when the vault collapsed. Or maybe not. Fracture in the right leg that had healed poorly, resulting in a shortening of the limb by well over an inch.

The bones—according to the doctor's report—were then cleaned and stored in a sealed crate that was turned over to the sexton.

She carefully reread the other list as well: four pieces of heavy fabric, probably gray in color; a belt buckle, two shirt buttons; five metal buttons; a flat metal fragment, ten by five centimeters in size; part of a thin, probably silver chain, eighteen centimeters long; other unidentifiable metal fragments, one of which was longer and bent at one end. And then a great many fragments of blackened wood, perhaps burnt. And all deposited in a second crate.

She stood there thinking, looking outside the window. A few minutes later she called the courthouse directly.

"This is Inspector Valenti, I'd like to speak with Prosecutor Arisi. Yes, thank you, I'll be in my office until noon."

When her two subordinates returned to the office she was still scribbling something on a piece of paper.

"So, how do you two think that guy ended up under all those rocks?" Stefania asked them point-blank.

The two policemen looked at each other as if they didn't know what she was talking about, but before they could open their mouths she added: "That bit of wall I saw still standing was on the hillside facing the valley, and there certainly was nothing else on that side because it's too steep. Whatever there was on the opposite side, if there was anything at all, must have already been torn down by the scraper. In front, on the lake side, there was nothing left, and therefore whatever there was had to have been in back, on the northern side. And there might have been something, theoretically speaking, since, among other things, there's never any sunlight on that side. And then, if, over the years, the land had crumbled over it, it might look like a natural slope. That makes sense, doesn't it? It gets covered over with grass and nobody imagines there might be anything under it. Assuming anyone was interested."

While Lucchesi and Piras were still mulling the first question, a phone call came in from the courthouse.

"Good morning, sir. About our inspection of that site yesterday in San Primo . . . yes . . . I called you to let you know that, according to the initial findings, we might be looking at a crime, and I also wanted to know whether . . . Yes, of course. Thank you."

After hanging up, Stefania looked perplexed.

"He didn't let me finish. He said only to follow Carboni's instructions, whom he talked to this morning. Needless to say, boys, I'll keep you posted. Please tell Marino to send the news-papers up to me."

She put the sheet of paper in a folder and wrote on it: *Unknown man: San Primo, March 19, 20***.

2

"Naturally we'll open a case file against unknown persons—that's the correct procedure. But the state's attorney's office is expecting a careful but quick investigation—and, above all, a confidential one."

Carboni spoke slowly, choosing his words carefully, with a cadence that was rather irritating, to say the least. Stefania watched him attentively without saying anything, but the questioning expression on her face must have been so visible that Carboni added: "In Lanzo they'll give you all the support you need concerning information gathering at the site, but you'll be the one leading the investigation. From here. And you'll report back to me alone."

An awkward pause.

Stefania decided to cast the bait to see if the fish would bite. She looked Carboni straight in the eye: "A *confidential* investigation? Who on earth would ever be interested in such a story? Tell me, Inspector, have I missed something, or are we in danger of finding the Monster of Florence hiding out in our mountains?"

Carboni, deep down, was not only a good person but an honest cop. He was surely no genius, but Stefania admired him just the same. And she worked well with him.

"That's right: *confidential*, just as I said. It's the same word Arisi used. That land, the woods above, the houses, the cottages, and everything else belong to the Cappelletti family."

So the truth comes out at last, Stefania thought.

"So what?" she asked, throwing up her hands in a gesture of disapproval.

"So we have to act with discretion, Inspector Valenti. The senator has every reason to want to avoid any more controversy after what the papers have been saying the last few months."

"How should we proceed?"

"Political issues are of no interest to us. You just try to figure out what happened, and then report to me. The rest is of no concern to us. We'll do what needs to be done, but without any brouhaha. And now you'll have to leave, because I'm busy."

Carboni just wanted, in one way or another, to end the discussion. The whole thing irritated him. Maybe he simply felt put out. The lot of them counted as much as the two of clubs in a game of *briscola* between retirees. The big game was being played higher up. She said, "Okay," and went out without further comment.

Descending the stairs lost in thought, she remembered the image of Senator Cappelletti from the posters of the last elections: tanned, good-looking, long well-groomed hair, blue blazer. "United for Progress" or something similar. Stefania didn't much follow politics in general, let alone local politics. She found it boring, of no interest.

On the other hand, she well remembered the Cappellettis' big house on the lake, Villa Regina, with its park climbing up the mountainside in terraces. So many years ago it was the dream of all the little children, including her, to scale the high walls and go in there, because of the aura of mystery that had always surrounded that magnificent house.

Her nanny, Zia Lucia Canzani, who used to do the ironing at the villa ever since she was a girl, would tell of embroidered table-cloths of fine linen for twenty-four settings that were changed daily for guests who would stay for weeks at a time. Translated into normal language, this meant that, in her opinion, those people were real *sciuri*.[1]

"Inspector, I've put the newspapers on your desk."

"Thank you, Marino. You're an angel," said Stefania. She was terribly fond of that simple, awkward man, who spent his whole day on the ground floor in the guard booth.

Closing the door to her office, she lit a Muratti and cast a quick glance at the local newspapers: nothing in the *Corriere di Como*, nothing in *La Provincia*, a few lines in *Il Confine*: "*Human Remains Found During Excavation for New Tunnel to Switzerland at San Primo Pass.*"

Following the intervention of the Carabinieri of the Lanzo station, coordinated by Assistant Prosecutor Arisi, the mortal remains were brought together and taken to the mortuary chamber of the local cemetery, awaiting identification. No leaks thus far concerning the ongoing investigation. Work at the site, by Valentini Roadworks Inc., has since resumed.

On the same page, not far from this, another article attracted Stefania's attention, mostly because it was accompanied by a large photograph of the worksite from a few weeks earlier: *"Valli's Intervention in the Province Will Not Halt Tunnel."*

The journalist wrote:

A stormy session of the Provincial Council yesterday evening. Councillor Luca Valli, known for his commitment to the environment, harshly criticized the work in progress at the San Primo Pass. It is "a useless, pharaonic project," the young councillor said, "that will forever change the face of our mountain."

This was followed by a brief interview conducted in the heat of the moment, right after the stormy session. Among other things, Valli said:

"The tunnel will fill the valley with even more cars and heavy vehicles, along a road system conceived in the early twentieth century and already congested and unable to handle even the local traffic. The utilization of one of the nearby mountain passes would have resolved the problem of the endless queues of tractor-trailers at the customs check. There was no need to sacrifice acres and acres of forest overlooking one of Italy's most beautiful lakes. We have gathered a list of signatures for a petition we will submit to the president of the region. In the event of a negative response, we will address our concerns to the Regional Administrative Tribunal."

Stefania remembered the strong scent of just cut grass, the deafening chirr of the cicadas on summer afternoons, and her

23

father's voice saying: "What you see down there is the lake of Lugano, and over there is the San Primo Pass, and those things above it are the flags at the border crossing. See the white flag fluttering?"

The wind would carry away the smell of his Turmac cigarettes and the scent of the woods and the sound of the cowbells in the pasture.

His hazel eyes had green highlights in the sun. Like hers.

～

Camilla's voice suddenly rang out over the phone.

"Mommy, can I go to the pool today with Vale? Come on, please, we haven't got much homework today. Her mother will take us, but you have to tell me where you put my blue bathing suit and my Snoopy towel."

"Just listen for a minute, Cami. Martina—"

"Don't worry, Mommy, Martina said she would lend me fifteen euros and that it's okay if I'm not at home today, because that way she can go and get her legs waxed and so everything's fine. Come on, Mommy . . ."

"But then you have to be home by six-thirty, because tomorrow—"

"Tomorrow's Saturday, Mommy!"

There was no way Camilla would ever let her finish a sentence. Whenever she got something into her head she was like a river in spate: unstoppable.

"Bye, Mommy, thanks."

I don't remember ever saying yes, thought Stefania. Then she called the other girl's mother.

"Yes, if it's all right with you I'll take the girls myself to the pool. I'll make sure they dry themselves well and I'll bring Cami back to you by dinnertime. For me it's a pleasure. Everything okay with you? I'll see you later."

So at five Stefania could go to the hairdresser. I'll follow Martina's example, she thought. Today we'll both slip away.

She cut out the two newspaper articles and put them in the file folder. Then she went down to the bar. It was empty at that hour. But there wasn't so much as a panino left. She settled for one of those round short pastries with a plastic cherry in the middle, which she hated.

She felt alone.

She'd known Giulio Allevi since her days at the academy. They were together for a few months, stuff of their salad days. Nowadays they talked often, even though they saw each other barely twice a year—at Christmas for the commissioner's party and in the summer. She called him that afternoon. With him she could speak openly, without beating around the bush.

"Listen, I need you to have some tests run on those bones that we found up in the mountains, along with a few other things: fabric, metal, wood, and whatnot. . . . By somebody good, because I don't really know where to start with all this."

Giulio had done well for himself. He'd gone from being a simple junior detective to becoming a high-ranking officer of the Polizia di Stato, landing a prestigious administrative position in the human resources sector. He came twice a week to Como, where there was a division of his department.

"Yes, the one that was found in San Primo. Call me on my cell phone, I get out at four-thirty."

Who knew how he'd found out that she was calling about the remains found at San Primo? News travels faster than the wind around here, she thought with amusement, especially when an investigation is supposed to remain confidential. An image of Prosecutor Arisi's frowning face and muddied loafers came back to her, and she felt decidedly better.

Before going outside she enjoined Piras to find a phone number for Luca Valli and tell him she wanted to talk to him.

"And what if he asks me why?"

"Just tell him that Inspector Valenti wants to talk to him. That should be enough. It's a confidential investigation, didn't you know?"

Piras never got a joke, but he was a good kid. And efficient, in his way. Practical. Trustworthy. A workhorse with an almost admirable sense of duty.

Giulio Allevi called back when Stefania was at the hairdresser's, with the strips of blond highlight paper still on her head.

"Okay, Monday morning we'll have everything brought down to you," she said. "Yes, I'll ring him first and explain a few things, or maybe I'll come down myself to say hi. Yes, thanks. I don't know what I'd do without you. When we turn sixty we'll get married; write it down in your agenda. Thanks again."

This had been a standing joke between Stefania and Giulio for quite some time. When we turn thirty we'll get married. Then the years would go by. We'll get married when we're forty. They had, in fact, gotten married, but each to a different person. Then each had had one child, he a boy and she, Camilla. We'll get married when we're fifty. Not on your life. Once was enough.

Age fifty wasn't that far away anymore.

"We're getting old, Stefania. This time, we really will get married—when we turn sixty," he'd said the last time they saw each other.

Getting old? thought Stefania. Speak for yourself.

Camilla would be spending the weekend with her father.

On Saturday Guido came and picked her up at two o'clock sharp, as always.

"Pack her a heavy sweater, because we may go skiing."

"Don't worry, she's got a purse the size of Mary Poppins's bag, from the series *Seven Days No Matter the Weather*."

"Bye," she said to her little girl.

"Bye, Mommy, I love you, don't be sad."

"Bye, my love."

Every time Camilla went away, the house seemed suddenly huge and empty, and a mess. This time, for example, it would have been a good idea to clean the kitchen and bathroom, pick up the toys and clothes scattered all over the place, wax the scuffed parquet floor, and give the cat some attention. Stefania had a look around, locked everything up, and went out. When she was already in her car and on the road, she phoned her mother.

"Hi, Mama, I'm coming over. Yes, I'll be eating with you. Polenta and *missoltini*[2] are fine. Yes, then I'll stay the night. No, Camilla's not with me. No, I don't know what time I'll be there, it depends on the traffic. Yes, I have the keys, don't worry."

She drove slowly, as she was in no hurry. It was a beautiful day, typical of the transition from winter to spring. The days were growing longer. She took the low road, which wended its way around the lake, because at that time of the year hardly anyone took it. She stopped for tea at La Vecchina, opposite the Imperialino in Moltrasio. At that moment the *Lario*, one of the bigger ferries in service on the lake, was passing not far away.

Half an hour later, as she was about to enter Ossuccio, where her parents' house was, she accelerated almost without realizing and kept on going straight, heading towards the main entrance to Villa Regina, which stood between Ossuccio and Lenno. In front of it lay the Isola Comacina, the only island in Lake Como. Pulling up outside the majestic cast-iron gate, she looked inside, as she used to do as a child, resting her head and hands against the bars.

The great cream-colored façade was the same as she remembered it, like the green shutters, the hedgerows on either side of the fountain, the soaring trees in the park looming dark in the background. All closed up, but not abandoned. The hedgerows were carefully pruned and the dead leaves of the plane trees had been swept away. The caretaker's house had the windows open.

"The masters are coming for Easter and will stay until October if the weather is good," Tata Lucia used to say. "The caretaker will be opening up the villa for the week of Palm Sunday."

Stefania stood there a long time, gazing at the stately property, until one of the two windows of the caretaker's house slammed against the wall in a gust of wind. She got back in the car, turned around, and headed back for home, where her mother was waiting for her.

Her parents' house was past the Spurano district in Ossuccio, in the hilly area above the tennis courts, a stone's throw away from the Romanesque bell tower of Santa Maria Maddalena in Ospedaletto, just opposite the *isola*. The view was to die for, one of the best on the whole lake, with the Zoca de l'Oli—the hill of olive groves over the gulf of Ossuccio—barely fifty yards away. Everywhere around, amid the houses and the cobbled streets and alleyways, the landscape seemed straight out of a dream. The absolute silence broken only, from time to time, by a barking dog or a trilling blackbird.

⌒

"So, Inspector, we're looking at some kind of firearm—a pistol, I'd say. The entry wound is the one at the back of the head, the exit wound is in front. Lower central position in the nape area, upper central position in the forehead, almost along the median line. A single shot fired from a short distance, but not point-blank. The respective positions of the two holes suggest that the victim's head was inclined slightly forwards, otherwise it would be difficult to explain this sort of trajectory. At any rate, whoever fired the shot took careful aim," said Selvini at the other end of the line.

"An execution?"

"Something very much like it, or perhaps, I should say, a coup de grâce. Death was immediate, but the victim was already wounded, though not fatally, when the shot was fired."

"Wounded?"

"To judge from the marks on the ribs and on one vertebra, I'd say shot in the lungs, from behind and from the left—several shots, perhaps from a machine gun. Nasty wounds, but not immediately fatal. He was finished off sometime after that."

"So you confirm that it was a man."

"Yes, a young man, not more than thirty years old, maybe less. Rather tall, very long hands, perfect teeth, and with blond or reddish hair."

"What about the right leg?"

"A nasty fracture, poorly mended, resulting in a shortening of the limb, but dating from a few months before death. It had nothing to do with his death. The young man probably had a pronounced limp and would have had trouble running."

"So when did this happen, Doctor? How long ago?"

"If I've understood correctly what you told me about the site where the remains were found, I would say that, to be in the state they were in, it would have to have been not less than forty years ago, maybe more."

"Could it have happened during the war?"

"Yes, quite possibly. That would make sense."

Selvini fell silent for a moment, then added: "I can't be any more precise than that, Inspector. I would have to have other evidence, like bullets, for example. Did you find any, by any chance? And I would have to see the site myself and take into account such factors as temperature, humidity, ventilation, the type of soil—I should probably have had a look at the place before they removed the skeleton . . ."

"Don't worry, Doctor, you've already been very helpful. I won't bother you any further for the moment. Giulio Allevi sends his regards."

After hanging up, Stefania sat there in silence. Then she looked at Lucchesi and Piras, who had heard the whole conversation on the speakerphone.

"What do you two think?"

"The guy was lying facedown, Inspector," said Piras.

"So what do you think happened?"

"If they killed him there, with a shot to the base of the skull, he very likely fell facedown or onto his side, and there was no need to turn him over to see if he really was dead, with that hole running right through his head. If he'd been hiding in there and they killed him when they found him, there was no need to shoot him first in the back."

True.

"But maybe he was wounded. Maybe he holed up in that cellar and they killed him after they caught up with him," Stefania commented.

"He could already barely walk when he was healthy, so you can imagine after he was wounded," said Lucchesi. "And if somebody breaks down the door and finds you hiding in a hole like that, where there's no escape even if you're healthy, you're not going to turn around just so they can shoot you in the back. If you're already wounded, they'll finish you off however they want to. You fall down and that's it."

"In my opinion, they brought him there after he was already dead, to hide the body," said Piras. "They shot him as he was running away, and since he was lame and couldn't run, they caught up with him, finished him off, and then dumped him there, or else they shot him from behind as he was walking, and when he fell they caught up to him and, seeing that he wasn't dead yet, finished him off and then brought him to that cellar," he concluded.

"What we still don't understand is how they got him down there, given that the place is entirely underground. It looked like there was a trapdoor, but there was no covering there now," Lucchesi objected.

"Listen, guys," said Stefania, "I want one of you to call Bordoli in Lanzo tomorrow morning and have him send you the photos and the workers' depositions." Then, turning to Lucchesi, "And have you found this Luca Valli?" she asked.

"Yes, I spoke with him in person. I got his office address from the editorial office of *Il Confine*. Apparently he's a land surveyor. He was very nice over the phone and even gave me this cell phone number," he said, handing her a folded piece of paper, "because he's seldom in his office."

～

She decided to go and talk to Luca Valli in person, among other reasons because she'd discovered that the environmental movement's headquarters was fairly close to her place and because Valli happened to be in that day. In reality she didn't have a clear sense of what to ask him or what to expect from their meeting. Maybe she was hoping to get some additional information that might point the investigation in a more precise direction.

"Signor Valli? Good morning, I'm Inspector Valenti."

Two dark, gentle eyes, a bit nearsighted, looked out at her from behind their lenses.

"Good morning. I can see that we've made some progress since the days of Inspector Maigret. Please sit down."

He looked at her as she crossed the room and sat down. The guy's never seen a female police inspector, Stefania thought.

"I've never dealt with a woman inspector before," he said a moment later.

"Is it a good thing or a bad thing?"

He smiled. He had beautiful teeth and a friendly smile. He looked about thirty, maybe a little older.

"It's always better not to have to deal with the police. You never know. In general, however, I prefer women to men, no offense. What did you want to talk to me about?"

Stefania smiled in turn. "Frankly, I don't know, Signor Valli."

"Well, let's have some coffee, then, just to pass the time."

"There was an article in *Il Confine* that talked about your actions at the provincial council concerning the new tunnel at the

San Primo Pass. I'm conducting the investigation into the human remains that were found by workers at the site."

He made no effort to meet her halfway, but merely waited for her to come up with the concluding statement by herself.

"There may be no connection at all between the two things—actually, in all likelihood there isn't—but nevertheless I'd like to ask you a few questions."

"Go right ahead, ask anything you like. Two teaspoons of sugar?"

"Yes, thank you. Where did the idea of building this tunnel come from?"

"That's something you should ask our political representatives. I think they wanted to promote regional growth—that is, economic growth within their electoral base—but they chose the worst possible way to do it, assuming, of course, that what the tunnel will bring could even be considered a form of local growth and not simply a profitable financial deal for a handful of people at the expense of the environment, which belongs to everyone."

"Are you always so polemical?"

"No. I limit myself to observing and cataloging."

"I read the article about your presentation to the provincial council, as well as the interview with you, and your interpretation seems essentially correct, but when you speak of the great interests and potential gains of a few against the interests of the many, who, specifically, are you referring to?"

Valli gave her a look of good-natured amusement.

"Certainly not to the restaurants that make polenta and mushrooms for the truck drivers passing through or to the German families on their way home from their vacation. I'm talking about the companies that have won the work contracts, the owners of the land whose value will multiply thanks to the new road, the owners of the lands that will be expropriated, and so on."

"I've heard mention that the Cappelletti family . . ."

Stefania hesitated, as though indecisive, but Valli looked at her and laughed out loud this time.

"Don't worry, Inspector. I don't know how it is in your neck of the woods, but around here the subject is public domain. The papers talked about it for a little while, even though the buzz soon died down. Now nobody talks about them anymore—about the Cappellettis, that is—but it's only right that we keep talking about the new road."

Well, we've talked about it in our neck of the woods, too, thought Stefania, but only "confidentially."

"But what do *you* think about it?" she asked.

"About the Cappellettis or the road?"

Stefania smiled.

"What I think is of no importance. It's a fact, however, that the road passes right through their property, and that the value of the land and chalets in that area has already gone up, and it's also true that the road project was approved after the senator's election, and not before. But that all might be a coincidence. What do *you* think, Inspector?"

Stefania had the impression he was good-naturedly pulling her leg and felt uneasy, but she decided, nevertheless, to continue the discussion. She said the first thing that came into her head.

"I think that wealth and power are like a drug for some people. They always want more, whatever the cost. These rich and powerful families . . ."

She stopped, sensing Valli's mocking gaze on her.

"Wiser words were never said, Inspector, but I'm afraid I have to disappoint you. This isn't some sort of Lake Como *Dynasty*—the Cappellettis' wealth doesn't go that far back in time."

"What do you mean?"

"My family is from Lanzo. I was born there and go back there whenever I can. Many in town know it, and some of the older folks even remember it."

"Remember what?"

"When they were a family like any other, maybe even poorer than the others, since they were in Pian delle Noci, a remote district that didn't even have a proper road leading to it at the time. A lot of children, like everyone else, a cow, a few chickens, and that was it. Their farmhouse is still there, but now there's a road leading there, a very fine road, and they've actually turned it into a vacation rental with Tuscan furnishings."

"I believe I've heard mention that the senator likes to proudly claim his humble family origins and talk about the struggle of surviving in a beautiful but impoverished environment."

"Yes, he talks about it the way the Americans talk about the Far West, but he usually leaves out one detail, which is that his family's wealth comes from smuggling."

Stefania assumed a jaded air.

"Well, around here smuggling's become some kind of epic tradition, with its legends and heroes. Nobody's shocked by anything anymore—actually, they write good songs about it."

"Sure, but they weren't all smuggling human beings."

3

"Hi, Cami, I just wanted to tell you I'll be home by six-thirty, so you wouldn't worry. Everything okay?"

"Everything's fine, Mommy. Me and Martina have done everything."

"What do you mean, 'everything'? Do you mean you've already done your homework and taken your bath and Martina has already made supper?"

"No, there's very little homework tonight, I'll do it later, and I can take my bath later, too, because we made a surprise for you that you'll never guess, but you'll see. Okay, we'll be waiting for you, bye," Camilla said, then hung up.

Stefania, feeling hardly reassured, accelerated. Or, she tried to accelerate, because in that traffic there was no way to go any faster than twenty-five miles an hour.

The last time Camilla said everything was fine and she had a surprise for her, Stefania had found all the furniture pushed up against a wall, the table chairs arranged in a circle, and her favorite bedspreads stretched across them, because "We were playing Indians, Mommy, and this is our tent." Needless to say, Martina and Camilla had painted their faces, and it had taken half an hour to clean the girl up.

What could they have done this time? Stefania wondered with apprehension. Guido, her ex-husband, said that in hiring Martina she'd merely taken on another little girl instead of a proper babysitter.

But Stefania liked Martina a lot. She was the eldest daughter of Consalvo, one of their senior police officers, who was getting ready to retire.

Years earlier, when Stefania was still pregnant, Consalvo had told her: "Don't worry, Inspector, when you need a hand I'll send my Tina over, she's a good girl and is very patient with little children. She has three younger brothers and takes care of them herself. She needs a little extra money for herself, poor girl. We can barely help her with her studies, and the rest is up to her."

Stefania had immediately fallen in love with the girl's smiling, round, makeup-less face, her black curls and slender figure. She wasn't much of a cook and didn't even know how to iron, but she just loved children.

And so Martina had now been with them for six years, cheerfully adding to the chaos of their household. Stefania wouldn't have wanted any other babysitter, although sometimes . . .

At the start of Viale Varese, she dived into the usual downtown traffic. Returning from Switzerland, where she'd gone to get gasoline and provisions of chocolate, was always like this. From Cernobbio on, there was an endless queue of cars. At any time of the day, in every season. From there, if all went well, it would take her at least another fifteen minutes to get home. She distractedly turned on the car radio.

Valli's words came back to her, along with images that those words called to mind: barely visible paths in the woods, hurried, silent steps, ears pricked up in the surrounding dark. A suitcase, perhaps, the past left behind, and an uncertain future ahead. Perhaps.

"Here," Valli had said, referring to the site where the remains had been found, "we're just a few steps from the Swiss border, and between '43 and '45 there were a lot of people traveling along what were traditionally the smugglers' trails. People fleeing persecution, political refugees, partisans, former Fascists, even. But mostly Jews, who were the most defenseless and who gave the most to those who took them across."

"Why's that?"

"Because they were no longer anybody: they used false names, false documents, they'd managed by chance to survive among families that had vanished onto trains as though into thin air, and they themselves risked vanishing into thin air. Nobody would know for a long time, maybe never again, whether they'd managed to get away or were captured. Who died and how. During those months the end of the war seemed so far away. And on top of everything else, the Jews paid, and paid well, all these intermediaries, these mountain guides, these cogs in the extragovernmental system of the contrabandeers—though there were, of course, a few who did it out of Christian charity or for political reasons. Some were probably even playing a double game."

"You mean they let them get caught?"

"Yes, or they demanded more money at a certain point during the escape, with the threat of turning them in if they didn't pay. Have you ever read Renzo De Felice? His book on the subject is quite exhaustive."

Stefania sat there in silence.

"Some more coffee, Inspector?"

"No, thanks, but if you don't mind I'd like to smoke a cigarette."

"Only if you offer me one, too."

Stefania smiled.

⌒

She opened the front door grumbling to herself because nobody had come to let her in.

"Camilla! Martina! Where are you? What the hell is going on?"

She stopped suddenly, stumbling over the carpet. The red cat meowed. The apartment was in total darkness and there was a sweet sort of burnt smell in the air.

"Martina! Camilla!" she called again.

She climbed the stairs at the entrance, her right hand touching the wall. From the landing she headed for the living room. At that moment all the lights came on. She opened her eyes wide. The apartment was full of colored balloons—on the floor, on the walls, attached to the paintings, on the ceilings, hanging from the door and window handles. Camilla and Martina ran up to her, laughing, and put one of those cone-shaped hats, covered with spangles, on her head.

"Happy birthday to you, happy birthday to you . . ."

Right! It was March 26 and her forty-fifth birthday. Nobody had remembered, not even Stefania, at least not until that moment.

Stefania felt a lump rise in her throat, but she smiled and didn't show it. Camilla and Martina took her by the arms and dragged her towards the kitchen table, where towered a huge, formless cake covered by a dense layer of sprinkles and a forest of precariously balanced candles. Popcorn, soda pop, potato chips.

"See what a nice cake we made, Mommy? We made it ourselves, and it came out perfect. Now you're supposed to blow out the candles!"

They started laughing and dancing and popping the balloons. As they ate the cake the sprinkles fell all over the place, onto the chairs and the floor.

When Martina left to meet up with some friends, Camilla threw herself down on the couch.

"That was fun, but now I'm really tired, Mommy, so I'm gonna watch a little TV."

"And what about your homework?" asked Stefania.

"Okay, I'll do it now." And she immediately fell asleep.

Stefania gathered up the remains of the balloons and everything else, and filled the dishwasher with the stack of dishes and pans cluttering the sink. Then she turned off the TV.

She took Camilla in her arms and carried her into her room. She didn't wake up even when she put her pajamas on her.

Stefania went out onto the balcony. It was a clear, cold night full of stars. She lit a cigarette, then buried her face in her hands and started crying, in silence.

～

"If you ask me, it would have been better not to waste a roll of film than to take pictures like this," Piras huffed as he opened the envelope that had just arrived from the Lanzo station.

Stefania examined them one by one. "Yes, they really aren't top-notch. Put them in the file with everything else. What's done is done. What about the testimonies?" Stefania asked her other colleague.

Lucchesi raised his chin to indicate a sealed envelope on the desk.

"We're gonna go, boss. We'll be outside the stadium till late tonight. The Italy Cup."

"Okay, guys, see you later. Go Como!" she exclaimed ironically.

She opened the envelope and started reading.

All the workers and the site foreman present at the scene when the remains were found had been heard from. Fifteen utterly useless depositions.

What imagination, thought Stefania. Only the clowns in Lanzo could think of getting testimonies from every single worker at a huge worksite, including those who were working two miles away that day.

But where the hell was the guy operating the excavator?

She pulled from the stack the deposition of one Giandomenico Vitali, "authorized machine operator specialized in earthmoving." Stefania studied it carefully. The style of the person taking the deposition was in perfect alignment with that of the workman.

"The foreman gave me the order to knock down whatever was left of the cottage and to load all the rubble onto the truck. After knocking down part of a stone drywall about four and a half feet high, I pointed the stick of the shovel at the foundation to load it up, but during the second maneuver I realized the bucket was coming up empty. So I got closer and noticed there was now a deep hole next to the wall. At that point I went into the hole and aimed my flashlight inside and saw bones and other stuff at the back. And so I informed the foreman right away." Read, signed, and approved.

Stefania thought about this for a moment, then took two photos out of the other envelope. The first had been taken in bright daylight from a few meters away from the ruin. On the left you could still clearly see the pile of rocks and earth freshly moved, corresponding perfectly with the scoop of the excavator. On the right, however, about three feet of wall was still standing. It was slightly hidden by the roots of a wild fig tree that had grown on top of it, which she'd already noticed when she was at the site. The right edge of the wall was sharp, and some of the stones might well be cornerstones. Curiously, however, the sharp edge, which looked like a corner of the house, plunged into the ground. The "hole," as the worker called it, was behind this length of wall, but the underground hollow extended a good ways to the right of the corner, because the little well, or whatever it was, was almost two meters long, and one of its sides went below and to the right of the corner.

The other photo showed the entire cottage—or rather, the entire ruin—from a certain distance, and enabled one to see its placement in the surroundings: the part where the length of wall rose above the underground chamber was without a doubt towards the mountain, but the underground "room" extended for a brief stretch farther to the right, into the part that must have been buried.

Yes, of course, thought Stefania: *towards* the mountain, not *into* the mountain. The other photos, shot inside the little underground room, were utterly indecipherable, black on black. You couldn't even see the man's bones and remains.

She grabbed the phone and called Giulio Allevi.

"Hi. Any news on those specimens I sent down to you?"

"Hi. You could at least ask me how I am."

"You're always perfectly fine, Giulio. You're a rock. Have you found out anything interesting?"

"Nothing special. It's not the most thrilling of cases, Stefania. Selvini left an envelope for you. He wants you to call him."

Giulio always knew everything about everyone.

"But where's the envelope now?"

"I've got it here, so you'll have to come and have it. Then I can get a good look at you once and for all."

"Around ten-thirty okay?"

"Okay, I'll be waiting. And when are we getting married?"

"Later, after you give me the envelope. Be sure you're ready."

Downstairs she ran into Marino, who was busy distributing the mail.

"Good morning, Inspector. Carboni's looking for you. He said that if I saw you I should tell you—"

"Except that you never saw me this morning, Marino," Stefania said hurriedly, winking at him.

"And what about your mail?"

"Read it yourself and tell me about it later."

She went out through the garage door and took a squad car, telling a colleague that she was going to see Allevi. Not that she didn't want to talk to Carboni, but, first of all, she had nothing concrete to tell him, and second, he might not have approved of what she had in mind. Carboni was someone who tried to avoid trouble as a matter of principle. But he always ended up doing the right thing.

It was better to wait and present him with a fait accompli.

⟡

"Nice. Panoramic position, breathtaking view of the lake. With a little fixing up, it could be the perfect place. But is it right for us?"

"Don't be silly. It's the cottage at San Primo where we found those bones," said Stefania.

"Then I'm not interested."

"Come on, look at that piece of wall on the left."

"I see it. And so?"

"Does that look normal to you, for it to end that way, at a right angle against the embankment? Doesn't that look to you like the corner between the side and the back of the cottage?"

Giulio studied the photo, bringing it up to the tip of his nose.

"You're right, it looks like the rear corner—but that wouldn't make sense, no stone mason would build an outer wall right up against an embankment, without leaving a little air space in between."

He looked at the photo a third time, then looked at Stefania, who pressed him.

"Okay, and so?"

"And so I can imagine that the cottage was originally freestanding on that side, too, and that later, for whatever reason, the embankment slid down, enveloping the whole back of the house, maybe even bringing down some other walls with it. And time and the vegetation took care of the rest."

Bingo! thought Stefania.

"Right. If you walk past it without paying attention it almost looks like a natural slope. You see the crumbling walls, it could be just about anything. Nobody's going to imagine that there's an empty space underneath, a cellar, a *nevera* or whatever it is— also because you don't see any door leading to it. And of course there was no trapdoor leading to it from the inside, because in that case we would have seen at least some kind of opening in the vault, even if the wooden lid had rotted in the meanwhile."

"Okay, I've got that, but where do you want to go with this?"

"I want to be able to say that that young man was killed and then put in the *nevera*. But whoever killed him had a reason for not wanting the body to be found, so he managed to make the embankment behind the house collapse, completely covering the rear entrance to the cellar, below the ground and the floor level of the cottage. At any rate, whoever it was, they also brought down part of the outer wall, even though there was no need, since at that point the house looked as if it was up against the bank."

Giulio looked pensive.

"But if we assume people were looking for a missing person, might they not have thought of looking in that very place, seeing that the embankment had collapsed and maybe even the walls, even if they only thought it was all an accident?"

"If anyone was looking for a missing person and suspected he might be in that area, then, yes, at least at first, people who knew the area might have thought of it. But there's also the possibility that nobody knew that person was missing, or could have imagined he would be there, for whatever reason. At any rate, time passed, and meanwhile the vegetation grew and memories faded."

"Okay, Inspector, so far, it makes sense. But what about the owners of the cottage? Maybe it was inhabited, at least in the summer. And what if they had wanted to rebuild it? They would have found the corpse inside."

"I thought of that, too, and I must say that your argument has merit. Unless . . ."

"Christ, you're right. Unless!"

They exchanged a glance of understanding. The two of them would have worked well together, because they reasoned the same way. Stefania, deep down, would have liked that. When the opportunity had arisen, however, she hadn't put in the request. She'd been afraid that standing shoulder to shoulder with him day in and day out, she might no longer be able to keep their relationship within the limits she wanted, since her limits were not the same as Giulio's.

"Aren't you going to look at the other photos?" he asked her. "Wasn't that the reason you came?"

"I almost forgot."

She opened the envelope. It contained a packet of numbered photos mounted on cards. Top-notch work. Selvini wasn't only a forensic pathologist and photography expert but a sort of genius at the disposal of the forensics department who knew how to do a bit of everything. This was why Giulio had turned to him. On each card was a label summarizing the basic facts of the object photographed. She put on her glasses and started studying them. Had she not known that these were things found beside the dead body, she would have had trouble recognizing them: they'd been cleaned, weighed, measured, analyzed, and, in certain cases, identified, even in detail.

"Very fine work indeed. I'll look at this carefully over the course of the day. Aha, he wore glasses: here's a metal earpiece. Have a look at this, Giulio. What could it be, in your opinion?"

She handed him the card with *Exhibit no. 11* written on it.

"Metal object, eighteen-carat gold, 4.722 grams, maximum diameter 3.5 centimeters, identified as handmade jewelry, the cover for an oval locket with a portrait inside."

"Yeah, I've seen that kind of thing before. My grandmother used to wear one with a photo of my grandfather and her young son who died at age two. There was a little spring latch on the side, and an empty space inside for photos. I think these things were rather common at the time."

"Sure, for those who could afford gold jewelry. And look at this other one!"

Giulio examined card number 18 and its images. The "flat metal object" in it turned out to be a slender silver cigarette case, a bit crushed and dented, but still intact. Inside were the blackened remains of a few cigarettes.

"The hand-rolled kind that people used to smoke," she added, studying an enlargement of the specimen. "Have you seen the cover?"

"Yes."

Etched in a simple but elegant cursive, the letters *K* and *D* were clearly legible.

4

Contrary to habit, Stefania went out for lunch that day. Slipping the envelope with Selvini's photos into her backpack, she hopped on her bicycle and headed off towards the lake.

She crossed the entire walled city, starting at Porta Torre, taking care to avoid pedestrians and turning her gaze every so often to the balconies of the houses giving onto the cobbled alleyways. When she got to Piazza San Fedele, she stopped briefly at a brand-new bookstore right in front of the Romanesque church, its entrance under a long-storied portico. She ordered the book by De Felice that Valli had spoken about, also casting a glance at the art books, her real passion. Her visit over, she traveled the last stretch of the historic center of town, passing the cathedral and the Broletto. At last she was in Piazza Cavour. The Metropole Suisse was where it always was, in one corner of the piazza. Across the street, the lakefront was looking as best it could, with a boat putting out and some Japanese tourists pointing cameras. Her favorite spot was a short distance away, secluded, on Viale Geno, near the little square with the cable car for Brunate. She found a free bench and sat down to watch the seagulls. The sun was shining, and she decided to go down to the lakeshore.

It was still chilly outside, and the lakefront wasn't crowded. She felt sheltered by the wall separating her from the promenade. The sun caressed her face with its warmth. She lit a cigarette and closed her eyes.

Ever since she left Giulio's office she couldn't get one image out of her mind: that of a young, blond man taking a hand-rolled cigarette out of his case and smoking it while looking at the horizon, unaware that death is lurking behind him. Her father, too, used to sit down alone and smoke while watching the lake. As a little girl, Stefania would sometimes sit down beside him, entering his silence without saying a word. Neither of them knew that death was lurking behind them and watching.

She felt bad for having been a little brusque with Giulio.

"Care to join me for a snack?"

"No. You know I never go out with married men."

She could at least have said thanks, or even accepted. But she'd run away with the usual excuse: no time, the office, and all the rest. But that silent appeal, that unexpressed question in his eyes, bothered her, irritated her, made her uneasy. She was sorry about it. For his sake, not hers. The only effect Giulio's wishes had on her was to make her want desperately to run away.

She sighed, then shrugged. A motorboat took off noisily nearby.

She reopened the envelope with the photos and looked at them all one by one. The eighteen centimeters of chain were real silver, of simple links appropriate for a man. The enlargement featured the last link in the segment, misshapen at both ends, as if the remaining part, which must have been another twenty centimeters long, maybe more—given the circumference of a man's neck—had been torn away.

"Assuming it was in fact torn away deliberately and not accidentally, and that it was around a man's neck and not, for example, in one of his pockets," Giulio had said with his proverbial rationality. "As for the locket, it was not a piece of male jewelry, and it was in fact unlikely that man had worn it around his neck, especially attached to a silver chain."

"But the average male taste in jewelry is inferior to your own, and our man might therefore have worn a gold locket hanging from a silver chain without any problem," Stefania had countered.

But it might also have been a gift from a loved one—say, his mother—and the man might have decided to wear it in any case, keeping it perhaps hidden under his clothing.

"Why not? Or maybe he'd stolen both locket and chain, our Mr. K.D.—assuming the cigarette case was his and he didn't steal that, too."

"You're insufferable, Giulio."

"No. I'm a policeman."

Stefania took a quick glance at the other exhibits. Most of the remaining metal fragments hadn't been identified, not even after they'd been cleaned and photographically enlarged. All but two: the first, which looked like half of a stud from a purse; and the second, which could have been part of an eyeglass frame. An earpiece, probably. The last card display, number 24, featured photos and enlargements of some pieces of wood. The label, however, said only *Wood: Still being tested.*

Stefania noticed that some of the fragments had a greenish sort of patina.

What could that mean? she thought. She really must talk to Selvini again this afternoon.

The first person she ran into while ascending the stairs was Carboni.

"Ah, there you are, Valenti, just the person I was looking for."

"Really? Nobody told me, sir."

"The prosecutor's office wants to know what point you're at in the investigation."

"Which one?" Stefania asked disingenuously.

"The one concerning the human remains found at the Valentini worksite."

Carboni seemed to be in a bad mood.

"Ah, yes, of course. Well, preliminary examination of the evidence leads us to believe that—"

"I know that already. I spoke with Piras and Lucchesi, since I couldn't talk to you. What I want to know is what you intend to do now."

"Find the owners of the cottage, naturally."

"But it's just a ruin! Who knows how long it's been in that condition!"

"Yes, but it must have belonged to somebody when it was still standing. If we could find the owners, we could ask them a few questions. After all, it's not every day that you find a corpse in your cellar."

"You are aware that that whole area, ruins and cottages alike, belongs to the family of Senator Cappelletti?"

"Indeed, I would like to start by talking to them."

"But they're the current owners."

"Clearly, and for that reason they'll know who they bought it from, no?"

The chief inspector seemed resigned.

"Agreed, but please proceed with extreme caution, and keep me informed of any new developments."

"Have no fear. Would you like a coffee?"

Carboni gestured no and disappeared into his office, shaking his head.

"Whichever of you two spilled the beans to Carboni is going to go on a hike in the mountains tomorrow," Stefania said as she opened the door to her office.

Lucchesi and Piras turned around in surprise. They looked like they'd just been having an argument.

"Tomorrow morning I want one of you to call Bordoli up in Lanzo. Then you should make an urgent appointment at the town hall with the municipal engineer or the councillor in charge of construction. Have them pull out all their past and present cadastral plans, old blueprints, relief maps, deeds. Everything they've got, in other words. We want to know the names of the current and prior owners of all the huts and cottages in the San Primo area. I want a detailed chart of all the property transfers from, say, the early twentieth century until now. Is that clear?"

Piras blushed, cleared his throat, and said: "Inspector, I'm sorry, but I actually have a doctor's appointment tomorrow, at two o'clock."

"Why, is something wrong with you, Giovanni?"

"It's not for me, Inspector, it's my wife. She doesn't want to go alone. It's a delicate matter."

Stefania looked at him and smiled. "But this is the third one in seven years, Piras. If you keep on at this rate, you'll end up having to change jobs."

"The fourth, Inspector, God willing."

"Yes, God willing. And you, Lucchesi, does your wife need you tomorrow, too?"

"But I'm not even married, Inspector!"

"Right, so you'll go instead. Do you have a clear sense of what we're looking for?"

"Yes, Inspector, I've written it all down."

"Good, then we're on the same page. And by the way, it's best if you go in plainclothes, but don't bring your girlfriend along, otherwise you'll end up like Piras. But if you like, you can drop in at the Locanda del Notaio in Pian delle Noci; they make excellent venison salami and have a huge wine cellar. And you," she then said, turning to Piras, "check and see whether the prosecutor's office has signed the authorization papers for the interment of the bones at Lanzo cemetery, then call the institute and ask when they can have the casket ready for transport. Okay, that's all. Now, if you'd please clear out of here, I have things to do."

After they left she opened the file, put the packet of photos back in, crossed out the words *Unknown Person*, and wrote *K.D.* in their place.

She saw the young man again. Sitting with his back to her, smoking in silence in front of the lake. We don't know much about you yet, my boy, but we'll get there, don't worry.

⌒

The following day Stefania decided to delve further into the articles of evidence.

"So, in your opinion, Selvini, you think it's painted wood, if I've understood correctly."

"Yes, they're chips of a board that was originally painted—green, I think. Beech wood, I'd say. One of the pieces has two rather visible holes. From large nails, no doubt. I'd told Dr. Allevi to have you call me, but only because I hadn't managed to finish the final entry in time."

"The work you did was superb, Selvini. I don't often get the chance to work with people as meticulous and professional as you. One last question: are you therefore certain the wood wasn't burnt?"

"Absolutely, yes. There's no sign of combustion whatsoever. Given the data I have, I can tell you that the wood fragments spent a long time underground, in rather humid conditions— and not the best quality wood, either. Over the years it would probably have rotted from the effects of rain and frost, even if it had been above ground."

"I won't waste any more of your time. You're very kind."

"I'm happy to have been of assistance, Inspector."

⌣

"Bingo!" Stefania exclaimed after hanging up the receiver. "We've found the door."

She lit a Muratti and opened the telephone book. No Cappellettis who could be traced in one way or another to Villa Regina.

She could understand why the senator might not want his number in the phone book, but how was she going to find him now?

For a moment she weighed whether to turn to the Carabinieri station in Lenno. Then, remembering her "colleagues" from Lanzo, she decided to wait. A moment later she remembered Tata Lucia, her former nanny.

Let's hope she didn't forget to turn on her hearing aid, otherwise this might take forever. She dialed the number.

"Who is it?" yelled a shrill voice at the other end.

"This is Stefania, do you recognize my voice?"

"Germania?"

"Stefania!"

A tomblike silence, followed by a din of voices and chairs.

"Pina, come here. There's somebody on the phone but I can't figure out who. See if you can tell," Stefania heard in the background.

"Hello, who is this?"

Pina was a few years younger than Lucia, meaning she hadn't yet reached the age of ninety-one that Lucia had so brilliantly passed. At the venerable age of eighty-two, Pina was still considered the baby of the family.

"This is Stefania. Hi, Zia Pina."

"Hi, Stefanina, how are you?"

"I'm fine, how are you?"

"We're old, but what can you do? The Lord doesn't want us yet. And how's your little girl? How old is she now?"

"Eleven, Zia Pina, going on twelve. Listen, I wanted to ask you something."

"What's your daughter's name again? I don't remember."

"Camilla. Her name's Camilla. Listen, Zia, do you remember the Cappelletti family, the ones who lived at Villa Regina? The *sciuri* where Tata Lucia used to go and iron when she was young . . . ?"

"Where are you living these days? I saw your mother at Mass, you know, and she said she has arthritis in her hands now and can't sew anymore."

"Yes, Zia, but do you by any chance know how I could get in touch with the Cappellettis?"

"What Cappellettis?"

Stefania realized she had to take the bull by the horns.

"Listen, Zia Pina, I'd like to come and see you in the next few days."

"That's a good girl. Will you stay for dinner?"

"No, Zia, I'll come after dinner."

"Good, I'll make you risotto with perch, the way you like it."

Forget I ever asked, thought Stefania. But deep down the prospect of spending an evening in the company of Tata Lucia and her two sisters didn't displease her. Two hundred fifty years and some between the three of them.

I have to remember to tell Giulio that women who don't get married live longer, she thought.

⌒

"Were they just giving you the runaround, or did they really not have anything? Because if all you need is a little help, we can have Prosecutor Arisi call them directly."

"I don't think so," said Lucchesi. "I was there the whole afternoon. They pulled out a truckload of papers, but the only town plan they have is from twenty years ago. They have cadastral maps of the municipality, but the oldest are already from after the war. Before that the mountain cottages and huts weren't even assessed, or maybe one out of ten at the most."

"So what have you got to show for yourself?" Stefania asked huffily.

"This."

Lucchesi handed her a binder with an industrial quantity of photocopies and an envelope with some photographs in it. Stefania put on her glasses and started examining the papers one by one, arranging them in orderly fashion on her desk.

After a few minutes of this she raised her head and looked up at Lucchesi over the tops of her glasses.

"I'm going to recommend you for a promotion, Antonio," she said.

Lucchesi looked at her in shock.

"I found out you requested to be transferred to that nice little station by the sea near Palermo. I could put in a good word for you . . ."

"But I didn't request any transfer to Palermo, Inspector. I'm Tuscan. If anything I would request a transfer to Massa so I could be a little closer to my family . . ."

He trailed off and then blushed, smiling feebly.

"Do you like puzzles, Lucchesi?"

"I don't know, really. I've never done puzzles."

"Well, then it's time you started. There are eight plates here. The plan probably measured a meter and a half by eighty centimeters, a sort of Persian rug with the altitudes. You did a good job, Lucchesi, but you had them photocopied in handkerchief-sized pieces and didn't number them. And you forgot the list and the general index. So now you're going to sit down here and put all these plates together. I'll be back in a couple of hours. If you want you can call Piras to give you a hand."

Lucchesi looked at his watch and sighed.

"If it's not all finished and on my desk when I return, you'd better get your towel and sand bucket ready for the beach."

"The beach?"

"Palermo beach," said Stefania, without adding anything else.

When she was in the hallway she smiled to herself. She was fond of those boys and wanted them to grow into their profession. She would rather intervene personally to correct whatever little mistakes or naïve blunders they made from inexperience than let the matter spill out of their office and come to Carboni's attention.

She went downstairs and into the guard booth.

"Hello, Marino. Listen, I'd like to make a couple of phone calls from your line."

She called the café nearby.

"Ciao, Isa. This is Stefania Valenti. Could you send a stuffed focaccia and a beer up to my office for Lucchesi? And the usual coffee for Marino, of course. I'll come by later to pay. Thanks."

She hung up and dialed a second number.

"Raffaella, this is Stefania. Shall we say at your office, in an hour?"

Raffaella Moretto worked at *La Provincia di Como* and edited the paper's cultural page with intelligence and passion. In the past, however, at the start of her career, she had also covered local crime, and they'd met in those circumstances, on opposite sides of the barricade, giving rise to a lasting friendship, even outside of work.

A year earlier her newspaper had published a series of articles, under her stewardship, on the most beautiful churches and villas around the lake. Stefania remembered having seen something about Villa Regina and asked her to pull up the article from the archive.

Normally on these occasions they would go into town to have lunch together. This time, however, Raffaella already seemed in a hurry over the phone. Another engagement, perhaps.

After parking her car, Stefania entered the bright, glass-encased lobby. The newspaper's office, brand new and very high-tech, was in the hills outside the city. A futuristic, colossal construction. The paper had a daily print run of forty-five thousand.

At the reception desk she gave her name and went up to the second floor, where the editorial offices were.

"So, Raffa, how are you?"

"Like a flower, can't you tell?"

"No, I can't: I forgot my glasses again this morning."

Raffaella made a face and then embraced her.

"Want some watery coffee with milk and cream, Swiss style?"

"Sure, thanks."

"When are you northerners ever going to learn how to drink coffee properly?" she resumed, waving her arms. That's how Raffaella was. She could never keep still. She gushed energy from every pore, like a volcano in continual eruption.

"Listen, darling, I've laid it all out for you on the table. So sit down and make yourself comfortable, and do whatever you need to do. Our very own Anna is next door, at your service, if you need copies or anything else. Now, there are a couple of things I have to tell you while we're having our coffee, but then I have to go."

"No sugar for me," said Stefania.

"Here's the article we published," Raffaella continued. "And here's the complete file. I also pulled out an issue of *Grandi Dimore* from a few years ago that featured something on Villa Regina. In the pictures you'll find some of the villa's prior owners. These, on the other hand, are the villa's current owners, a really lovable lot. Here: the official portrait of the family in full regalia. Last Christmas, give or take a few days. But why are you so interested in the Cappellettis?"

She pointed to a color photograph, also reproduced in the article.

"Here are some other photos taken the same day—but which the family later didn't 'approve.'"

"Stop for just a second. You're making me seasick. Who's this guy? And this lady?"

"I don't know them all! I only spoke with the matriarch and

an American nephew. . . . 'Spoke' in a manner of speaking, since he didn't know a word of Italian. The snobbery, I'm telling you . . . They were all so irritating. I practically had to pull the words out of them, and in the end they told me to tell the usual lies, the ones everybody knows."

"No surprise. You probably got them upset with your constant jabbering, as you always do. Of course, they, too . . . Who are they, anyway? Did they land here from Mars? Do they have to give their approval or disapproval for everything?"

"Down to the smallest detail, darling. When they agreed to grant an interview after numerous requests, they stated in writing—I swear—that they had to see the article as well as the photos of them and the villa and approve them before we could publish them."

Stefania shrugged.

"Just imagine, when they gave me back the text of the article it was so changed I hardly recognized it."

"And what's the villa like?" Stefania asked in curiosity.

"It's very beautiful. Both outside and in. And it's almost unknown to the public. Anna," she said to the secretary, "please call Dr. Rivolta and tell him to come here and meet a friend of mine."

Stefania looked at her affectionately. Raffaella never changed: small, plump, always moving. She was never quiet for a minute and was always doing three things at once, laughing and dashing about in an office packed full of papers and books. She alone could find things in that chaos.

"But why do you want me to meet Rivolta? Aside from the fact that I'm not in the hunt at the moment, I really don't see the point . . ." said Stefania.

"What, are you crazy? He's game, don't you worry about that. This'll arouse his curiosity, and maybe something'll even come of it. Anyway, when are you going to run into another one like him? And he's available, on top of everything else."

"No, no . . . I mean yes, of course. . . . It's not that I don't like him. I'm just not interested."

"Just leave it to your Lella. As my granny used to say: 'The fish you can't sell the day it's fished you'll never sell.' Nobody'll have it the next day. Dr. Rivolta!" Raffaella then said dramatically to a graying man who'd appeared in the doorway, "Please come in so I can introduce you to a dear friend of mine, Inspector Valenti."

Stefania turned around abruptly towards the door and turned as red as a poppy, not knowing where to rest her eyes.

Let's hope he didn't hear anything, she thought.

As she was shaking Rivolta's hand, she saw another person come out the door of the archive room, which was in front of them. The face was familiar to her. The glasses, too. She would never have expected to run into him here.

Valli, too, seemed surprised to see her:

"Our favorite police inspector. How are you?"

"Not too bad, and you?"

"A little tired. I'm glad Easter's on the way. I need a few days off. Just so long as nobody comes along in the meantime to bust my chops."

At that point Rivolta took his leave and, muttering some excuse, went back to his desk.

Raffaella, meanwhile, had stepped forwards. She wasn't the type to get easily discouraged.

"Did you know our friend Valli has a house on the lake like you?" she said to Stefania.

"Actually, it's my parents' house, and it's in Lanzo, in the mountains. There's a view of the lake in the distance. Lake Lugano."

"Where's your place, Stefi?"

"Ossuccio, a bit higher up."

"Well, what a lovely coincidence. Our adviser has a passion for hiking in the mountains, just like you. It must be so beautiful. It would do me a bit of good, too, let me tell you, but what can you do? I'm always shut up in here. You'll have to invite me another time. But when are you going up?"

"I have to wait for Camilla to get out of school tomorrow, and then we'll head up."

"And you, Valli?"

"Unfortunately I can't get away until Saturday. We have a provincial council meeting on Friday evening."

"So, what's on the agenda? I'll be in the cathedral listening to the Requiem being sung by the Schola Cantorum of the Ticino. Sorry, Stefania, I have to go now. It's getting late."

"You come with me, Valli," she added.

She planted a noisy kiss on Stefania's cheek, winking, took Valli by the arm, and disappeared into the elevator with him.

Good God, thought Stefania, let's hope she doesn't make any more trouble for me.

5

Built in 1765 at the behest of Ludovico Antonio Borsari, marquis of Stabio, Villa Sorgente (as Villa Regina was originally called—ed.) was enlarged by Borsari's son, Giovanni, with the addition of the lemon-house, a labyrinth, and the Grotto of the Nymphs in the spot where, at the time, water sprang from the spring that gave the house its name.

In the latter part of the nineteenth century the gardens were expanded and embellished with fountains, and the monumental dock with its overhead balcony with nymphs and naiads was built. In 1812 the villa was included in the dowry of Enrichetta Borsari, who was to marry Count Prospero Parravicini later that year. The couple soon created the park with its English gardens farther up the mountainside and acquired broad tracts of forest and vineyards.

In 1862 Maria Giulia Parravicini had a number of greenhouses built for growing camellias and eventually gave her name to the famous camellia called Rosa Julia, which passionate floriculturists still appreciate today. When the countess died in 1878, leaving no heirs, the villa came into the hands of Leopoldo Parravicini, her second cousin, who never moved in and let the property fall into neglect. Indeed, such was its condition that when the villa was put up for auction to cover the gambling debts of the same Count Leopoldo in 1896, the new owner, Luigi Davide Montalti, of the noted Milanese banking family of the same name, had to intervene and refurbish large sections of the structure.

Over the course of the next twenty years the new owners restored the villa to its former splendors, however sacrificing a good deal of the land up the slope, which was sold to cover the immense costs of shoring up the structure. The new owner changed the name of the villa in homage to his eldest daughter, Regina, who was born in 1902.

In 1924 Regina Montalti had a driveway installed linking up with the state road, calling it the Allée of the Plane Trees, as well as a stately entrance gate in wrought iron.

In the mid-1940s the villa became the property of the Cappelletti family. Today the villa's interior, aside from its forty perfectly restored rooms and salons, houses a precious collection of French Impressionist paintings belonging to Durand Antiques of Geneva.

In the photo, Germaine Durand Cappelletti, in the villa's Imperial Salon, with her four children. Two of them live in the United States. One of them is a well-known lawyer, while the fourth, Paolo, is a senator of the Italian Republic.

All that's missing is the family accountant, thought Stefania.

She quickly skimmed through the rest of the article, which described the villa in every detail, down to the stuccos, marble statues, frescoes, tapestries, and architectural peculiarities. No more mention was made of either the Cappelletti or Durand families.

She examined the contents of the folder and found three drafts of the article, each with a different date. "Good thing they printed them out," she said, thinking of the many times she had written over original drafts of reports on her computer.

They must have been quite a pain, she thought, wondering how Raffaella had managed to put up with that family.

The oldest proof must have been the original version of the piece. She compared it with the one that was eventually published in the newspaper; in the section that had most drawn her attention, a number of sentences had been changed:

At the end of the war the villa was acquired by Remo Cappelletti, but the family didn't move in definitively until 1947, when the eldest son, Giovanni, married Germaine Durand, who came from a prosperous family of Genevan antiquarians. All four of the couple's children were born here: Paolo, now a senator of the Italian Republic; Marie Claire and Augusto, who have followed in their grandfather Gustave's footsteps and manage the family's vast network of antique shops in Switzerland and the United States; and Filippo, a well-known criminal lawyer at the Forum of Milan. Upon the decease of Giovanni Cappelletti in 1979, Germaine Durand moved permanently to Switzerland with her daughter.

On the right, the Cappelletti family in a photo from 1944. On the left, Germaine Durand Cappelletti in the Imperial Salon.

So, what's so different to warrant changing the sentences? Stefania asked herself.

If they're happy, everyone's happy.

She took a quick look at the photos of the villa that hadn't been published, and in this instance the choice made by the owners was quite effective, in the sense that the selection served to highlight the great house's outstanding features while hiding its small defects.

As for the photo of the Cappelletti family, Stefania studied it closely. It was hardly the height of glamour, but it wasn't a bad shot, either. From the image you could see that the Cappellettis were a family that still bore the signs of sudden wealth. Certain details would never escape the trained eye: they were dressed in quite dignified fashion, no doubt, but their overall bearing, the expressions on their faces, and the overall tone had a good dose of embarrassment and a kind of woodenness in front of the camera. In a word: they lacked the elegance—even physical elegance—that instead distinguished the members of the Durand family. There was no greyhound crouched at their feet, of course; only the pathetic floral background of a nouveau-riche family from the provinces.

To make up for it, the Cappellettis were almost all quite good-looking; two in particular, male and female, probably brother and sister, were unusually beautiful, still diamonds in the rough. The same could not be said of the Durands, who were elegant and extremely refined but, except for Germaine, decidedly plain.

Stefania thought she'd like to get to know them better. She glanced at her watch and gave a start. Maybe the Durand family was a little embarrassed of their ever-so-inelegant relatives.

She slipped the photo into her pocket, left a note for Raffaella, and quit the newspaper's editorial offices with a hurried step.

Back at her office, she grabbed the reassembled blueprints that Lucchesi had stuck together with tape and numbered. He'd done an excellent job. A Kinder-brand Easter egg, wrapped in pink grocer's paper, sat on her desk. There was no need to read the attached note to know that it was a present from Lucchesi and Piras.

She smiled to herself. Before returning to the office, she had gone to a pastry shop and ordered a huge ice-cream cake for all present and future members of the Piras family, and a little chocolate bunny each for Lucchesi and Marino.

She lit a cigarette and began studying the material. It was the plans for the construction of the road and colossal viaduct in the San Primo area. The Valentini Roadworks logo was quite visible at the top of each page, along with that of a well-known engineering design firm from Milan, people who sprang into action only for great works.

The city hall of Lanzo had provided Lucchesi with copies of the relief maps of the current state of affairs—that is, the state before the start of the excavations and demolitions. One plate in particular marked the presence and location of peasant dwellings in the area affected by the construction.

After searching for a few moments she found the cottage where the body had been found. She circled it in red pencil, tacked the sheet to the back of the door, sat down about six feet away, and started studying it.

The cottage was in a rather secluded area: the nearest hut was no less than a kilometer away, based on the scale provided in the key.

How odd, thought Stefania.

All the others were close together, almost forming a small agglomeration, a sort of rural village at the top of the mountain, and lined up as though along the old mule track that went up to the pass. She remembered that old trail well: it climbed almost straight up towards the mountain, cutting directly across several of the main road's winding turns.

The cottage in which the bones of "K.D." had been found was instead not only far away but stood on the other side of a dense triangle of woods at the bottom of a small depression. The vegetation was rather thick around there, at least for three quarters of the year, until the leaves started to fall. It must have served as a sort of protective screen for the house, making it practically invisible to the other cottages and stables.

In addition it was the cottage closest, as the crow flies, to the fence marking the border, which around there blended in with the woods.

It was also the house farthest from the border guard station, thought Stefania.

A short distance to one side of the cottage, another thin strip of woods led towards the steep slope of the valley, which at certain points plunged straight down in sheer drops to the torrent below. Apparently there were no mule tracks or trails connecting the house to the other cottages, or at least not according to the map. Whereas on the side of the torrent you had to be a goat to manage it.

There probably used to be a footpath, Stefania concluded, perhaps a small one now forgotten.

It occurred to her how some things can be imperceptible when seen close up and then emerge as plain as day when seen from a different perspective.

Her meditations were interrupted by Beethoven, third-millennium version.

"Mommy! Did you hear the ringtone I put on your phone? Martina changed it for me. She said it's called *Elise.*"

"It's called *Für Elise*, as far as that goes, but don't tell me you called me just to tell me that."

"No, I wanted to tell you that I also changed my own ringtone and that they charged me five euros for it and so—"

"So they used up your recharge money. Well, it doesn't matter, you'll just have to economize. What's the problem, Cami?"

"That's just it. Is it a problem for you if I call Papa?"

"Of course not, every so often. Okay, bye, love. I'll see you this evening."

"No, wait, Mommy: I invited Vale to come with us."

"You invited Vale? To come where? Sunday's a holiday, and we're leaving tonight to go and stay three days with Grandma."

"In fact I told her that if she stays the night with us tonight and part of tomorrow, we'll take her to Gravedona ourselves."

"Gravedona?"

"That's where her grandparents live."

"Naturally. Couldn't you have told me this before? Just to let me know? Is her mother okay with this, at least?"

"Of course. We called her and she said it was okay with her if it was okay with you. Could we lend Vale some of my pajamas?"

"So you're not coming with me to Tata Lucia's tonight?"

"But Tata Lucia's such a bore, Mommy! She always asks me the same things: How old are you? What grade are you in? How's your grandma doing? Anyway, she's so deaf she won't even notice."

"She may be deaf, but she can see just fine, and she'll be sorry not to see you. Anyway, I think she has a present for you."

"No problem, Mommy. She can give it to you to give to me. All right?"

Stefania started laughing.

"Okay, okay. Just be sure the two of you are ready by five. We'll be leaving right away, because there'll be traffic."

"Bye, Mommy."

Stefania looked at her watch: it was almost two thirty. At three there would be the annual office party at the commissioner's, as usual a few days before the actual holiday. She had barely enough time to change into her uniform.

"Marino!" she called over the internal line. "Come upstairs for a minute, would you? I want to give you something, and I need somebody to make the knot in my tie."

The cell phone rang again. GIULIO ALLEVI, read the display.

"Hi, Giulio. Of course I'm coming. As if I had the option to turn down the invitation. Okay, you can tell me everything later. No, I'm not in a bad mood. Maybe it's because of the hors d'oeuvres. You know I can't stand them."

The lobby was mobbed. After meting out handshakes and smiles, she'd almost made it to the other end of the hall, where she could nonchalantly position herself right next to the emergency exit. By now she was familiar with the ceremony and knew well that once the commissioner had made his speech of greeting, most of her colleagues would throng around him to pay their respects. The rest of the crowd, however, preferred taking up positions around the buffet table. Stefania was hoping to seize the right moment to get out of there as quickly as possible.

She felt someone take her by the arm.

"Ciao, Inspector, you look quite fetching in uniform. You should wear it more often."

Giulio did it on purpose, knowing full well that Stefania couldn't stand wearing a uniform.

"You're right: I look good in blue, and it's so comfortable."

"Have you looked at the program I sent you of the course?"

"Looks nice. And Amalfi must be glorious in spring."

"But you're not coming."

"What am I supposed to do, drop everything, my daughter included?"

"Is it that you can't or you won't?"

At that moment the commissioner appeared. Stefania made a sign to Giulio.

Good, she thought. The moment has come.

Then, before her colleague could resume the discussion, she slipped behind a couple of other coworkers.

Happy Easter, dear Giulio.

She dashed back to her office to change. Luckily she didn't run into anyone. At that moment she saw a huge bouquet of orange roses. Giulio's card, unsigned, said only: *Happy Easter. I'll wait for you. In Amalfi or somewhere else.*

Why do you do this, Giulio?

You make everything more difficult.

～

The lake road was more unpredictable than the London weather.

To travel the distance from her house in Como to Ossuccio,

where her mother and three aunts lived, it could take Stefania anywhere from thirty-five minutes to an hour and a half, especially if she got stuck behind a truck or camper or bus at one of the narrow points in the road.

That day everything went quite smoothly. They left at five thirty sharp and got to Ossuccio at seven, having made a long stop for hot chocolate and *maritozzi*[3] for the girls at the Pasticceria Manzoni in Menaggio and then backtracking.

After dropping off the girls, the cat, and the luggage at her mother's, she headed off for her tata's house.

The timetable at Tata Lucia's house had been a very rigid one for at least the past sixty years: dinner at seven o'clock sharp in summer and six thirty in winter. Everything had to be washed and put away—dishes, pots, and pans—by nine thirty, because by ten o'clock the three sisters were already in bed, after reciting a decade of the rosary.

Their home was in the center of town, inside an intricate labyrinth of little streets and densely packed houses. Stefania headed up the steep cobblestone streets on foot, laden with parcels and victuals of every sort.

Every time she went to see her former nanny she felt like she was going back in time: the same stone walls, the same inner courtyards paved in gray flagstones, the little cellar windows with cross-shaped iron bars, and the smell of must, mildew, and dampness that reminded her of the places of her childhood.

For years she'd been in the habit of always giving the same presents: Chicco d'Oro coffee beans, felt slippers, floral-print aprons, helanca stockings, Virginia-brand amaretti, rhubarb candies, hairnets, and barrettes. All things that you could no longer find at the supermarket.

Sliding open the bolt of the little gate, she went into the courtyard and headed for the kitchen, which was on the ground floor. It was all open, as usual, as it had always been. When, in the spring, the sisters worked in the garden behind the house, the kitchen would remain closed, but the key was always there, over the door.

"Come, it's all ready," said Zia Pina, standing at the stove. "Look who's here, Milin, it's Stefania. You go out now," she said to the old house cat.

Zia Ermellina, whom they called Milin, could hardly see and was almost always seated beside the fireplace, reciting litanies or listening to Radio Maria. On rare occasions one saw her in the courtyard under the pergola, with the cat, from whom she was never far apart.

Stefania took a long glance at the old house, then looked over at her aunts. She wished she could freeze that moment so she could come back to that haven of peace whenever she wanted.

"So, Stefania, how are you?" Zia Pina began. "And how old's your little girl now? What grade is she in?"

After the perch risotto, they would inevitably have cheese from the local mountain farms, some steamed vegetables, and stewed pears.

"Did you make me stewed fruit?"

Zia Pina nodded, smiling through her wrinkles.

After dinner she helped her aunts unwrap presents and then sat down beside the fire. Milin was dozing off. Tata Lucia's hearing aid was screeching a little.

"Tata, look at this photograph. Can you tell me who these people are? I don't know them," said Stefania, showing her the photo she'd taken from Raffaella's desk.

Lucia put her glasses on, looked carefully, and exclaimed: "*Ossignur de Còmm!*" Then she started naming them one by one.

"These are the *sciuri* Cappelletti! This is Caterina, the mother, who died after the war from a heart attack. This is poor Remo, her husband. This instead is Margherita, the youngest daughter. Look how pretty she is, she was still wearing braids and woolen stockings. And this one in the back is Giovanni, the son, Margherita's brother, before he married the *francesa*."

"And who are the others?" Stefania asked, starting to take notes in a small agenda.

"This is Battista, the other son. Poor thing, he wasn't completely normal. He had the falling sickness, but he never hurt anyone. And this, I think, is Maria, the eldest daughter, the one who never married.

"How many children did they have in all?"

"Well, things certainly weren't the way they are now. Caterina *had made* six or seven, but some of them died, and even I lost track. Remo would stay away for months at a time and when he came home, you know how it is, the boys and girls would come as fast as the good Lord could send 'em."

"And they all lived at Villa Regina?"

"No, Caterina didn't want to stay at the villa because she said it was jinxed. She was always up in the old house with Battista, who nobody wanted at the villa because he yelled when he talked. The daughter-in-law, the *francesa*, used to say he should be put in an asylum, but Caterina wouldn't allow it. She loved Battista."

"Why did she say it was jinxed?"

"Because of the girl who died there, Margherita. After that happened, Remo was never the same again. Poor Caterina, she saw her own daughter and husband die and then died herself from grief."

"What happened to Margherita? She was still young."

"She wasn't yet twenty-two when she died. She was the only one who got along with the French girl because they were about the same age. During the years Giovanni was engaged to her, the *francesa* would come and spend summers at the villa, and the two girls, Margherita and the *francesa*, would always be together. The young lady taught her how to curl her hair and wear silk stockings and tight skirts like her."

Whenever Zia Lucia would say "the young lady" or the "*francesa*" or the "French girl" she would wrinkle her nose and gesticulate.

"I guess you never liked the *francesa*, eh?"

"I was just there to iron clothes and keep to myself. But it's true, the young lady used to give herself such airs with her silk undies and her embroidered linen sheets. . . . Nothing was ever good enough for her."

"In what sense?"

"On the day her dowry arrived from France, they needed three porters to unload the truck. She had just got there and already she wanted to change the curtains, the wallpaper, everything. A week later she called the Bargna people to have them build a personal bathroom for her in her bedroom."

"But the house wasn't hers yet."

"I'm telling you, that girl was born to give orders. And to think there was even a moment when it seemed like the marriage was going to go up in smoke!"

"What happened?" Stefania asked, curious.

Her auntie lowered her voice as if there were someone

around who might hear them. Milin, meanwhile, was sleeping on the ottoman and gently snoring, while Pina was still busy washing the dishes rigorously by hand.

"Look, nobody ever told me anything. But when Margherita died people started talking a lot in town. You know the type, the ones who want to make trouble at all costs, envious people. It was wartime and there were other things to think about. But those ones always had time to speak ill of others."

Stefania waited for Zia Lucia to finish her little rant and get to the point.

"In short, there was sort of a scandal, and the young lady didn't come that summer. Her excuse was that the roads weren't safe. A pack of lies, I say—she just wanted to wait and see how things settled down before marrying into the family."

A brief pause before continuing.

"But the stuff was there," she said, rubbing her index and middle fingers against her thumb, "enough to tempt even a snob like her."

"How did Margherita die?"

Her aunt lowered her voice.

"They never really found out. They brought her home in a closed coffin, and nobody was ever allowed to see her, not even the town doctor. They said the sight was too awful. Poor Margherita, she was so beautiful!"

Stefania started to grow impatient.

"But what happened to her?"

"Some people said the partisans killed her, up in the mountains. Others said it was the Germans. Who'll ever know? But from that day on, Remo, who was the head of the family, went insane, talking to himself, going up the mountain and calling Margherita's name, and he always went around in his shirtsleeves, rain or shine. He seemed crazier than Battista. And then one night he fell. . . . The bad luck of that man . . ."

Lucia wiped away a tear.

"Starting the very next day, the young lady took control of everything, even though the house belonged to the Cappellettis. Giovanni had a heart of gold and let her give the orders. She had Battista put in an asylum when his mother, Caterina, was already hospitalized, and they never even told her. Then Caterina died. And not even a year after Remo died, they got married. You tell me if there's any respect for the dead anymore."

Zia Pina called out from the kitchen:

"Stefanina, would you like some coffee?"

This was the signal that the evening was drawing to a close, because anise-flavored coffee always represented the official ending of their social encounters.

Stefania took advantage of the final moments to explore a question that had caught her attention.

"You said Remo fell, if I understood correctly."

"Yes. With him always roaming about up the mountain, day and night, in the rain and in the snow, one morning they brought him home dead. He'd slipped down the cliffside to the torrent. Maybe he hit his head, I don't know. But when we dressed him up his head was all wrapped. He was a great big man who'd withered to skin and bones."

"I wrote you a note, Stefanina," said Zia Pina, taking away the espresso cups.

"What about, Pina?"

"Didn't you ask me for the Cappellettis' telephone number? You should call Armando, who's the caretaker, and make arrangements with him. But call him early in the morning, because by six thirty he's already outside."

"Before six thirty on a holiday?"

Pina gave her a reproachful look.

"The cows have to be milked every day, including Easter," she said, setting down a small chocolate bunny with a bell. "This is for your little girl," she added, holding out a packet of Lindor chocolate as well, "and this is for your mother."

She headed off for her parents' house, where her mother was waiting for her in front of the TV set. The girls were still playing with the cat, for whom they'd built a sort of little house out of a cardboard box. The only problem was that Ron didn't want to hear about going inside it.

Feeling overwhelmed with fatigue, she went out on the terrace. It was pitch-black outside. A very fine freezing rain was falling. It felt almost like melted snow.

She turned up her jacket collar and, shuddering, went back inside.

She thought about the evening she'd just had.

On the way back from her visit with her aunts she'd driven along one side of the park of Villa Regina.

On that side, which jutted out a bit with respect to the main entrance, there was a small iron gate that she couldn't remember ever having seen open, not even when she was a child. In autumn she and the other children in town used to pass by often. They would go there after a strong wind had been blowing, because there was a chance they would find hazelnuts and chestnuts fallen from the centuries-old trees inside the park.

She looked out her window again: the rain was still coming down, inexorably.

An image came back to her, of a man wandering in the rain oblivious to the fact that he was soaked and chilled, a man who could think only of his Margherita. He looked for her every-where, but she was gone, and that great house seemed more and more hostile to him with each passing day.

Till tomorrow, Villa Regina, she said to herself before getting into bed.

6

~~

The following morning, voice still hoarse with sleep, she remembered Tata Lucia's recommendation: to call Armando. She felt uneasy: she wasn't in the habit of importuning people at that hour.

Summoning her courage, she decided to try anyway. It was seven A.M.

When somebody finally picked up at the other end, she felt as if she'd tapped into an anthill at rush hour. In very quick succession her call was passed on to first the greenhouse, and then the stables.

"Armando was here, but he's over with the horses now. Try again later."

A booming voice then emerged from the background.

Stefania looked at her watch, feeling the need for a coffee.

"Hello, Signor Armando, my name is Stefania Valenti—yes, Pina's niece, the one who works for the police."

"What do you need, signora?" the man asked brusquely.

"I would like to meet with Signora Cappelletti, Germaine Cappelletti, for an informal chat."

"The signora will be coming to see the horses this morning at nine. I'll tell her myself. I give you an answer this afternoon. Call me around two, at this other number."

"You're very kind, thank you."

After taking down the man's cell phone number, Stefania lay back down in bed for a spell. But she was no longer sleepy. In the end she got up, went into the kitchen, and made coffee.

The scent filled the whole house. Her mother was still asleep. Stefania would never admit it, not even if tortured, but she was tense.

She looked out the window.

It was already getting light. The sun had just popped out from behind the Legnone. The lake looked calm, the mountains dark in the background. A light fog was floating just above the surface of the water, and there was deep silence all around. A clear sky, cleansed by the rain, promised a beautiful day.

The girls were also still asleep. They would be allowed to stay in bed as long as they wanted that day, to play and chatter.

She put on an old pair of jeans and a cable-knit sweater, small boots, and a striped scarf. She left a note for her mother saying *I'll be back soon,* and went out.

Twenty minutes later, after passing through Ossuccio, she was at the Sport Bar of Lenno, a beautiful café with tables outside, right on the lakefront. You could smell the scent of freshly made pastries from the street. She sat outside, with the *Corriere di Como* folded on her lap, distractedly watching the early tourists strolling along the lakeshore.

She finally felt like she had some time to herself, and it was a nice feeling. She had nothing to do until at least ten thirty. Almost three hours. An eternity, compared to her usual rhythms.

She ordered an apple *sfogliatina* and half closed her eyes like a cat, watching from a short distance away the hydroplane *Voloire*, which was engaged in docking maneuvers at the pier opposite the Hotel San Giorgio. Five people came out, a family, consisting of father, mother, and two small children—clearly foreigners, probably British—and a solitary passenger.

She was about to light her first Muratti of the day when she was overwhelmed by a gust of chill air that smelled of cologne. She looked up distractedly.

"Inspector, what are you doing here at this hour of the morning?" said a familiar voice.

"I could ask you the same thing. I'm practically at home here."

If she hadn't already seen him more than once, she would have had trouble recognizing him in his corduroy knee-length shorts, blue sweater, and checked shirt, with a camera slung across his chest.

But behind the rectangular lenses of his glasses his teasing, dark eyes were still the same, as was the elusive smile.

"What are you doing by the lake all dressed up like a scout, Valli?" Stefania asked with a smile.

"To tell you the truth, I've just escaped from boarding school."

"Off the balcony down a rope made of bedsheets tied together, that sort of thing?"

"More or less. We had a rather eventful evening yesterday at the association's headquarters."

"I see. So your only option was to flee out the window."

"Exactly. And my escape was a success, mostly because I turned off my cell phone. A true liberation. Nobody—except you—knows I'm here. And I don't want to hear from anyone about anything, at least not until Tuesday. Nothing but hikes in the mountains until then."

A pause. Then Stefania, with a spontaneity that almost surprised even her, pushed out the chair beside her.

"You can count on my discretion, unless there's a big bounty on your head. Care for a coffee before you head up the mountain? The apple *sfogliatine* here are out of this world . . ."

She stopped, blushing slightly, and said no more. Luca Valli, on the other hand, didn't seem the least bit embarrassed. He took off his backpack, set it down on one of the plastic chairs, and sat down. Then he looked at her and smiled.

"An apple *sfogliatina* is certainly not something to pass up lightly. How are you? You seem well, but if you hadn't turned your head this way, I wouldn't have recognized you. You're a little different from last time."

"Let me tell you something: even police inspectors go on vacation. But you're right about one thing. When I come here my life and mood suddenly change."

"Maybe it's because everything around here is so beautiful. Normally we feel better when we see beautiful things."

Another pause. This time it was Valli who smiled. They both looked out at the lakefront.

The sun was lightening the brown of the still-leafless woods on the other side of the bay, where Villa Balbianello stood.

"You'll be here the whole weekend?" Stefania asked.

"Yes, today we're going up the mountain, and tonight I'll be sleeping at the house of some friends, in Plesio, which is above Menaggio. Tomorrow morning I'll hop on a bus and go up to see my parents in Lanzo. Like a young student. My car is at the mechanic's until Tuesday. And what will you be doing?"

"Oh, me? Nothing, really. I'm at my mother's place with the children. We don't have any precise plans."

Stefania started wondering why, in the presence of this man—who in reality seemed like a boy next to her—she was unable to string together three proper sentences and keep her usual cool. She decided to take matters onto neutral ground. Professional ground.

"Listen, this afternoon I may be going to pay a call on Signora Cappelletti . . ."

"Really? Well done, Inspector. It's not so easy for the rest of us to be received by someone in the family. You must have a saint in heaven looking after you."

"I certainly do, and a very powerful one: my tata Lucia and her two sisters, who are almost a hundred years old."

Valli laughed. Stefania thought he became handsome when he laughed. His face brightened and he looked like a little boy.

"But aside from the indubitable pleasure of speaking with Madame Cappelletti, hopefully in French, what do you expect to gain from the encounter? If I remember correctly, the last time we spoke you were concerned with a corpse that was found in a mountain cottage."

"And you're wondering what the connection is between the two things, is that right?"

"Yes. I was wondering that even when you came to talk to me at the association."

"It's just a feeling I have. A sense of smell. Feminine intuition, perhaps. At some point in this affair I started thinking that there had to be a connection between the family that owned the villa and the young man who was killed in that cottage. I don't know why— I mean, I don't know yet, but I can sense it. Bearing in mind of course that the family also owns the cottage in question, and therefore wanting to know what they know is . . ."

"All in the line of duty?"

"Exactly. Actually, I could have called them in for questioning, but I'm convinced that not only would they not have come but they would have sent me the usual insufferable lawyer to tell me the usual things—namely, that the family has no connection to the affair and so on. I would rather see them up close and hear them speak. And provoke them, if necessary. A little improvisation, in short, without too much advance planning."

Valli looked at her, nodded, and said nothing.

They sat there gazing at the lake and the lakefront promenade, which was slowly coming to life. The first tourists. Families with children. Some elderly nuns, all hunched.

The blare of a horn interrupted that moment of pleasant absorption. An SUV had pulled up in front of the café.

"Here are my friends to pick me up, Inspector. I'm going to go say hello to them and then head up to take some pictures of a church at the top of the mountain, but I'll probably go up there alone. They never want to walk anywhere."

"Okay, have a good hike, Valli. See you around."

"See you, Inspector. Have a good weekend."

As the Jeep Cherokee was leaving, a hand waved good-bye out of one of the windows.

⌐

A butler in a white jacket and black trousers came to greet her at the front door.

"Madame is waiting for you, Inspector. Please come in and follow me."

Coming down the majestic allée at the entrance to the property, Stefania had felt as though suspended in air. It was as if she'd been catapulted into a Visconti film or a nineteenth-century French novel. Armando had been faster and more efficient than all of her fellow policemen put together. He'd set up the appointment for five in the afternoon. Teatime.

Following the butler's elegant caracoles, Stefania passed through silent rooms and anterooms on the ground floor, then ascended an imperious marble staircase to the second floor. She crossed a splendid veranda, then a sort of glass gallery open onto the lake, and finally came to a small sitting room hung with pale green floral silk.

"Please make yourself comfortable. Madame will be with you momentarily."

Left alone, Stefania looked around. In contrast to the severity of the ground-floor rooms, which were monumental but a bit cold, the space she was in now was warm and welcoming, with a few small armchairs in soft colors, a low table covered with small silver-framed portraits, and generally lovely furnishings. A few white gardenias faced out from a cachepot on the side of the room closest to an enormous lighted fireplace.

She went over to the window, which gave onto an interior courtyard, a sort of small, rectangular cloister with slender columns. Everything was centered around a fountain in the middle, half hidden behind some boxwood hedges.

That part of the villa seemed uninhabited: all the windows on the courtyard side were shuttered. And the hedges around the fountain looked like they hadn't been pruned for ages. Only a trained eye could perceive, at various points, a complex geometric design of wedge shapes in sequence and intersecting—juxtaposed triangles, perhaps, or stars. She had a sense of déjà vu: the design was in some way familiar to her, as if it reminded her of something she'd seen before.

She went back to the fireplace and stood there warming her hands before a blazing log. Oak, no doubt. At that moment she noticed the painting hanging over the fireplace, in a splendid gilt frame. It so struck her that she had to put her glasses on to examine it better, from up close. She was so engrossed she didn't notice that a door had opened behind her.

"Do you like it? It's an old family memento," said a voice at her back.

Germaine Durand must have been a rather attractive woman in her youth.

Slender, above average in height, and haughty, still today. Her eyes were a rather unusual shade of blue.

Okay, down to business, thought Stefania, absorbing without blinking the condescending gaze of those two eyes, which looked her up and down in an instant. The woman was leaning on a cane, but her character must have been the same as in her prime.

"Do you like Paris in autumn, my dear?"

"Yes, though sometimes it seems sad to me, or maybe just a little too black and white. Like Venice with its canals, really."

"Not everyone who comes into this room sets his eyes on that painting."

"Let's just say it's not every day that you get to see a Sisley from up close. Outside of a museum, I mean."

Madame Durand fell silent and observed her some more, this time with interest, as though sizing her up. She seemed stunned, but wasn't the type to let it show. Stefania turned again momentarily towards the painting, for the specific purpose of letting herself be observed. Then she said:

"Thank you for agreeing to see me today. I hope I haven't

disturbed you. I only wanted to ask you a few questions. Grant me ten minutes, and I'll leave you to your family."

Madame Durand proceeded as if Stefania hadn't spoken.

"There are other such paintings in the house, but this one was my father's favorite. He never wanted to resell it after buying it at auction in Berlin. He turned down every offer, even by our best clients. And so, in the end, it stayed here. In the family, so to speak."

Stefania wondered what she'd meant by that last comment, since she knew that the family didn't actually live at the villa. But she didn't say anything. There was no point in pressing Madame, since, at any rate, she would say only what she had in mind to say.

Madame Cappelletti sat down in an armchair, adjusted the shawl over her shoulders, and gestured to Stefania to sit down in the chair facing her. Then, in a tone of polite detachment, she asked:

"What did you want to ask me, Inspector?"

The scorn she put into her utterance of the word "Inspector" was the first sign that a clash was imminent.

"I believe you were informed that about ten days ago, during the demolition of a ruined cottage on your property in the San Primo area, around the worksite for the construction of a tunnel through the mountain pass, some human remains were found that we haven't identified yet."

"Yes, the caretaker mentioned that to me. But he also said that it would all be properly taken care of."

Properly, thought Stefania: an adverb that Carboni would have approved of.

"If you're referring to the fact that the remains have been reassembled and taken to the ossuary of the Lanzo cemetery, then, yes, I think it's been properly taken care of. Now we're trying to give the lad a name."

"Lad?"

"Yes, Madame. A young man, in all likelihood. Do you know the spot where we found him—that is, the cottage and its surroundings?"

"Not really. Actually, not at all. It's been years since my legs allowed me to do what I would like to do. So you can imagine how often I go up the mountain. . . . My husband was always the one looking after that land and anything else to do with his family's possessions. He, the family business manager, and our caretaker. I never got much involved with any of that, I must say."

Stefania took note of the way she said "his family," referring to the Cappellettis.

"Have you never seen those other properties?"

"Just a few. When the kids were small they used to spend part of the summer holidays here. During excursions to the Sighignola we would sometimes stop at one cottage or another for a glass of water."

"But the cottage in question wasn't on that road."

"I repeat, I really don't know those areas well. Cottages, huts, ruins—for me they're all the same. I don't think I can be of much use to you, I'm sorry. Perhaps Armando, our caretaker, is the best person for you to talk to. He knows these mountains well, he's always lived here, and he's been working for our family for more than thirty years. You should see what he has to say, if you wish. By this hour he should already be back at the villa."

Her assertion had a tone of politeness and dismissal at once.

"Yes, that would be helpful, thank you."

"Good. Then I'll send for him. Would you like a coffee in the meanwhile?"

"With pleasure," Stefania replied, not too certain whether she'd opened a breach in the woman's defenses.

Madame rang the kitchen and ordered them to serve coffee. Then, with the pager, she called the caretaker.

"Armando, would you be so kind as to come up into the green sitting room? Yes, right now, thank you."

Madame spoke somewhat softly, and in a gentle tone, and yet every word, every phrase, sounded like an order. Essentially her every gesture conveyed authority, a familiarity with power. Her tone was one that allowed no objections.

A few moments of silence passed.

Stefania turned back towards the painting.

"To return to things of beauty, I can understand how your father, having the good fortune to own something like this, might never want to part with it, preferring to keep it for himself and his loved ones."

"All the same, he surprised everyone when he gave it to my husband's sister. That's why it's here, in Margherita's room, where it's been ever since."

A shudder ran up Stefania's spine.

"So your sister-in-law also loved the French Impressionists?"

"Well, not really. Margherita didn't know anything about the Impressionists when I first met her, but she had an innate sensitivity to beautiful things, and that helped her instinctively to understand art. She *perceived* beauty, if I can put it that way. She was attracted to it. My father was very strict with everyone. But there was something special about her, an innate grace. Something that made all of us fall in love with her the moment we first met her, right here in this room."

Madame Durand fell silent for a moment and looked out the

window. Leaning on her cane, she took one of the portrait frames and handed it to Stefania.

"This is Margherita, in a photo by Hoffmann. She and I were the same age."

Stefania looked at the photograph: a pair of dark eyes looking into the distance, a luminous face framed by chestnut hair hanging loose to the shoulders.

"Her father," continued Madame Durand, "my husband's father, came only once to Geneva, and then, when my father opened his business in Lugano, he used to come into the shop every so often, always alone, and often after closing time. We knew nothing about the family until I came here with my father in the spring of 1943. That was when I met Margherita and Giovanni. This house was very different then."

A housemaid came in and set down a tray with coffee on the small table. Stefania stared at the portrait for a few moments. Margherita had been photographed in a light-colored summer dress and was wearing only one piece of jewelry, a sort of pendant hanging from a ribbon. She looked at it carefully, but the details weren't very visible. It was oval, in all likelihood. Smooth and rather thick. So this elegant girl, portrayed by a famous photographer, was the same girl as in the photo that Raffaella had shown her in the editorial office. But in the photo Stefania was looking at now, she was slightly different, and even more beautiful.

Madame Durand sipped her coffee in silence. Stefania, who would have given anything to continue the conversation, said the first thing that came to mind.

"What a beautiful girl."

"Enchanting."

"With a kind expression."

"Yes. Losing her was a terrible tragedy for all of us."

No dice, thought Stefania, with a sense of disappointment. End of show. She couldn't think of anything appropriate to keep the conversation going.

Madame Durand turned her gaze towards the window. Her eyes seemed to caress the lake.

"Armando," Madame said to the caretaker, who'd just come in, "Inspector Valenti would like some information on the cottage where those mortal remains were found. I haven't dealt with any of that property for many years. Do you know the place?"

"Yes, Madame. It's in an isolated area, practically overhanging the torrent. There isn't even a mule path leading there. Nobody ever passes that way anymore. It's been years. Or maybe a hunter or two, every now and then. As far as I can remember, it's always been like that—a ruin, a few crumbling walls here and there. The woods had covered it up so much that anyone who didn't know about it would never have imagined there was anything there."

"All right," said Stefania in a determined tone, "but up till when was it used? And who used it?"

"Nobody, as far as I can remember. Those cottages and huts up there were only used for summer grazing. Our farmers would take the animals up there in summertime, but the rest of the year they would sit empty. Anyway, that particular cottage, I don't think I ever saw it in one piece, and I've been going by that area for more than thirty years."

Stefania did a mental calculation. The caretaker's memory only went back, at the most, to the early 1970s.

"And before that?"

"You'll have to ask somebody else about that. When I first came to work here in '71, the old caretaker took me around to show me all the huts that were still in use. The ones rented to local peasants. There already wasn't anything there."

"And does the business manager know anything about it?"

"It's only since my husband died that we have someone overseeing the administration of the different properties," Madame Durand intervened. "Before that he saw to everything himself."

Germaine Durand had been following Stefania's conversation with the caretaker with a bored expression, twice looking at the pendulum clock beside the fireplace.

"I guess the former caretaker's been dead for a while," Stefania said with a note of irony in her voice.

"Yes, for more than ten years. Did you know him?"

"No, I just did the math."

Without realizing it, she'd made a faux pas. And a bad one.

Stefania felt as if she were in a blind alley—or rather, that these two people had led her down a blind alley. She smiled, cleared her throat, set the coffee cup down, and stood up. She cast a last glance at the portrait of Margherita.

"I don't know how to thank you for making yourself available to me, Madame. And for the coffee, too. But now I really must go. Sorry, again, if I inconvenienced you. There are still a few formalities to be finalized, but we can talk next week, if you're going to be in Italy for a few more days yet."

Madame stared at her, then asked in an indifferent tone:

"A few formalities?"

"The usual stuff, paperwork. Required procedure, as we call it. It'll merely involve signing a statement declaring you have no idea who the person found in the cottage might be. Inspector Carboni might even have you look at a few objects. Formalities, in short."

"Objects?" asked Madame Durand.

Stefania realized that the fish was finally biting, and she congratulated herself for her well-calculated bluff. Were Carboni to find out, he would certainly give her a tongue lashing.

"Some of the man's personal effects, found with his remains. No cause for any concern, of course."

Germaine Durand eyed her with an indecipherable expression.

"We're at your disposal, Inspector. See you soon."

The butler saw her to the door. Armando, in the meanwhile, had stopped off in the study, together with the lady of the house.

You'll see me soon, all right, Madame, thought Stefania. You can be sure about that.

7

When she came through the front door it was past seven thirty.

"Where've you been?" said Camilla. "We've already had dinner."

Camilla and her friend Valentina were playing video games lying on the rug in their little bedroom, amid an indescribable chaos of clothes and shoes.

"I thought you were having a clothes war. Too bad, because I brought you these," she said, showing the boxes with pizza. "I guess me and Grandma will have to eat them ourselves."

"Pizza? I guess we could still have a taste. Well, not me, but let Vale have a taste, because I think Nutella for dinner is something new for her. Okay, Mommy?"

"Okay, I'll get it ready in the kitchen."

"Can't we eat it in here, so we can keep playing?"

"Cami, the only thing that's missing in this room are pizza crumbs and oil stains on the clothes and inside the shoes, then we'll be all set. I'll be waiting for you in the kitchen."

She left the room to keep from laughing, then went into

the kitchen to set the table for four. The moonlight coming in through still-open windows in the hallway sparkled on the surface of the lake, which was stirred up by the wind.

Her mother was in the kitchen watching TV with the sound turned off, the radio on, and the cat dozing on the windowsill. The pans on the stove still gave off a scent of roast beef and potatoes, leftovers from lunch. Stefania lay down on the sofa beside the window, letting her thoughts caress her. She felt serene.

The following day passed quietly.

Late to rise, breakfast with *maritozzi* from the Manzoni bakery in Menaggio—hers plain, the girls' with whipped cream and marrons glacés. Grandma was busy at the oven all morning, preparing a traditional roast lamb with potatoes. The scent of rosemary and garlic filled the kitchen. They all had lunch together and then, before fatigue and sleep got the better of them, they went for a short walk to the little park with tennis courts, where there was a small, charming café. Sitting at a table outside, they watched the motorboats come and go in the lake area between the Isola Comacina, which was right in front of them, and the gulf of Sala Comacina. Guido called to know how things were going and to say hello to his daughter. Later that afternoon they drove Valentina to her grandparents' house in Gravedona, in the Alto Lago district. The drive back was very slow, due to the heavy traffic of tourists' cars that had invaded the local lakeside establishments.

When they got home it was getting dark. Nobody felt hungry for a proper dinner. A cup of broth for everyone, a little chat with Grandma about minor matters in town, while Camilla, who had spent the afternoon running and jumping around, fell asleep in front of the TV with cartoon images on the screen. Stefania struggled to carry her in her arms to her room. Time was flying and Camilla was growing up. In just a few years she would no longer be a little girl.

When she returned to the living room, it was empty. Her mother, too, had gone to bed. The house was now enveloped in silence. It was a good silence, made up of familiar sounds: the ticking of the pendulum clock in the hallway, the drip of the faucet in the kitchen, and, in the distance, the sounds of the valley, which during the day were drowned out by the noisy bustle of the household.

The bells began to ring at the sanctuary of the Madonna del Soccorso, which stood on a nearby hilltop and was reachable only on foot, by way of a tortuous path dotted with Stations of the Cross, one of the most ancient Sacri Monti in northern Italy and a destination for tourists and the devout in all seasons. Stefania counted the chimes and was surprised to learn how late it was. It was Easter, but for who knew what reason it made her think of midnight Mass on Christmas Eve.

For years Stefania had been promising herself to go to midnight Mass. But with each passing year she postponed it, perhaps because going to midnight Mass alone was like admitting one's own failings.

This time, however, was different. She no longer had any doubts.

This year, I really will go, come hell or high water. This was her last thought before falling asleep.

Easter Monday morning arrived without any hurry.

Camilla would be going to see Monica, a friend from elementary school who lived a short distance away in Ossuccio. She wouldn't come home until late afternoon, and for once it would be her friend's parents bringing her back.

Stefania got up late and was in a good mood that morning.

After seeing to her household chores, she looked in the closet for her Invicta backpack. She made a sandwich and grabbed an apple, a pair of binoculars, a novel by Camilleri, and a pack of Muratti Lights. She went out to the section of the street that led uphill, taking a small path that cut through the planted fields behind the house, and went up towards the Sacro Monte.

Halfway up she stopped for a moment to take in the lake and the mountains. From that height she could see the *presqu'île* of the middle basin from Lezzeno to Bellagio. She could clearly make out the Ponte del Diavolo and the secluded Villa Lucertola below it, and then, towards Bellagio, the Villa Melzi d'Eril, and the Spartivento point that divided the lake into its two main bodies.

Past Bellagio, on the Lecco side, she could just glimpse Varenna and, a short distance to the north, the mountains of Valtellina and their pure-white glaciers. To the south, on "her" side, lay the tiny Isola Comacina, the monumental Lavedo di Lenno, a sort of natural promontory that hid Villa Balbianello from view. Reinvigorated by this natural spectacle in all its splendor, she instinctively headed for the trail to San Benedetto.

She knew the trail well, having traveled it many times in the past. And every time she did, once she rounded the corner of the rocky ridge plunging straight down into the valley, she would stop and admire the stark and vaguely sinister silhouette of the Santuario della Madonna del Soccorso, just above.

That day the church's silhouette against the spring light looked to her like some sort of miracle. She closed the top button of her jacket and resumed her climb. She didn't feel tired. In fact, she felt as if she were gaining strength and youth at each new turn.

A little more than an hour later, she'd reached her destination. Sitting down in the sun in a clearing near the church, she rested her back against the outer stones of the apse, which were as ancient as the mountains themselves.

She savored the silence of the place, quietly collecting herself, inhaling the scent of resin from the woods behind her. The dry heat of the stone, the sharp profile of the stone-tiled roof—everything in this secluded place called to mind a distant past, and one could easily lose oneself in it, cradled in that evocation of remote epochs. The peace of such places penetrated to the innermost regions of her soul.

For years she'd felt an unspeakable aversion to crowded churches on high holy days, with the people all noisily gathered in the churchyard, and the bother of having to say hello, smile, and listen to anecdotes she cared nothing about. All the distraction made it hard to collect herself. On the other hand, whenever she had the chance she would go up to the Madonna del Soccorso, where a sixty-year-old priest would say Mass to some fifteen or so people. Collecting herself in meditation felt natural to her in such a place, perhaps because the long climb up the Sacro Monte put her in a state where she felt like a pilgrim from some past century, or more simply because the place and the austerity of the church made it impossible to feel otherwise.

San Benedetto was instead a sort of piece of the Middle Ages that had remained intact into the twenty-first century. It celebrated Mass only once a year, due precisely to the secluded site where it had been built many centuries ago, right in the middle of the valley, squeezed between two mountains in absolute silence.

Only the sound of cowbells in the distance, or sometimes of ax blows or, in summer, of sickles, and a few lone voices in the fields and huts, shepherds calling their dogs, laughter along the footpaths . . . But these things did not disturb; on the contrary, they kept you company. As her father had once said many years earlier: "In these mountains you're never alone, and never shoulder to shoulder."

Stefania remained engrossed in the silence for a few minutes, eyes closed, feeling the sun on her skin, smelling the chimney smoke coming from who knew what refuge. She was just about to nod off when she heard some hurried steps behind her. Before she knew what was happening she found a yellow Labrador jumping all over her noisily, sniffing her neck and trying to open her backpack with its paws.

She'd never been afraid of dogs. And the animals realized this and let her pet them. This one, however, though perfectly harmless like all Labradors, was too large a specimen to be wandering around alone without a leash.

"Tommy! Tommy!" she heard its owner calling.

The voice was familiar, and when Tommy's owner appeared at the edge of the clearing, Stefania recognized him at once. After all, if she'd headed off for San Benedetto, there must have been a reason, however unconscious. She started to walk away. She didn't want it to look as if she'd gone in that direction in the hopes of meeting anyone.

"Don't be afraid, he won't harm you. Don't worry."

It was too late to leave. She had to stop and turn around.

"Good morning, Valli. Long time no see. I think maybe it's time we dropped the formalities . . ."

He smiled in shock, seeming happy to see her.

"Good morning. What are you doing out this way?"

"I could ask you the same thing."

They looked at each other and started laughing, remembering the words they'd exchanged at the café opposite the pier.

"Still running off, I see."

"Now I'll stop for a spell. Tommy was the only one who wanted to come out with me today, but he's made me run the whole way. I'm out of breath."

He took off his backpack and sat down beside her, heaving a sigh of relief. Tommy was also tired. Moments later he lay down at their feet, whimpering with satisfaction.

"It's very beautiful here," said Valli.

"Isn't it? I really like it, too. I come here whenever I get the chance—just to think, or just to have a few quiet moments alone."

"So I'm intruding."

"You're not intruding at all, Luca. In fact I'm glad to see you, especially because I'm hoping you have a light."

Valli smiled and took out a box of wooden kitchen matches. Stefania thought again that he had a nice smile. She noticed his hands as he was holding the match: they were large and protective.

They smoked in silence. Then, suddenly, Valli asked:

"Everything okay, Stefania?"

Stefania looked at him with a combination of astonishment and gratitude. In any other circumstance she would have reacted rather stridently to what could have seemed a deliberately nosy question.

Smiling wanly, she replied: "Things could be better, actually."

Valli waited for her to decide to continue.

A few seconds passed, then Stefania added: "At certain points in a person's life, work becomes particularly important—it becomes a kind of acid test, a confirmation of many things, a means of escape. But I don't want to bore you. I'm working on a case at the moment for which no concrete hypothetical solution has emerged yet."

"A normal police detective, Stefania—I mean a good, scrupulous investigator, not a character in some mystery novel—even while doing her job well, that is, in conscientious, dedicated fashion, can still sometimes find herself unable to conceive a solution at the drop of a hat. And sometimes, in professional life, one never actually finds any solution at all, however hard one may try. I don't think there's anything strange or bad about that, do you? And anyway, I doubt it's the only case you have on your hands at the moment."

"There's no lack of scam artists, petty thieves, hoods, and purse snatchers, if that's what you mean. But when faced with someone who was killed, for whom justice was never done, my self-assurance starts to totter a little."

"I don't think it's the first time that's happened in human history. Isn't justice in God's hands, after all?"

"It's also in mine, if you'll forgive the lack of modesty. And I've managed to do absolutely nothing about it so far, and that upsets me. I find it unbearable."

"Are you referring to the case you came to see me about?" asked Valli.

"That's right. A few aspects of the case have been brought to light. But details are useless if you don't have the whole picture. In the present instance, *all* that's missing—so to speak—are three things: who he was, why he was killed, and by whom."

"But the first time we saw each other, actually all you wanted from me was information on the mountain pass project and the family who owned the land where the work is taking place. That means, therefore, that since then, you've been following a specific lead."

"In reality, the initial hypothesis was rather banal: a man's remains were found in a ruined hut privately owned and belonging to a certain family. I tried mostly to figure out whether this family knew anything about the affair and whether they were in some way involved in it. And thanks, in part, to your help, I was able in the end to talk to that family."

"And so . . . ?"

"For the moment the signora hasn't given me any useful information. And so we're back to square one."

"Maybe you're on the wrong track. Maybe the investigation will continue on other fronts—or rather, on *additional* fronts. No?"

"That's precisely the problem. At the moment I have no other leads. And anyway, I'm convinced, you see, that there is *some* relationship between that family and that corpse—a connection, a precise link. I think the family knows more than they're letting on. Just some sixth sense of mine: I can feel it, but I have no proof."

Stefania looked at the sun-caressed valley with a slice of lake in the distance, then said in a soft voice:

"Don't you see? It's as if I already had the pieces to a puzzle in my hands. I have them all, but I have no model to show me how to begin to put it together. What image do I want to reconstruct? Which piece should I start with?"

She fell silent for a moment, as Valli seemed to be thinking. Then she added:

"Sometimes I wonder whether I'm just being presumptuous: a classic case of the detective's delirious sense of omnipotence. Maybe I just like to think that this is really the way it is and I'm unconsciously neglecting to explore other avenues because I know they wouldn't lead anywhere."

The silence was broken only by the sound of a match being

struck. Valli had lit another cigarette. Stefania thought that, for an environmentalist, he really was one of a kind. Then, before even smoking half of it, Valli stubbed it out against a rock and put the butt in a pocket of his backpack. Then he turned to Stefania and said:

"Listen, I know it's none of my business and I shouldn't meddle, and of course I would never presume to give you any advice. However, if I were you, I would move a little on all fronts, without, however, neglecting the lead you're already following, and without ruling out any of the others. I would cast a very wide net, in short, in the hope that the fish you're seeking will sooner or later end up in it."

Without realizing it, Valli had lightly grazed the back of Stefania's hand.

"For example, I would dig further into the local history of that time: look at newspapers, archives, city hall, records offices, parish archives. The family is well known. The whole area must have been shaken up a few times by newsworthy occurrences, if only because it was simultaneously a theater of partisan struggle and, being a border region, a nucleus for smuggling and refugees. Something of note must certainly have happened. For example, there were some barracks for *repubblichini*[4] and Germans, representatives of the regime; they surely must have left some souvenirs, however horrific. Then you should start looking for people who still remember that period, living witnesses. They'll all be over eighty, but there must be some around, after all. People around here live a long time."

Stefania looked at him, and he stopped talking. Then, a bit confusedly, he said:

"I'm sorry, I got carried away, I let my enthusiasm get the better of me."

"You're really something, you know, Valli," Stefania said, smiling. "I'm glad I met you, I mean it. And now I guess I should thank you. But, please, let's change the subject. Would you like half a prosciutto sandwich, for example?"

"I'll gladly trade it for this half sandwich of leftover roast and mayonnaise and a tangerine."

"Getting into the refined stuff, I see. Okay, then, I'll make it up to you by telling you everything I know about this church, so that next time you'll think twice about following me."

"But I didn't follow you. It was Tommy who found you."

⌒

"Why do I *have* to go to school? I've been going to school for so long, I'm tired of it. Why should anyone have to go to school after they've learned how to read and write?" complained Camilla.

"What are you talking about?"

"I'm talking about all the other useless things they make you study."

"So what would you rather do?"

"Certainly not spend my afternoons studying how to find the area of an isosceles triangle."

"Would you rather have a job?"

"No, I'm too little to have a job."

"So if you don't want to study and you don't want to work, what would you like to do? Who's going to support you?"

"What's that got to do with it, Mommy?"

"A lot . . ."

Whenever Camilla returned to her daily routine of school and homework she had trouble getting her bearings back, especially after a vacation. She'd started complaining as soon as the alarm clock went off, and she hadn't stopped for a second. Stefania, between wet laundry, the meowing cat, and the ringing telephone, listened to her with a distracted ear.

"Have you had breakfast?"

"I don't like Mulino Bianco plum cakes."

"Then get something else."

"Like what?"

Stefania looked at her watch. "At this point you can't have anything else. It's too late. Have you brushed your teeth?"

"Not yet."

"Well, what are you waiting for?"

"I was waiting to eat breakfast, obviously."

"You're so pleasant this morning."

"Look who's talking."

For Stefania, too, coming home to Como was always an ordeal.

Suitcases to unpack, a half-empty refrigerator, not knowing whether Martina was coming or going with her university classes . . . Life as usual, in short, starting up again.

They slipped into the downtown traffic and got to Camilla's school a split second before the first bell.

"Don't forget to come pick me up this afternoon!"

"Bye, love. Hugs and kisses."

Entering her office, she tossed her purse onto the chair, cast a glance at the metal in-box, then picked up the phone.

"Ciao, Raffaella, this is Stefania. I need a big favor from you—I need to consult your archive. Local news from the thirties to the fifties, more or less."

"Is that all?" asked Raffaella in a mocking tone. "What about the Vatican Archives, and the gestapo's?"

"If you also have a historical photo archive, I'd like to look at that, too. And I could also use a list of the associations and foundations that collect the testimonies of survivors, partisan fighters, ex-military types . . ."

"What's got into you this morning, darling? The Easter holiday didn't do you any good, I'm afraid. Take a deep breath and tell me clearly exactly what you need. We can't very well go digging randomly. The archive is endless."

"Shall we meet at your office in an hour?" asked Stefania.

"Yes. Coffee and brioches for me, thanks."

Raffa laughed and hung up, giving her no time to reply. They could understand each other with a mere gesture or inflection of the voice.

Stefania went down to the bar behind headquarters. She'd never seen it so crowded. After a cigarette with Marino, at nine thirty she headed for the editorial offices of *La Provincia di Como*. She was almost in a good mood, but didn't know why.

Raffaella was waiting for her at her computer. It was ten o'clock.

"Alone?" asked Stefania.

"The others never come in before the editorial meeting at ten thirty."

She told her everything calmly, trying to proceed in orderly fashion. She left out a few details, such as her encounter with Valli.

Raffaella listened attentively, but when Stefania had finished her account, she remained rather unusually silent, as though perplexed.

"Well?" asked Stefania. "Why are you making that face?"

"I'm happy to lend you a hand, it's the least I can do. But I get the impression that you're floundering a little. I don't get exactly what it is you're looking for."

"Shall we start with the archive?" asked Stefania.

"The eighties?"

"No, earlier."

"How much earlier?"

"The thirties and forties. Weren't you listening when I told you over the phone?"

"It's all on paper. In those days they made bound volumes of I don't know how many editions. Great big tomes."

"So you're saying I should pitch a tent in the square outside."

"Come on, let's go down into the main archive. All we've got on this floor are the last twenty years."

8

Stefania started with the bound volumes of the first few months of 1935. After just a few minutes, she went on to the following months in rapid succession: 1935, 1936. As the hours went by, history passed under her fingers—history with a small *h*, that of the provinces, and real History, that of Fascist Italy, as seen from a peripheral, privileged point of view. She turned the pages one by one, went through each edition, casting a quick glance only at the front page and those concerning the lake and the surrounding valleys.

July 17, 1936: A leading article on the Spanish Civil War. *"Fascist Youth Games at Menaggio Attended by His Excellency the Prefect."* The death in prison of the notorious Clemente Malacrida, nicknamed Ul Màtt, the Madman, king of the local contraband circuit.

January 11, 1937: The economic crisis reaches the textile industry, all the fault of the sanctions against Italy following the Declaration of Empire. Parade of Youth Brigades of young Italian women at Lanzo for the anniversary of the founding of

Rome. Housing crisis. Great public works celebrate the glory of the regime: inauguration yesterday of the Casa della Madre e del Bambino. Inauguration of the offices of the Fascist Union of Industrial Workers. New barracks for the Fascist militia at Cernobbio: group photo in front of a bust of the Duce. Replacement of the old nineteenth-century cars of the funicular. After two years of state collections, Como figured among the top Italian cities for donating gold to the Fatherland. The new urban development plan: hygienic reclamation of the Cortesella finally under way.

January 11, 1938: The race laws.

June 10, 1940: Italy enters the war.

Stefania gave a start when her cell phone started ringing. It was Raffaella.

"You're still there? Do you know what time it is?"

"I've just started the forties. We just went to war in the last issue."

"Think we can manage to eat a sandwich before they start shooting, darling? I doubt you're going to want to stay there till nightfall without ingesting so much as a coffee."

Stefania would gladly have stayed on, but she didn't want to seem impolite. Raffaella had been very nice to help her out.

"I'll be there in five minutes. I would like to get at least to the first microfilmed issues before four o'clock."

"Why, what happens at four o'clock?"

"I have to go pick up Camilla."

"And when do the microfilmed issues start?"

"In 1945, I think."

"So we're all set, then."

Stefania was back hunching over the bound volumes before two o'clock. The lunch break had only made her more restless.

The early war years, 1940–41: Indispensable commodities rise sharply in price. *"Exhibition of Autarchic Radios at the Broletto a Huge Success."* Agreement reached with Swiss customs authorities to suppress illicit traffic across the border; group photo of finance police at the San Primo Pass.

Stefania gave a start, then cast a quick glance at the article, eyes gliding over the page. Nothing of interest. She sighed and kept turning the pages. News on crimes in the areas of concern to her were very rare. She desperately wanted a Muratti but chased the thought from her mind; smoking, at any rate, would not have been possible, especially in that sort of underground bunker.

June 26, 1941: The glorious Sixty-seventh Regiment, back from Albania, on parade in Via Plinio. A number of instigators discovered among the workers at Omita in Albate, order quickly reestablished. Fugitives and deserters arrested at the Italian-Swiss border; numerous Jews arrested with large quantities of gold and precious stones.

She stopped to read the article, which was accompanied by a photo, but it didn't concern the San Primo Pass. Increasingly discouraged, she carried on.

Pages and pages of news from the various war fronts; bread lines; ration cards; increasing difficulties for the population, which was beginning to tighten its belts, notwithstanding the regime and its mouthpieces constantly blaring triumphalist optimism.

Floral festival at Menaggio: Young women of Italy gathered at the picturesque lakeside locale throw flowers at the spectators, a floral homage to the wives of the authorities on the stage.

She was starting to get a backache. She skimmed the pages quickly, reading only the headlines before moving on. She rang headquarters twice to keep abreast of two ongoing investigations.

July 1943: Mussolini deposed.

September 8: Chaos breaks out. Public meeting in Cathedral Square, with prominent anti-Fascists on the stage.

September 12: The Germans invade Como. Large photo of Piazza Cavour and the Hotel Suisse, which has now become the command headquarters of the Wehrmacht.

There started to be some issues missing. The time measured in the pages of the newspaper seemed to be rushing towards the grand finale.

1944: The bigwigs of the quisling Repubblica di Salò continue to display optimism. Photos of party officials in villas around the lake with children dressed in sailor suits and maids in starched caps.

German soldiers billeted in the villas, small German trucks parked beside the statues of Venus at her bath and at the foot of monumental staircases. Group photos of Nazis, *repubblichini*, and local administrators, all smiling.

She stopped, drawn by a full half-page photo showing a group of German soldiers, doctors in long white smocks over their uniforms, other military men in uniform seated in carriages with their heads and legs bandaged, and candy stripers and nurses in front of vans bearing the Red Cross symbol. Behind them, plain as day, Villa Regina.

"Find anything?"

"Yes, this."

Raffaella looked at the page Stefania held out for her.

"Lovely. What the hell is it?"

"An article from spring 1944. It talks about Villa Regina. It says that the villa had been serving for several months as a hospital for German soldiers wounded on the various fronts. The salubrious lakeside serenity and climate, the loving care of the military doctors and candy stripers, and so on. Officers interned at Villa Regina would recover their physical strength and spirit in a hurry and go off again to serve the glorious Third Reich."

"Wonderful. Is that some sort of news you can use?"

"Who can say? Maybe. At any rate, it's more than enough for today. I'm going to pick up Camilla now, and then drop in again at the office. In the meantime I'll think about this. I'd like to come back here early tomorrow morning. From this point on, everything's on microfilm. It'll all go more quickly, both the research and the printing."

"I'll be here as of nine thirty."

"Perfect, you're a sweetie. By the way, I asked Anna to look for the original print of the shot reproduced in the newspaper—provided it still exists, of course—and to make me a copy of it. Or else the negative, at which point my own photographer can take care of the rest. Provided that it still exists. I told her to leave it with you. Is that all right?"

Raffaella smiled.

"See you tomorrow, then," said Stefania, blowing her a kiss and dashing headlong down the stairs.

As soon as she got into her car, the cell phone rang. It was Giulio. She hesitated for a moment, then decided not to answer.

I haven't got time right now, Giulio, she said to herself. In reality she didn't feel like talking to him. Halfway to Camilla's school the phone rang again. One ring, then two, then three. I'll call him later, she thought.

When she pulled up in front of the school, she gestured to Cami to get in the car.

"Hi, Mommy, today I actually got a good score in math."

The girl's voice was interrupted by the phone ringing a third time. He can be really exasperating when he wants to be, thought Stefania. She grabbed the phone with her free hand and answered.

"Giulio, what is it? I don't have time right now. When I don't answer there's usually a reason. I've just picked up Camilla at school and we're already running very late. I'll call you later, okay?"

There was nothing at the other end. She was about to hang up when she heard a hesitant voice.

"It's Valli, Stefania, but maybe it's not the best time."

"Valli—I mean, Luca, I'm sorry, I thought you were someone else," said Stefania, blushing.

Camilla, meanwhile, was huffing and puffing in the backseat, as she always did when her mother wasn't at her complete disposal.

"Who are you talking to, Mommy?"

"To a friend. We're talking about work. Be quiet for a minute, Cami. I'm sorry, Luca, I was saying that I'm right outside my daughter's school and—"

"No problem, we can talk later, more calmly. Oh, and thanks for that 'friend.'"

Stefania remained silent for a moment, trying to think of a reply. Meanwhile Valli had hung up.

"So who's this Valli?" Camilla asked in an inquisitorial tone.

"He's a friend, as I said."

"So you could have let me talk. You always let me talk to Giulio."

"But it wasn't Giulio. So, how'd it go today?"

Camilla started telling her about all the new things that had happened and quickly forgot about the phone call. Martina was already waiting for them at home. That evening it would be Gran Pizza–brand pizza by the slice and Esselunga-brand woodland fruit meringue because the refrigerator was still empty and Stefania wouldn't have time to do any shopping.

"But why do you have to go back to the office?" asked Camilla.

"It won't take long; I'll be back for dinner. If I'm a little late you'll be with the babysitter and you can eat together. But maybe leave me a slice of pizza."

She grabbed a packet of crackers and dashed off as the baby-sitter yelled into the stairwell: "I have to leave by nine o'clock, nine-thirty at the latest."

By ten past five she was at the office. Piras and Lucchesi had vanished. She sat down at the desk and started opening her e-mails, feeling tired. She lit up a Muratti and went over to the window, looking distractedly over the expanse of rooftops and balconies between Via Italia Libera and Via Cadorna, past the boundary wall of police headquarters.

She dug out of her pocket the article she'd had photocopied, reread it, and then examined the photo through a magnifying glass. The reproduction was too grainy, the details getting lost despite her efforts to coax them out.

She kept thinking about things. The place equipped for of-ficers to convalesce. A perfect spot for the Germans, no doubt. Perhaps the villa had been confiscated, but where were its owners? Were they pro-Fascist? Had they sold it? Had they been chased out?

She picked up the phone and dialed Raffaella Moretto's cell phone number.

"Hi, it's Stefania again."

"Long time no see, darling."

"Could you check the proofs of that article you wrote on Villa Regina to see whether there's anything on the period in which the house was occupied by the Germans?"

"What?"

"You know, after the Montaltis and before the Cappellettis. What happened between '44 and '47?"

"I'll go and check. Is it urgent?"

"No, no, take your time. At any rate, I'll be here at the office until at least seven."

"So, taking my time would mean before seven o'clock, if I've understood correctly. Whatever you say, then, Inspector. Your wish is my command."

She hung up. But she was laughing. Luckily, Raffaella was a very good-natured person.

A few minutes later, the cell phone rang.

Good God, that was fast, thought Stefania.

"What's up?"

It was Giulio.

"I'm working, naturally. Unlike you, who are always doing nothing with the excuse that you're forever continuing your education."

"Sooner or later you'll have to take these same courses. But why didn't you answer earlier today?"

"Why, did you call?"

"Twice."

"I guess I didn't hear the phone."

"Any news?"

"No, unfortunately," said Stefania, who had decided to play her cards close to her chest as far as this case was concerned. Giulio's interest was starting to seem suspicious to her.

"I went and talked to Signora Cappelletti," she continued, keeping to the essentials, "but she didn't tell me anything in particular. Then I did a little research in the archives of *La Provincia*, but haven't found anything of interest so far. It does turn out that Villa Regina was occupied by the Germans in 1944. They made it into a military hospital. At the moment I'm waiting for a call from Raffaella Moretto, who's checking the archive for more details, such as what happened to the Montaltis, the family that owned the villa before the Cappellettis."

"I don't see what use that would be to you. I also don't understand the point of following this lead. For now, at least, there's no link between that dead body and these families, or the villa, or the Germans occupying Italy during the war, or anything like that."

Stefania remained silent for a few seconds.

"Actually, I have a question for you. If I'm able to get my hands on a photograph or a negative to be printed and enlarged as much as possible, do you know whom I could ask—for quality work, that is?"

"I'll think about that and let you know. But I believe Selvini can do that sort of thing, too. Now I have a question for you. If you pass this way in the next few days, could you drop by my office?"

~

Stefania had been struck by Giulio's straightforward reasoning. What he said was true: nothing of what she'd found out so far meant anything.

Maybe the mere fact of having read news of refugees, soldiers, and wartime had played a dirty trick on her, catapulting her back into that era like an engrossing film.

But the real question was: What did Giulio have to tell her?

He was one of those people who when he talked about work never said anything out of the blue. Apparently the phone wasn't the right place to discuss the thing he wanted to talk about.

She would have to think about this tomorrow.

Maybe she could pop over there during lunch break.

She was still lost in thought when she heard the door open behind her.

"Don't people knock before entering in your neck of the woods?" she said in irritation. Unfortunately it wasn't Lucchesi or Piras. It was Carboni.

The chief inspector froze in the doorway, as though surprised. Stefania looked him straight in the eye, over the tops of her glasses, and then, to change her tone, added:

"Good evening, Inspector."

"Sorry to bother you, but it's important."

"No bother, go ahead."

"To hell with preambles. The prosecutor's office has been asking me repeatedly what point the investigation into the human remains found at the Valentini worksite is at."

"You can confidently tell them that we know it was a Caucasian male, a young man, who did not die of natural causes. A homicide, in other words. We've reconstructed the cause of death and identified a few objects found with the mortal remains. We've collected some information on the cottage where the body was found and have spoken with the current owners. That's all for now. But you already knew all this, I imagine."

"Yes, and what I'm asking you now is whether you have any concrete hypothesis as to the identity of the victim, the motive of the killing, and the time period. Anything at all."

"No, nothing so far."

Carboni sat down. He took off his thick, magnifying eyeglasses and rubbed his eyes. He was visibly tired.

"Listen, Valenti, we've been working together for years now—me, you, the boys. I know how you work, and I don't want you to think I don't appreciate what you're doing. But we need something right away, if we don't want this case shelved. We need clues, evidence, facts. We have to report to Arisi with something specific, to give the impression that the investigation is going somewhere. That is, going in a specific direction, with a specific goal in mind. Is that clear?"

"Perfectly."

Carboni stood up and started to leave. Then, with his hand on the doorknob, he turned around and made a gesture as if to say "I mean it."

Stefania came to her usual conclusion: he was a good man.

"Thank you, Inspector."

She went back to the window and lit another cigarette. She'd been smoking more than usual of late. And deep down she couldn't really blame Carboni. In his shoes, and fulfilling the same function as he, she would probably have acted the same way.

Okay, but what would she do now?

She glanced at her watch. Raffaella hadn't called back yet, but that didn't matter. She would see her again the following morning. As for Giulio, she was certain that he would ring sooner or later.

She thought of Luca Valli.

It was time to go home.

She'd ended up staying quite late again.

Sighing, she wearily climbed the stairs to her apartment. Martina had already left an hour earlier after texting her a message on her cell phone.

Dinner OK. Camilla watching dvd. Laundry to dry. Pizza in the mw.

Stefania wondered whether she would have the time the following day to leave work at four, pick Camilla up at school, take her home, and wait for Martina. She thought of her mother, who had taken care of her granddaughter many years earlier. Maybe Guido would take care of things. It wasn't as if he lived a hundred miles away.

She would take care of it tomorrow.

She went immediately into the little girl's bedroom. Camilla was sleeping in front of Winnie the Pooh jumping around in the Hundred Acre Wood. She turned off the DVD player and tucked in her covers, then stood there watching her sleep for a moment. She was beautiful, with her long eyelashes and apple-colored cheeks.

My little girl, she thought.

The pizza in the microwave was hard and cold. She opted for the meringue, hot and melting on her plate. She was scooping up the blackberries floating in cream when her cell phone rang.

"Leave the photo with Selvini's secretary. If you have the negative, that's even better."

"Excuse me?"

"The photo you mentioned to me. Wake up, Stefania, Selvini! The guy you used last time? He'll see to passing it on to the photography department. Got that?"

It was Giulio, and it was almost eleven. Efficient at all hours, day or night. She could call him at three o'clock in the morning, and he would still answer calmly and rationally. And he would be able to get to the police station in half an hour dressed in coat and tie.

"Tell me, Giulio, do you sleep in your coat and tie?"

"What are you talking about?"

"Nothing, it was just in a manner of speaking."

"Are you okay? What were you doing?"

"I was just fishing some blackberries out of a puddle of cream."

"Sounds like fun. Maybe you need to get some sleep, Stefania."

"I do. Good night."

"Call me if you need anything. And be sure to drop by my office tomorrow."

"Yes, I'll see if I can. Bye."

Before going to bed it occurred to her that if Giulio was so insistent about this, there must be a good reason for it.

She turned off the light and fell asleep.

9

Consulting the old editions on microfilm was very easy: one button for going forward, another for going back, one for enlarging, and another for reducing. The pages slid by two at a time before Stefania's eyes, making an even hum.

1944: Essential foodstuffs grow scarce; people turn to the black market; cross-border smuggling; more than six hundred reports filed by Swiss customs agents in the first ten months of 1944; escapes across the border, dozens of people arrested, many of them Jews; photograph of the outside of the former Lamberti dye works, now functioning as a "gathering" center; barracks of German soldiers at Cernobbio, SS command center.

Stefania paused a moment to look at the photos outside the barracks' entrance, which showed groups of people being escorted by German soldiers. They walked in silence, lined up, luggage in hand. She gave the order to print and moved on.

Strikes in the factories: the Comense and Castagna dye works in Como, the Burgo paper mills in Maslianico. Some strikers arrested. Number of draft resisters grows.

Partisan resistance groups were forming in the mountains around Lecco and Como. This could be gathered even by reading between the lines of the many articles about "deserters," "spies," and "brigands." Attacks on military convoys and barracks. Favored objectives: munitions depots, through swift acts of sabotage.

Stefania noted with some curiosity how, over time, the meshes of the censors—normally very careful not to let through any mention of common criminality (on the strict orders of the Duce's own secretariat)—had gradually expanded.

She started reading more carefully, because by now almost every edition reported on activities in the mountains, despite the hypocrisy of the writers of such articles, who never mentioned the word *partisans*. She enlarged the images in order to read the names of the places where the clashes had taken place.

Proclamation of General Alexander, October 18, 1944: *Dragnet to be performed in the Pizzo d'Erna area above Lecco.*

She was so engrossed in her reading that she didn't hear Raffaella come in.

"Find anything? I didn't call you back yesterday because I didn't find anything in particular. There was another packet of photos of the house that the owners had discarded, and so we couldn't use them for the article. I'll put them here—I took everything back out for you."

"This tiny print is making my eyes fall out. Have you by any chance found the original photo of Villa Regina, the one from 1944?" asked Stefania.

"They made a copy for me, I'll bring it to you later. Blind detectives, though, should be whisked into retirement! Want a cup of coffee? Salvatore's just back from Salerno with an Easter cake that's out of this world."

"All right, that way I'll take the photo and look at the rest."

She didn't mind taking a break. She had trouble looking closely at things for long stretches of time. Which, translated, meant a terrific headache after two hours in front of a computer screen. As they were drinking the coffee, she carefully examined all the contents of the folder.

"Want another slice? That way you can take some to Camilla."

"Thanks, if there's any left. Here, have a look at this."

"A little courtyard with little columns, in a state of abandon. So, what about it?"

"I saw it when I was at the villa. You're right, it looks abandoned. Look at the hedge around the fountain. It's quite incredible how things change in appearance depending on the moment you see them and your point of view."

"Meaning?"

"Last week, when I was looking at that hedge from inside the house, I thought I could still make out the design of the pruning through the branches that had since grown wild: a sort of motif of wedge shapes that looked familiar but which I was unable at that moment to associate with anything. This morning, when thumbing through your newspaper, I saw many of these same shapes again. They're stars, Raffaella, interwoven Stars of David."

"So, Jews, in other words?"

"Exactly, but we should also verify. At any rate, however, the iron gate Regina Montalti had built in 1924 also has a subtle frieze of the same motif. It's hard to spot it because it's lost in the rest of the decoration, which is as detailed as lace. When I think of all the times I've passed in front of that gate . . ."

"And so?"

"And so nothing. I was simply thinking about the fact that there are often things right before our eyes that we don't see.

Or rather, we see them without understanding them. Yesterday, for example, I read an article I found in the news ten times, but only now have I become aware of a certain detail."

"What article?"

"A March 1944 article. At that moment Villa Regina was in German hands, and they turned it into a sort of clinic. But there's already no trace of the former owners. Not a word is mentioned about them. It's as if they'd vanished into thin air. And, wouldn't you know it, it turns out they were probably Jewish. In the proofs of your article you wrote that in '44 the villa became the property of Remo Cappelletti. As you mentioned to me, the family revised your article before it was published. There is no longer any mention of this acquisition in the final version."

"Maybe they bought it for themselves as a Christmas present, who knows? Though I can understand why they might not want that side of things to be known, if it involved Jews. Many years have passed since the end of the war, but not a hundred. There might still be someone around who remembers."

"Or else, more simply, there was something they wanted to keep hidden. Because it does involve a rather strange transfer of property, you have to admit. But I'm going to get back to work, otherwise I'll be here till nightfall again."

She grabbed the envelope with the photo and went back upstairs to the archive. Eyes burning and refusing to focus on the smaller print, she got back to work.

Offensive graffiti and gunshots fired at the Casa del Fascio and the barracks of the Guardia Nazionale Repubblicana. Roundups and reprisals.

She was reminded of certain clips from films and documentaries on the Resistance, with the image of partisans wearing a sign saying BRIGAND around their necks as they hung from the scaffold, barefoot, with the swollen faces of men subjected to torture after arrest.

December 1944: Acts of sabotage at Pian dei Resinelli, in Valsassina, and at Mandello and Bellano, in the Grigne. Guerrilla fighting engulfs the Lariano triangle: Canzo, Sormano, Erba, Monte Palanzone.

The lake's western shore had likewise become a theater of civil war: the news from Gera Lario, Menaggio, and the Val d'Intelvi was unequivocal in this regard.

January 21, 1945: A company of Black Brigades[5] surprises six sleeping young partisans at Cima di Porlezza: shot on site. A few days later, a partisan detachment falls into an ambush on Monte Bisbino. All members of the group killed at the Murelli.

Now she was going very slowly, in part because she was tired, in part because of her eyes. She had the distinct feeling that something was about to happen, there, at that moment, in her mountains. Any day now, at any moment, like a fire set to the autumn brush that spreads inexorably, one meter at a time, until it gets so close you can feel the heat. By this point it was clear that the partisan struggle was well organized even there, in that winter of '44–'45, and every day was a good day for fighting. And dying. On both sides. On the right side and the wrong side. Assuming you can talk about the wrong side when talking about twenty-year-old boys.

It's unjust to die young, thought Stefania, no matter which side of the barricade you're on.

She kept sending print commands for all the pages that had anything to do with those mountains, "her" shore of the lake, if only to avoid the risk of missing something, considering that by now she could barely read anymore. She stopped to examine a few images showing a column of German soldiers on the move:

a small number of officers, only light weaponry, a few vans, a sidecar, an open truck behind them. Other soldiers aboard the truck, perhaps wounded, sitting with their backs against the side bars, and behind them, an ambulance with a red cross. The road, at first glance, had looked to her like a lake road. Now she recognized it: it was the old Regina road. Stefania could not be mistaken; she knew every inch of it. Two curves past the villa, in the direction of Ossuccio. She pressed the print command without stopping to read.

Her cell phone vibrated, but she knew it was only the alarm. It was three o'clock—time, that is, to pull up her tent, gather her papers, and leave, because Camilla would be coming out at four and there was nobody else but her to pick her up. Guido was an excellent father, but that day he could do nothing.

Five more minutes, she thought.

She tried to speed things up, but there were so many headlines to read; she couldn't very well limit herself to reading only the main ones, since what she was looking for might easily be tucked away in a side article on local crime. Her attention was drawn to a series of photographs showing some places she was able to recognize by some familiar detail or other: the crest of a mountain, the profile of a bell tower, a view of a lake. Filing past her eyes were the mountains of Grona, the old military grating, the Lago di Piano, the Dente della Vecchia, the cliffs of Val Rezzo.

Deserters captured and shot just outside the Swiss border. Gunfights between National Guardsmen and bands of guerrillas along the border.

At one point she thought she recognized the profile of the mountain above the San Primo Pass and a stretch of the passage's mule track in the background of a group photo of Blackshirts posing with SS men and dogs on leashes.

Now it really was late. She grabbed the folder of printed pages overflowing the tray and ran out.

It was one of those rare times when everything strangely went smoothly: green lights, little traffic, few driver's-training-school vehicles in front of her.

She arrived outside Camilla's school ten minutes early. She even found a parking spot and then leaned against the wall, waiting and exchanging a few smiles with some of the other mothers chatting among themselves.

Though she hardly knew anyone there, she enjoyed being in the others' company. The cold season was over and the azaleas in the school garden were in bloom. It was spring again, even if she hadn't fully realized it until that moment.

Cami came out of the school holding her down parka in her hand.

"Already here, Mommy?"

"It's vacation time! Want to go to Cernobbio for hot chocolate?"

They got in the car. Half an hour later they were seated at the Caffè Onda with a tray of pastries in front of them. Hot chocolate for Stefania, strawberries and cream for Camilla. The little girl talked nonstop, telling her all the latest news about her friends and teachers. Every so often Stefania would turn her gaze towards the window and the lake outside, which lay calm in sunlight. She felt good.

They went shopping at the Bennet supermarket in Tavernola and came home with a mountain of shopping bags. For once the refrigerator was stuffed full. There was no room left for anything.

"It's so nice to open the fridge and see all these good things," said Cami.

"Yes, but don't eat your Kinders now, because the pasta's almost ready."

Later they both got into the big bed to watch cartoons, falling asleep together. Around three o'clock Stefania woke up, stretched, and looked at the clock. It was still early. She fluffed the pillow under Cami's head, gave her a kiss, and went back to sleep. Ron was sleeping quietly between them.

～

The following morning the police station was silent and calm. Almost all the boys were out to provide security for the annual silk manufacturers' convention, and there was a coming and going of people and blue squad cars.

At the bar behind the station she ran into Lucchesi.

"Any idea where Piras has run off to?" she asked impulsively. The two were always together.

"He's on leave till Saturday."

"What about you?"

"I'm off to the market this morning."

"To buy what?"

"To the fish market, Inspector. For work. Last night the custodian was assaulted and two shipping containers full of oysters just in from Normandy were stolen."

"If you have any time when you're done, could you drop in at this address? It's just a five-minute walk from the fish market."

She handed him a piece of paper.

"It's the local Jewish Documentation Center. I want you to get every bit of information they have on a certain family, whose name I wrote down for you."

"The Montalti family?" he said upon seeing the name. "I used to know a Montalti; he had a bookshop near my parents' place when I was a kid, but I would never have guessed he was Jewish!"

"So what? It's not like they're a different color or something, Lucchesi. If we don't find anything there, I want you to go and visit your friend. I'll be in my office all morning."

She went back to the office, drafted a couple of reports in a hurry, and then took from her purse the photocopies she'd made at the newspaper office. The photo of Villa Regina slid out of the envelope and onto the floor. Stefania picked it up and started studying it. It was of course better than the picture in the newspaper; you could see a little more. Of the three military doctors, one had a huge dark mustache. Then there were two stiff-looking Red Cross nurses, one rather elderly, the other younger, in capes and uniforms with the cross motif, and three others, quite young, in white dresses with starched bibs. Then two wounded soldiers standing next to the doctors, one with a rather large bandage over his eye, the other with crutches sticking out from under his overcoat. The others were sitting in front of them, one with his arm in a sling, another in a wheelchair, a third with his right leg in a cast and extended in front of him.

The group was posing at the bottom of the grand staircase of Villa Regina, while in the background, against a cloudless sky, flew the flags of the Nazi swastika and the Red Cross.

Stefania tried to read the expressions on people's faces, the fine details, but there wasn't much to go on. Under the magnifying glass the outlines started to blur. With the naked eye, however, you could with some effort imagine other perspectives. One of the two doctors had himself photographed in profile, striking a stiff, somewhat comical pose, as in a ceremonial photo. The eldest of the Red Cross nurses was as stocky and puffed up as an old hen ready to be made into broth, with neck extended and nose in the air, also like a chicken.

The other nurses were really just girls: a little blonde with her hair still in braids, and a dark one with her hair down and wearing a sweet expression. The soldiers were all smiling but one, the one with his leg in a cast sitting in front of the nurses. He was blond, wore glasses, and had a pensive look in his eyes.

Let's hope the enlargement comes out better, thought Stefania.

At that moment she realized she hadn't yet given the photograph to Selvini to enlarge, and she remembered Giulio. Glancing at her watch, she thought she still had time to read the articles closely, take the photo to Selvini, and then go see Giulio. On the way back she would drop by the dry cleaner's to pick up her blue suit.

The office phone rang. A private number.

"Am I disturbing you? Hi, it's Valli."

"Valli!" exclaimed Stefania. "You never disturb me, on the contrary . . ."

She fell silent, fearing, as usual, that she'd said too much.

"Tomorrow evening at the Press Club there's going to be a presentation of a book that talks about our mountains: *We Went Smuggling: Stories of Contrabandeers and Mountain Guides.* A subject very close to your heart. I was wondering—if you have no other engagements—whether you felt like dropping by. It won't last more than an hour."

"I certainly don't have any engagements, but I'll have to see if Martina has."

"Is she your daughter?"

"No, she's the babysitter. For any after-dinner activities I have to reserve her in advance."

"I understand."

"I'll call you back later, if you don't mind."

"Let me give you my cell phone number."

Stefania smiled.

⌒

"What do you think?"

"It's an old picture of a column of German soldiers on the march, escorting a medical convoy."

"Yes, but where are they going?"

"Just read the article. *'For strategic reasons the military hospital that for nearly two years has welcomed the valorous soldiers of Germany wounded in action on various fronts is being closed. Those who can take up arms again have been requartered at Cernobbio.'*"

"Yes, but where are they at the moment the photograph is being taken?"

"I'd say about two or three kilometers from your mother's house."

"Just outside the gate of Villa Regina?"

"The one you pointed out to me last year? Probably. And so?"

"What they were evacuating at that moment was the medical facility they'd housed at Villa Regina. Look here, there's no doubt about it!"

She handed him the photo.

"Of course, to evacuate a place you have to occupy it first. Two years sounds a bit exaggerated, but in any case whoever wrote the article must have informed himself."

"So they were closing the 'lazaretto' they'd created at Villa Regina, and the soldiers still in fighting form had to return to the barracks."

"Sensational. But aside from the imaginativeness of calling

the circumstances of a veritable retreat 'strategic,' I don't see why this is news. Anything else?"

"Knock it off with that mocking tone and just read the article. It talks about deserters captured and shot as they were trying to cross the border, about shoot-outs and mountain huts being set on fire, about blowing up the lairs of brigands in cahoots with the deserters, and we're at San Primo! Here's the old mule path of the mountain pass! It's perfectly clear!"

"Fantastic. I think that during that period, and after the eighth of September,[6] that sort of thing was happening every day in that area."

"Maybe the deserters included some German soldiers who didn't feel like returning to battle."

"Sure, why not? Along with a good number of Italian ex-soldiers and a vast assortment of Jews, victims of political persecution, partisans, and so on."

"Why are you like that, Giulio?" asked Stefania.

"Like what? It's you who are 'like that.' Jesus Christ, you're a police detective, Stefania. You're conducting an investigation, you're not trying to think up the plot of a novel. Don't confuse reality with your imagination. Do you remember what they used to say at the academy?"

"Aside from 'about-face'?"

"That you mustn't manipulate clues to 'construct' a version of events. You must act critically, as if all possibilities were always open, right up until the moment when your hypotheses find concrete confirmation."

"What a fucking bore, Giulio!"

Giulio fell silent. He went over to the window and stood there looking at the rush-hour cars go by. Then, unexpectedly, he spoke again.

"Just be careful, please."

Stefania turned around abruptly.

"Careful about what?"

"Your excursions to lakeside villas and related courtesy calls have ruffled some feathers in the higher spheres, so to speak. Carboni also tried to make you realize this, but you weren't listening. You're going to be relieved of the case as soon as Arisi returns from his magistrates' convention. You've got a week, maybe two, and no more. And maybe it's a good thing."

"Why?"

"Because somebody somewhere, with a lot of power, told somebody else that you have to stop sticking your nose everywhere. You have nothing concrete to go on, and a lot of time has already passed. How long do you want to carry on with this business?"

"Good God, I've barely started! Some investigations go on for years. And that young man up there has been awaiting justice for sixty years."

"Well, you've been warned. If they transfer you to Pantelleria on forced vacation don't take it out on me, okay? Do you understand, or should I say it to you in French?"

"Given the circumstances, I'd prefer it in German, thanks."

～

"Damn, I guess you really did go to the fish market this morning," said Stefania, holding her nose.

"Of course, why do you ask?"

"Never mind. Were you able to go to that other place as well?"

"They kept me there for over an hour. A rather nice secretary spent a while looking on the computer, then printed up some pages for me. I left them on your desk."

"What else?"

"That's all. She said she could also give me some information of a general nature. But for other details—concerning people still alive, for example—you have to present a written request."

"I'll go and get them straightaway. Thanks, Lucchesi. Work well this afternoon."

Back in her office, she lit a Muratti and tried to collect her thoughts. She didn't have many days left. What could she do in so little time? The photo enlargement wouldn't be ready until the following morning, and at any rate she didn't even know whether it would serve any purpose.

She opened the envelope Lucchesi had left for her and started skimming through the pages.

Montalti.

An introduction to the origins of the name, followed by graphics representing the geographical distribution of the families that bore it. There were Montaltis all over the country, even in Tuscany, as Lucchesi had said; all the name's possible variants, the different branches of the family, the notable members. Jewelers, mostly, but also businessmen, professionals, and bankers.

On the Milanese banking Montaltis, there were three lines in all. The descriptions of the family's businesses ended more or less with the end of the nineteenth century.

Stefania felt miffed. At that time the Regina Montalti who would give the villa its current name wasn't even born yet. After a moment's calculation she had to conclude that this information wouldn't be of much use to her, either. Even Lucchesi, in the end, had only wasted her time. This was information she could have easily pulled off the Web.

She dialed the number of the Jewish Documentation

Center. A woman answered, and Stefania naturally thought, from the tone of her voice—polite and inflexible—that it was the same person Lucchesi had described to her.

"Inspector, as I said to your officer this morning, if you're look for something other than information of a general nature on the history of the Jewish people or of Italian Jews, you need to submit a written request. For example, if you needed information concerning a particular family still in existence, or concerning recent events, let's say from the twentieth century to now, you would need a letter of presentation specifying in detail the reasons for your request. Our center will then evaluate whether the reasons given are compatible with the purpose of our center."

"This involves an investigation," Stefania said bluntly.

"Of course, Inspector, and as soon as we receive your written request, we will do everything we can to provide you with the maximum cooperation possible, and an immediate reply by mail. Have a good day."

Stefania felt perplexed, then dialed an internal number.

"Lucchesi, come upstairs for a minute. We have to send a fax right away. I'll leave it on my desk. I'm going downstairs for a coffee."

On the stairway she remembered she was supposed to call Martina.

"Could you stay with Cami for a couple of extra hours tomorrow evening?"

Affirmative reply.

Then, after waffling for a few minutes, she dialed Valli's number.

"Hi, it's Stefania. So, tomorrow evening's okay. Let's meet directly there at nine. It's not far from my house."

Their quick conversation over, her thoughts turned back to the investigation.

She picked up the photocopied newspaper pages and reread for the umpteenth time the same articles she'd had Giulio read. She looked in the cabinet for the small folder in which she'd put together everything to do with the dead young man. On the cover of the main folder she saw the initials K.D.

She cleared her desktop and spread out all the sheets of paper, like pieces of a puzzle.

As a little girl she used to love puzzles. Her father bought her many. They would assemble them together, in a kind of family ritual. When she would get one that was particularly difficult and she didn't know where to begin, she would start with the outside pieces, looking for those with at least one flat side and especially the four that had two flat sides. Which were the corners of the picture, its foundation stones.

Then, starting from the sides, you went towards the center, one piece at a time.

An idea came back to her: *The stone discarded by the builders became the cornerstone.* Which was what she'd thought when first studying the photographs of the ruined cottage and the strange right angle of wall that ended inside the mountain, enveloped in the roots of a wild fig tree.

The only problem was that her investigation was proving more difficult than finding puzzle pieces with flat sides.

She started shuffling the pages around and lining them up in chronological order from left to right.

1944: Remo Cappelletti acquires Villa Regina, his family poses for a portrait taken by the town photographer. They're all there, with the head of the family standing, Caterina sitting and holding Battista close; then Maria, the old maid, and finally Giovanni and Margherita.

The same year, in March, the newspaper shows Villa Regina occupied by the Germans and turned into a hospital.

How the hell did that come about?

Raffaella told her that she'd gotten the information in her article in part from a prior article published in a different magazine a few years earlier, but that in any case the Cappelletti family had very carefully vetted the text.

The Cappelletti family—that is, Germaine Durand and her children, thought Stefania.

Because at the time, in 2001, her husband, Giovanni Cappelletti, had already been dead for a while. Raffaella probably hadn't bothered to dig too deep. After all, what could readers in the year 2001 have cared about such a detail?

On the upper right, she put the year 1945: Villa Regina evacuated, the Germans in retreat. Able-bodied men have to return to the front. Of those attempting to flee into Switzerland, some don't make it. Firing squads, cottages torched in reprisal or blown up with dynamite.

She double-checked the dates of the articles.

January 21, February 20, March 18, March 23, 1945: it was all coming down, the great tragedy was in its final act.

In 1947, however, something happened: Giovanni married Mademoiselle Durand, and the family "moved into" the villa.

Which family?

The married couple, and the children who would soon be coming, and an army of maids, nannies, farmhands, and laundresses like Tata Lucia. Everyone—except Caterina, Giovanni's mother, who'd stayed behind at her mountain house with her son, whom nobody wanted at the villa because he was a bother. Caterina never got tired of repeating that the villa was cursed.

Stefania remembered the disapproving tone with which Tata Lucia had said that "those two"—that is, Giovanni and Germaine—had got married "not even a year" later. They hadn't bothered to observe the period of mourning for Remo, who had died in early 1946, falling one night into a steep ravine made slippery by rain.

Remo, no less: the smuggler. Who should have known those trails better than anyone. Who fell while wandering around aimlessly, calling Margherita's name.

The daughter had died less than a year before. The Cappelletti family's tragedy had played out in the shadow of the great tragedy of the war.

With her pen she made a mark from 1945 to 1947. At that exact point, over the course of those two years, situated somewhere in time and history, lay the solution to the case. Clearly some pieces of the puzzle were missing.

Tata Lucia, who well remembered Giovanni's years of betrothal, always wrinkled her nose when speaking of the *francesa*. The elderly woman had told her how the minute the young heiress to the Durand fortune arrived at Villa Regina, she'd had the wallpaper and bathrooms changed, as though the house were already hers at the time.

"I'm telling you, that girl was born to give orders," she had added.

But then there was that moment when everything had seemed like it might fall through—the "scandal" that had followed Margherita's death. Everyone in town talked about it, Tata Lucia had said. The French fiancée had prudently decided to stay away for an entire summer, perhaps to see how things went.

Stefania, for her part, did not think that all the problems that were eventually resolved had involved money, as the silence of the local people might lead one to believe. Above all because as far as money was concerned, Germaine Durand had more than enough. So whatever scared her off at the time of Margherita's death must have been something else, perhaps the fact of being implicated in something unpleasant.

She thought again of her meeting with Madame Durand. Of that blend of tenderness and compassion with which Madame had spoken to her of Margherita in that green sitting room with the fine Sisley painting left out in full view, though worth millions of dollars, simply because it had, in a sense, belonged to the unlucky girl.

Margherita, Margherita.

In mere months Germaine had succeeded in transforming the wool-stockinged girl with braided hair of the earlier photo into the elegant young lady with the pendant around her neck in the portrait she'd seen in that sitting room. A couple of years at most, maybe three. From 1943, when Germaine and her father had first come to Italy—meeting Giovanni and Margherita, among others—to late 1945, early 1946.

Another question arose in Stefania's mind.

What had the Durands come to do in Italy right in the middle of a civil war that had set the country afire?

Something very important, no doubt, and this "something" must necessarily have had something to do with Remo Cappelletti, whom, moreover, they already knew, at least by reputation.

It certainly wouldn't have been a chance journey, at that particular moment in history. Business dealings to be continued in Lugano? Perhaps Remo was interested in antique furniture and fancy paintings? She found this hard to believe.

To judge from the family photo, one would never have known: a tall man, well built and sturdy in his hunter's jacket and boots, a determined expression on his face. His son, too, was tall, though more slender, with his mother's face, like Margherita. The other daughter, Maria, had instead taken entirely after him: tall and a little ungainly, with a voluminous bust and enormous hands. But no one ever took this daughter into consideration, though she could hardly have gone unnoticed. Even Tata Lucia, after all, had not graced her with the adjective *poor*, which she normally used when speaking of a deceased loved one.

Perhaps a simpler explanation was that Maria wasn't dead.

But if she was still around, how old would she be now? Stefania wondered, answering her own question at once: eighty, maybe more.

She noted the question in her agenda. She would ask Tata Lucia as soon as possible.

With her chin still in her hands, absorbed in thought, Stefania heard someone knock discreetly at the door.

"It's Lucchesi, Inspector. I've brought you the fax receipt."

"Put it over there," she said, gesturing towards a small table. "What time is it, anyway?"

"Three forty-five."

Camilla.

She grabbed her jacket and purse on the run and headed for the parking lot. At the first red light she rang the office.

"Lucchesi?"

"Yes, Inspector?"

"I forgot to tell you that there's something that needs to be done right away. You must call the people in Lanzo and tell them to go to city hall and ask for the death certificates of the following three people: Remo Cappelletti, Margherita Cappelletti, and Caterina

Cappelletti. With the cause of death, if possible. Tell them that Inspector Valenti wants the documents on her desk tomorrow morning before noon."

"Got it."

"Thanks, Lucchesi. Listen, Cappelletti was Caterina's married name; I don't know her maiden name. At any rate, she was the wife of Remo Cappelletti. Margherita was their daughter."

She hung up, feeling confident about Lucchesi's efficiency in dealing with red tape.

In front of the school the usual crowd of mothers and parents was lined up and waiting for their children to come out, their cars parked haphazardly here and there on the sidewalks, one right outside the entrance to the take-out pizza joint.

⌒

"But where exactly are you going?" asked Camilla.

"To a book presentation."

"But isn't it the same if you just buy it and read it at home?"

"In a sense, yes, but the author will be there, and people can meet him and ask him questions."

"And if you don't buy the book, will he get mad?"

"Of course not, he's not there to sell the book. But if you buy the book there, he'll even autograph it for you."

"So it's like going to class."

"Sort of."

"So it'll be dreadfully boring. How will you go there?"

"By car, or bus, or even on foot, however you like."

"No, I meant how are you supposed to look, what will you wear?"

"It's not a reception, Cami."

"So then why has it taken you the last half hour to get

dressed, and why have you already tried three different pairs of shoes and two different purses?"

"Cami, don't you have anything better to do?"

"And who are you going with?"

"With Mr. Valli, whom you don't know."

"The guy who called the other day?"

Camilla had an elephant's memory that worked best when it wasn't supposed to.

"That's the one. I'll be back by eleven-thirty. Be good, both of you."

As soon as she was outside she quickened her step.

When she got to the offices of the cultural association, Valli was already in the lobby waiting for her. Light-blue shirt, velvet jacket.

"I hope I didn't make you wait," Stefania began.

"I just got here myself. Would you like a coffee?"

"Gladly."

"There's nobody in the conference hall yet."

"Are you sure this is the right day?"

Valli laughed.

"One should never arrive on time. The way to do it here is you arrive, wait outside, and exchange greetings and gossip with people. That way you can work on the relationships that matter to you, and every so often cast a glance into the conference hall."

"To know a little about the book?"

"Just to have an idea. There's a cafeteria right outside here, just a couple of steps away."

"I get it, you need a cigarette," said Stefania, smiling.

They sat down at a corner table looking out onto the lake. It wasn't warm enough yet to stroll about in the evening, and the lakeside promenade was almost deserted, apart from a few young men ducking into the little bars cluttering that stretch of lakeshore.

"You look good, a little different from last time. But then you look different every time I see you."

"Do you prefer the afternoon edition or the evening edition?"

"I'd say I like both."

"Well, I see you're in your evening edition as well, though those knickerbockers didn't look bad on you at all. They would be perfect with a pair of leather suspenders with Alpine stars embroidered on them."

"A felt hat wouldn't hurt, either."

They laughed and chatted for a while. Stefania was a bit at loose ends, and she couldn't even have said why. She felt light-headed, and a little out of place. She was aware of his eyes on her, and this had a strange effect. No longer accustomed to such attentions, she nevertheless liked the feeling. After coming out of the cafeteria they stopped and sat down on a bench to smoke a cigarette. The lake was ever so lightly ruffled by a gentle wind, and they were unable to keep the lighter lit. Finally Valli managed to cup the flame with his hands, and she leaned forwards to light her cigarette. At that moment her hand grazed his, and as she raised her head she looked into his eyes from close up, for only an instant. A scent of bitter almonds.

"We'd better go now, or else we risk missing the end, too," said Stefania.

"That's the best moment, anyway. Normally they're drinking to the book's success."

They continued laughing and chatting, hearing only the last comments in the debate in the reception hall. At that point Stefania looked at her watch: it was almost half past eleven.

"Good God, I have to go. I even have to drive Martina home. I'm sorry."

"Shall I give you a ride?"

"No, you stay, that way you can tell me how it went."

"Do you really have to go? I'm so sorry. It's been a lovely evening."

Valli squeezed her hand as Stefania was getting up out of her chair. When she was in the doorway she stopped for a moment and turned around. He was watching her. She smiled at him and waved good-bye. Then she went out.

When she was almost home she got a message on her cell phone.

Good night, Stefania. Thanks for a lovely evening.

10

"There was a call for you this morning, Inspector, but they didn't leave a message."

"Thanks, Lucchesi, have you already had coffee?"

"No, ma'am. If you want, I can have someone look for the number of the person who called."

"Wait, it may not be necessary. Let's have a coffee and then you can have the switchboard call the same number back and put the call through to me. Any other news?"

"Piras is back on duty and apparently has some very good news. Dr. Allevi came by asking about you."

"At what time?"

"Seven thirty. I'd just come in."

"One last favor: Call our friends in Lanzo and tell them to hurry up with that information we asked for, the death certificates for those three people. Before noon, if possible."

She went back into her office and rang Giulio.

"Here I am. Were you looking for me?"

"You should contact Selvini or someone from that department. It would be even better if you went there in person. The overall enlargement of that photo is ready, but now you have to let them know which details, people, or things you're interested in. They can make further enlargements of specific areas, as with a zoom lens."

"But can't they just send the stuff to my office? I have a lot of urgent things to do this morning."

"They could also dismantle their two-hundred-thousand-euro processor and send it to your office, preferably with two rented technicians. But you'll have to ask them yourself, okay?"

"Giulio . . ."

"Yes, my dear."

"I was also thinking they could make bigger prints."

"The kind you hang from wires with clothespins in a darkroom?"

"Go to hell."

"I will, my dear, but after you. When are we going out to dinner?"

Stefania laughed and hung up. Giulio was incorrigible.

She was still busy looking for Selvini's number in some lost corner of her desk when a call came in from the switchboard.

"What is it, Marino?"

"There's a call for you, Inspector. The same person who called for you this morning. A certain Montalti, if I heard right."

"Put him on."

A bustle in the background, then a voice at the other end.

"Inspector Valenti?"

"In person. With whom do I have the pleasure of speaking?"

"I am Paolo Montalti, I'm calling from Geneva. I was told you were looking for me."

The man spoke calmly, in a somewhat detached fashion, with a vague French accent to top it all off. He sounded quite old.

"The secretary at the Jewish Documentation Center in Italy passed on your request for information, Inspector. I have to admit we were a little surprised."

"Surprised? Why?"

"It's the first time anyone has ever asked us for information concerning Villa Regina."

"Really? From what I'm told, it's a home of tremendous artistic value."

Stefania was hoping her interlocutor would keep talking, and limited herself to feeding him cues to this end.

"No doubt about it, but surely you must know it hasn't belonged to us for many years. What in particular did you want to know?"

"Mr. Montalti, the first question I'd like to ask you is: when did the transfer of property between your family and the current owners—that is, the Cappelletti family—take place? What were the circumstances of the sale? Assuming, of course, that it was indeed a sale."

"It happened during the summer of '43."

"I'll make a note of that. Are you certain?"

"I don't recall the exact date, but it was definitely in June or, at the most, early July, of 1943."

"Excuse my bluntness, Mr. Montalti, but according to documents in my possession, the villa was taken over by troops of the German occupation force."

There was a long moment of silence.

"It's true, but the villa was sold right around that time. The contract was drawn up in Milan, after having been worked out in Geneva, at the firm of the lawyer Durand. They don't have notaries in Switzerland, you know, there's a lot less bureaucracy here. At any rate it was a proper sale in every respect, though subject to some unusual conditions."

"The lawyer Durand, you say," Stefania said indifferently. "I know some Durands who are antiquarians in Geneva."

"It's a branch of the same family," said Montalti. "I think they were first cousins. The deed of sale was drafted in their law office, between my father, his two brothers, and Signor Cappelletti."

"Was that when you met Signor Cappelletti?"

"No, I'd met him some time before."

"Did you also know the Durands who were antiquarians?"

"Personally, no, at least not all of them. My father had spoken about them often. I met Auguste Durand in person at least twice—the first time at our house in Milan, the second time actually at Villa Regina."

"I have another question for you, Mr. Montalti. Why, in your opinion, would the Cappelletti family have later declared that they acquired the villa after the war?"

There was a long pause, interrupted by some rustlings.

"Inspector, I have just activated the speakerphone. Beside me are some other members of the family who would like to listen directly to what we're saying. You don't mind, do you?"

"No, go right ahead. But please answer my question."

Stefania was certain that Paolo Montalti hadn't forgotten her question, but she just wanted to avoid any stonewalling.

"You just said you'd met Auguste Durand. Was someone in your family interested in antiques at the time?"

A rather lively buzz in the background.

"My uncles and my grandfather Davide were clients of the Durands. They were known to everyone and had been art merchants for generations, being one of the most prominent families during those years. But I want to make this clear: at that moment it had nothing to do with interest in antiques."

"Then what did it have to do with?"

"You see, Inspector, at that particular moment in history, we Montaltis, like many others, were forced to get rid of a great many precious objects. Paintings, furniture, jewelry. In a way, the Durands, during that period, took back a lot of what they'd sold our family in prior generations. It's odd, don't you think?"

"So there must not have been much sympathy on your part towards them, I imagine," Stefania commented.

"Please don't misunderstand me, Inspector, but sympathy or lack of sympathy had very little to do with anything in this case. Auguste Durand was an art dealer, one of the most skilled and competent around. But however cultured and refined he might have been, he was still a businessman. He certainly wasn't tender with us, but, to our great fortune, he turned out to be quite fair. An honest man, in his way."

She heard more bustling.

"The whole thing was obviously a very good deal for him, Inspector, very advantageous. But just to give a complete picture of the situation, I have to add that he did not behave like a cutthroat. Especially compared to some of the other characters we had the bad luck to cross paths with during that period. The agreed price for the villa was certainly less than its market value at the time, but it was paid in full, down to the last cent, and right away, just as we'd requested."

"So, in essence, Mr. Montalti, you're telling me that your family turned to Durand in those circumstances because you'd already had prior business dealings with him."

"That's correct, Inspector. And also because, thanks to him—and this was very important for us—the money obtained for the villa was paid out mostly in Switzerland, to a trustee of ours. I think you can understand, Inspector, that at a moment like that, the physical and economic survival of our entire family hinged on such things."

"Yes, of course I understand. What is truly surprising is that someone was able, in the middle of a war—and on top of that, in the middle of the German occupation of northern Italy—to buy, in Italy, a great quantity of priceless antiques and export them abroad, across borders that were under very strict surveillance. But what kind of man was this Durand, anyway?"

"An exceptional man, in his way—or, better yet, exceptionally clever. We knew we could count on his cleverness, and indeed the whole thing was organized to perfection. There wasn't the slightest snag. I've always maintained that that man must have had some very important connections, friends, and protectors in Italy and all over Europe."

"Apparently so. And so you felt grateful to him, or at least so it seems to me."

"It would be more accurate to say that our interests and his happened to coincide at that particular moment, to the satisfaction of both parties. Most probably if we'd turned to someone else, I wouldn't be here talking to you now, and neither would much of my family. I was little more than a lad at the time, but I remember him quite clearly, with his reddish mustache and his tall, lean figure always dressed in gray. He would look over our things, our precious objects, one by one, taking notes all the while. I still remember the wooden smell of the straw-filled packing crates in our garage. The whole thing took many hours, the time I saw him in Milan."

"And after that you saw him at Villa Regina. Was it for the same sort of business?"

"Yes, in a way, because it again involved money. The circumstances, however, were quite different."

The man remained silent for a few moments. None of the other people with him—however many there might be in the room he was calling from—uttered a word.

Stefania was beginning to grasp what it was in the man's words that interested her, but she realized that it was best not to force things. And so she said, in a sympathetic tone:

"I'm sorry if this reawakens painful memories for you. If you prefer we can continue another time."

"No, there's no need, but I thank you for your tact. For a certain period of time Villa Regina was a sort of way station, a temporary depot for the crates that were going over the border, while we waited for the right moment to conduct the operation. Things went on in this way for a while, then I think some problems arose, or at any rate crossing the border became more difficult. At that point the last things to come out of our house in Milan, which by then were almost exclusively furnishings, were simply abandoned inside Villa Regina—some in the second-floor rooms, others piled up in the attics."

"But what point was there in bringing all those things to Villa Regina? It still belonged to you, and it would not have been difficult for someone to find them there if they'd wanted to."

"Your observation is correct, Inspector, but you have to bear in mind that a portion of the furniture sold to Durand at some point had to remain in Italy, because it had become too dangerous to take things out. And if everything hadn't come to a head so suddenly, the flow would probably have continued."

"Even so . . ."

"At a certain point things changed radically. We ourselves became the 'objects' to be exported, and the antique furniture faded into the background."

"Meaning that you were forced to expatriate?"

"By the start of the war some of us had already moved to Switzerland: the grandparents, my aunt Regina, other close relatives, some cousins. The youngest kids were sent to study in the finest Swiss boarding schools. At that time crossing the border into Switzerland, with car and luggage, was basically child's play. Others, however, had remained in Italy despite the difficulties and hardships. For years many had thought they could get by inside their own country. But that turned out to be a grave error of judgment."

The tone in which Montalti had said "their own country" did not escape Stefania's notice.

"And did Villa Regina figure as well in your expatriation plans?"

"You needn't worry about speaking openly, Inspector. You can call it an escape, since that's what it was. I, along with my mother, my sister, and two cousins more or less my age, was already up at the lake by the start of the winter of '43. We'd been expelled from the Italian schools. Things quickly got worse. Without warning, my father and his brother came to us one evening. It was night, I remember it well: they told us straight out of the blue to put on our mountain hiking clothes and get ready. We could bring only what would fit in a backpack, no more."

There was no longer any sound at the other end. Stefania, too, was holding her breath.

"The villa was in total darkness and silent. We all gathered in a room on the ground floor that faced uphill, one of those that give onto the park. We waited a long time and then, at a certain point, we distinctly heard sounds of footsteps and subdued whispers. Someone tapped lightly on the windowpane. Through a secondary door, a man I had never seen before came in: tall, well built, in boots and hunter's jacket, with a rifle strapped across his back. He exchanged a few words with my father, then signaled to us to get up and come with him. We all went out in silence and single file, and headed towards the property's boundary wall, in back, where there was a secondary exit with a small gate that was never used. This second exit gave onto a dark path. Waiting there outside for us were three other armed men. They gestured to us to remain silent. They brought some wooden crates inside the gate, hastily arranging them in the woodshed."

"I assume they weren't antique pieces . . ."

"I doubt it. But actually we were all in a kind of trance. We didn't know why those men were bringing in those crates. Everything happened very quickly. Once the crates were hidden behind a stack of firewood, they bolted the woodshed shut and two of them came with us. The third, the youngest, remained on the property. The last thing I remember about Villa Regina was that gate in back and the bolt that locked it. I have not been back there since."

"The man who came to get you was Remo Cappelletti, wasn't it?"

"Yes, Inspector. Obviously there weren't any introductions or niceties and everything happened very quickly. My father told us to be good and do everything he told us to do."

"Then when happened?"

"Cappelletti told us to follow him. None of us must talk. We walked for a long time, for hours, in silence and the blackest night, going always uphill to boot. I think he'd decided to take a roundabout route to avoid the town. We passed villages and woods and mountains, and at the first light of dawn, after having made only two very brief stops of a couple of minutes each, we reached a clearing with a few huts and stables. There we encountered other men who were waiting for us. They exchanged a nod of understanding with Cappelletti and set us up in a hayloft. For me it was sort of an adventure, in a way. Before that I had never slept in a farm cottage before."

"What sort of impression did Cappelletti make on you?"

"A decisive man, surely. During the entire journey he said barely a few words. And he addressed only my father. As soon as he'd set us up in the cottage, he disappeared back into the woods. Probably someone had stayed behind nearby, on guard, a short distance away. But we didn't see anybody. We holed up in the cottage for many hours, almost a whole day."

"Were you able to tell where you were?"

"It's impossible to say, though through the apertures in the hayloft you could see part of a lake in the distance. The cottage was on a small grassy slope, but everything else was a succession of very green, dense woods. I think there must have been a torrent passing somewhere in the area: I could clearly hear the rushing waters, though far away. Otherwise there wasn't a soul anywhere. Late that afternoon a girl came with some bread, cheese, and a pail of milk. She was very tall, with an angular face and red cheeks and a rather graceless way of moving. She didn't say a word, either. My father later told us she was Cappelletti's daughter."

"Was she a pretty young girl with dark hair?"

"Pretty, I really wouldn't say, Inspector. Young, yes, but as tall and big as her father and just as brusque. She told my father we had to remain in hiding. She would come back and get us as soon as darkness fell."

"And what happened next?"

"At around nine thirty or ten o'clock, Cappelletti and the two armed men from the night before knocked at the door. We went out with them, and our journey resumed."

"Where were you headed?"

"We didn't know. We walked in the dark, always uphill, and sheltered by the woods, always in silence. That night we didn't go as far as the day before. Our pace slowed down because we were no longer following an actual path, but walking along the forest bed, between the roots of the trees, behind our guides. Long afterwards my father said that we crossed the border at San Primo that evening, pointing out the exact spot on a map."

"Then what happened?" asked Stefania.

"At some point Cappelletti finally signaled to us to sit down and wait in silence. There were fewer and fewer trees. By the first light of dawn we began to glimpse stretches of green, open meadows. Cappelletti kept an eye on his watch by matchlight. He went up to my father and under his breath indicated a place to him, repeatedly making the 'two' sign with the fingers of his hand. My father turned to me and my uncle and told us to get up and quickly cross the field in front of us. He embraced me and told me to run as fast as I could. We mustn't stop until we'd passed a row of trees just visible in the distance. There were about two hundred meters in the open, maybe more. Past the trees, down a path hidden from view, we would find a car waiting for us. I remember the exact moment my father kissed me on the forehead and then patted my uncle on the shoulder. And then it was all over, at least for that time."

"What do you mean, it was all over?"

"The two of us crossed the border, and five minutes later my mother and sister crossed as well. Then my two cousins, and finally my father. We found the car, as we'd been told. Cappelletti had done a good job. And that was it. It was over, and we were in Switzerland, safe and sound."

"Did you know the man who was waiting for you with the car?"

"He was the same man that Durand had sent to our home

in Milan to pick up the most valuable items. A right-hand man of his, obviously."

There was a pause of silence, which Stefania was the first to break.

"Signor Montalti, I realize I'm taking advantage of your co-operation, but it's important to me and to the investigation I'm carrying out. Two more things. Let's go back for a moment to the sale of Villa Regina. How did this happen, considering the cir-cumstances?"

"Do you mean how could we conceive of 'selling' something that we had to leave behind when we escaped?"

"Exactly. I'm interested in knowing who could think seri-ously of buying something from you that, practically speaking, no longer belonged to you, since you didn't know if or when you would ever be able to regain possession of your properties in Italy."

"My father and his brothers were thinking the very same thing when Durand asked them shortly thereafter if they wanted to sell Villa Regina. He was offering a price that was less than one fifth of its actual value. They, however, decided it was an opportunity they shouldn't let get away, if only because Villa Regina would be expropriated in one way or another just the same. After all, it went a lot worse for many of our Jewish ac-quaintances. Many of them lost everything. They were unable to save anything except their own skins. That was how my father decided to accept Durand's offer. What was needed most at that moment was money: for the most basic necessities, and to help others of us try to get out of Italy. Like my mother's family, for example. The ones who did get away managed to do so thanks, in part, to the money from Villa Regina, in a sense."

"When did you learn that Villa Regina had been occupied by the Germans?"

"Months later, even though I don't remember that detail very clearly. You probably also know that the villa, at least at first, was requisitioned by the government and granted to a few local Fascist leaders who settled there for a while with their families."

"Actually I didn't know that detail."

"From what we were told, the regime's police raided the villa just a few hours after we fled."

"A close call, then. Was it only a lucky coincidence?"

"My father told me he'd been informed by a person he trusted. That was why he came to us that way, in the middle of the night, and told us to get ready to flee. At the time we didn't know that both my father and my uncle had already been living for some time under false names in Milan, and that our house had already been assigned to other people, along with everything inside it. In short, Inspector, when my father was told that Villa Regina had been occupied, he thought again that it was a good thing he'd sold it, or, at least, a lesser evil. But this, too, in retrospect, was a serious mistake. But the times being what they were, it was very hard to know what the future would bring. Everything seemed as if it would end in a great catastrophe. One thing is certain, however, and that was that Durand didn't make the same mistake. It's possible he knew—as so few did at that moment—what might happen not long thereafter."

"Wait. I'm afraid I don't quite understand what you just said to me, Mr. Montalti."

"Think about it, Inspector. Imagine a prominent person, well placed in the right milieux, in the closed circles of economic and political power in Europe and outside. . . . Anyone at that moment of history had the means to see that the war was lost by then. The

Third Reich and the Fascist regime were on life support. It's natural that some people were already thinking of the future, of war's end, of reconstruction. Once the war was over, the large properties would be returned to their legitimate owners or their heirs, perhaps damaged but none the less considerable. Many of the Jews who got away, in fact, had means and acquaintances that helped them to recover what had been taken from them."

"And so?" Stefania asked, still not having fully grasped Montalti's line of reasoning.

"And so it's better to buy when the price is low while it's still possible, in order to resell as soon as the price goes back up—it's a basic rule of economics. Obviously one had to have the means to do so, but that certainly was not a problem for Monsieur Durand."

Stefania realized that the conversation had already gone on too long and she didn't want to overdo it. She still had a couple of other things to ask him and figured that she had the time to settle everything calmly. And so with a tone of conviction, she said:

"Yes, that's quite clear. But you keep referring to Durand. Wasn't it the Cappelletti family to whom you sold Villa Regina?"

"Of course, and the deed of sale will attest to this, but the money came from Durand. While Cappelletti had enriched himself with his smuggling operations, he didn't have that kind of money available. But he was the ideal person for Durand: trusty, resolute, and anything but stupid, endowed with that quintessentially peasant shrewdness that certain people of the lake area possess. Cappelletti immediately realized that Durand might represent his big break, the key to a leap forwards in the quality of life of his whole family."

"I get the impression you don't think very highly of either one of them."

"On the contrary! There is no doubt in my mind that Durand was a genius in business, and the fact that Cappelletti represented his armed force was perfectly logical. Neither of the two had a great deal of scruples. But don't misunderstand me, Inspector. They weren't scoundrels. Durand needed a lieutenant, a trusted person capable of managing, on his own, the transfer of antique pieces out of Italy and across the border. Who better than Remo Cappelletti, one of the most famous smugglers in the region? And at that time Cappelletti exported goods just as skillfully as he imported them. Let's just say that everyone, on both sides of the border, was a client of his. The rest just came naturally, what can I say? The circumstances were favorable, and the two men were very good at not missing opportunities."

"So who else?"

"Victims of political persecution, Jews like us, deserters— people who wanted to get out. Anyone who was in a position to pay became a client of Cappelletti's enterprise. And then there was the weapons business."

"Weapons?" Stefania asked in surprise.

"Of course. Weapons destined for the partisan struggle, however strange that might seem to you. My father told me that Durand had excellent business relations in the United States as well. The weapons may have come from there, but we'll never really know. My uncle, perhaps under the influence of his excessive passion for spy novels, used to say that Durand was actually in the pay of the Allied military secret services."

"What a pair, those two."

"You can say that again. Cappelletti, by staying in Italy, controlled Villa Regina and everything that was in it. By that point it already belonged to him and to Durand, even though nobody knew yet. And while he was supplying Fascist officials with chocolate, at the same time he was letting weapons destined for the partisans into Italy. In short, he did business with everyone. Though his masterwork was clearly something else."

"And what was that, Signor Montalti?"

"As he was bringing weapons clandestinely into Italy, having them pass through Villa Regina itself—in other words, right under the noses of the Fascist officials—Cappelletti got a rather brilliant idea. When the Germans arrived and things started to get complicated with all those soldiers around, making his work more difficult, his daughter discovered her vocation as a Red Cross nurse and moved into the villa, briefly becoming a sort of administrator of the German hospital."

"You mean Margherita, correct?"

"No, not Margherita, but the older one. I believe her name was Maria."

"Please continue, Signor Montalti, I'm listening."

"The young lady in question, as I was saying, managed the other nurses, oversaw the military doctors, and provided the German commanding officers with whatever was available via contraband. As she was doing all these things, she kept an eye on and protected what already belonged to her family, and managed to keep Durand's and her father's business far from prying eyes and ears. In the end, when things started to go bad for the Germans as well, I think more than a few of them, too, were hidden and helped to flee the country."

"There's one thing I don't quite understand. Why didn't a shrewd man like Cappelletti try, so to speak, to set himself up on his own? His business was prospering, after all."

"Actually, I think that that was his real masterwork. By that point old Remo was aspiring to something more: to take his family and his business to a higher social level."

"With a good marriage, for example?"

"Precisely. I met Mademoiselle Durand in Geneva. A very elegant young lady, an only child, though rather unpleasant, in my opinion. But also quite beautiful."

"So this is the question. Why would a beautiful, rich girl from an excellent family consent to marrying into a family of so low a social rank?"

"Who can say, Inspector? Maybe it was love. Why not?"

"Of course, why not?"

Stefania fell silent. Moments later Montalti asked:

"Was there anything else you wanted to know, Inspector?"

"One final detail, Mr. Montalti, I'm sorry. Just now, in describing your escape across the Swiss border, you used the words 'that time.' I was wondering, were there other times as well?"

"Yes, there were two other times. A few months later Cappelletti brought two of my uncles on my mother's side, with their families, across the border in an entirely different area. Seven people in all, with two small children."

"That must have been dangerous, with two small children who might start crying at any moment."

"I imagine it was, and indeed the price was proportional to the risks."

Again there was a lively buzz in the background, as at the start of the telephone conversation.

"Is there a problem, Signor Montalti?"

"They're suggesting I tell you about something that happened the time after that, also in connection with the price of life."

"I'm all ears."

"Several months later, towards the end of the war, Durand was arranging for the escape of my uncle Heinrich, who was a colonel in the Luftwaffe."

"Your uncle was a Nazi?"

"Absolutely not. He was a career military man. He came from a family that had provided Germany with soldiers for generations. Men of solid, upright character. He was never a Nazi—on the contrary, his career ended the moment it became known that his wife was Jewish. He was released from the army. My aunt fled to Switzerland, while he, thanks to his family's influence, was reintegrated into the service, even though there was no longer any chance of making further career advancements. But that's irrelevant. Anyway, once he was injured in combat he was sent to recover in Italy. First to Rome, then to northern Italy, where he ended up at—"

"At Villa Regina?"

"Exactly. But don't think it was yet another coincidence. My aunt was in close contact with Monsieur Durand. My uncle was losing his eyesight and needed urgent care. And the fact was that Uncle Heinrich also wanted to leave the country, and so Cappelletti had him cross the border at night, exactly the way he did for us. Heinrich, his young attendant, and two ex-Fascist officials."

"A diverse little group, in short."

"Well, it certainly wasn't the most pleasant company, but Cappelletti was a businessman. Politics didn't interest him. He would work for anyone, as long as they paid."

"And so what happened?"

"I'll tell you exactly what I was told. It was a slower journey than usual, because my uncle and his attendant kept falling behind: the one because he couldn't see, the other because he limped, due to an injury to his leg. At a certain point they were joined by a woman, who took Cappelletti aside to talk to him. They had an animated discussion, and the woman gestured to a point behind them, looking at the young man. At that point

Cappelletti and his men told my uncle and his soldier to stop. It was because of them, they said, that the group was moving so slowly. They told them they would let the others go across first, and then come back and get them afterwards, if there weren't any hitches. They took them to a cottage and left them there with a man on guard."

"Was it the same cottage where they left you and your group?"

"I can't say with any certainty, since I wasn't there. My uncle's eyesight wasn't very good, but his attendant told him that at dawn he'd seen the lake in the distance. So it may have been the same place."

"Did they ever come back to get them?"

"The following evening, but there was still the same problem. The old man and his young caretaker walked too slowly. The young man often stumbled and fell, and they would have to stop. One of the guides told him quite openly that if he didn't hurry up, they would leave him behind to the mercy of the partisans."

"The woman you mentioned: who was she?"

"My uncle told me that when they were still in the cottage, the young man told him that another person might be joining them. He was always looking around impatiently. As for the woman, my uncle didn't say much else, except that he'd already seen her at Villa Regina."

"And then?"

"At a certain point everything became a mad rush. The sun was rising. Time had been lost due to the two Germans' slowness, and it was getting late. Two guides grabbed my uncle by the arms and practically dragged him along, while the young man stayed behind. My uncle never saw him again."

Stefania held her breath inadvertently, as though waiting for the epilogue.

"When it came time to cross the border, they told my uncle to walk always straight ahead, because there weren't any more obstacles. When he asked about the young man, they answered that he was a short distance behind them and would cross over shortly after him. And so he crossed. Waiting for him on the other side was my father, who'd been expecting him since the previous evening. You can imagine the situation. My father wanted to leave at once, but my uncle wouldn't hear of it. Seconds later they heard shots in the distance, and then deep silence. My uncle stayed there, waiting. An infinity seemed to pass, my father said. When the sun was already high in the sky they heard an explosion, a big one, and then saw a column of smoke rising. At that point they decided to leave."

There was a very long silence.

"Inspector? Is there anything else you want to know?"

"No, Mr. Montalti. Thank you for everything. You've been very helpful, too helpful."

Stefania sat there looking out the window, an elbow on the desktop and her hand under her chin. It was a gorgeous spring morning, and if she looked up she saw only sky. She thought of her mountains and the trails through the woods, those known only to people who were born in the area. A scent of stables with hay and the sound of rushing mountain torrents came back to her.

Montalti had seen the lake and heard the sound of the waters from the barn in which he'd spent the night before his decisive escape. He'd walked through woods that didn't even have a path all the way to the border. K.D. had also seen the lake from afar, perhaps for only an instant.

Many details were still missing. She needed to think the whole thing over calmly. She knew those places well. Every trail, every footpath.

She thought of when it rained heavily at the lake in summertime.

In an instant the trickle of water in the stream became a river of mud and broken branches rolling on down to the lake, carrying everything it encountered along with it. Then the rain would stop, the torrent would slow, and the ripples on the lake would, little by little, carry everything that floated back to shore.

And whatever was there you could see very clearly.

11

There was a discreet knock at the door.

"Inspector?"

"What is it, Lucchesi?"

"The fax from Lanzo came in."

"Well done."

She snatched the pages from his hands and started reading them carefully.

The first two were a copy of Margherita's death certificate with what looked like the medical report attached:

Margherita Luisa Cappelletti, daughter of Remo Cappelletti and Caterina Novi, born at Lanzo d'Intelvi on December 13, 1923 . . . deceased there on March 6, 1945. Multiple bullet wounds in the abdomen and side with profuse hemorrhaging . . . given the condition of the mortal remains, it is recommended that the casket be immediately sealed.

Stefania sat there staring at the elegant loops of the handwriting used by the records office clerk.

Margherita hadn't reached her twenty-second birthday at the time of her death.

Stefania then started examining Remo Cappelletti's death certificate:

> ... *death occurred in the Prati di San Primo zone on November 20, 1946. . . . Bone fractures of the neck and cranium from accidental fall.*

Caterina, Remo's wife, died in 1949 of natural causes, from "acute heart failure." Someone had affixed to her death certificate another document dated three months later. It told the story of Battista Cappelletti, twenty-seven years old, handicapped, interned at the Santa Maria della Pietà Institute for the Mentally Disabled, near Bergamo, with the consent of his brother, Giovanni, and his sister, Maria. In front of Maria's name there was a little mark whose significance was unclear; it may have been only a stain or a stray stroke of the pen. Upon more careful observation it seemed to look like a small *s*.

Stefania stopped to contemplate these latest developments.

Caterina hadn't made it, and so Battista had been left on his own. Caterina had always said that Villa Regina was cursed, and to judge from what happened to her family, she was clearly right.

Along the way to Selvini's office, a unit of the forensics police that also housed a photography department, Stefania kept thinking about the wake of death that had engulfed the Cappelletti family in the space of just a few years. Meanwhile it had gotten late: it was almost one o'clock, but she still hoped to find somebody at the office.

They were still there. Selvini came out to meet her.

"Inspector, you should start looking at those we've already printed. That way, hopefully, we can better home in on the details you need. We can print more limited fields and bigger enlargements. We can't exactly work miracles with an old photo, but we can certainly improve it. So you can take your time. We're going out for a sandwich and will be back in an hour."

Stefania sat down at the window so she could examine the enlargements in the best possible light. The details had now become clearly distinct: the flowers in the large vases beside the staircase, the groups of palm trees, the details of the soldiers' uniforms. Everything looked completely different.

With the help of a magnifying glass she studied the people in the group. Now she could even see the expressions on the different faces. She focused first on the candy stripers, then on the nurses. Her attention was drawn by the young one, then by the other one, the tall, dark woman.

She grabbed the telephone.

"Marino, get me Lucchesi or Piras, would you? Whichever one you find first. Quick. I'll stay on the line."

A few moments passed.

"What is it, Inspector?" asked Piras.

"Go into my office, and on the desk you'll find a folder with the letters K.D. on it. Bring it here to me at once. I'm in Selvini's office. Come as quickly as you can."

She lit a cigarette and looked out the window. She'd had an intuition, and she was quite sure about it—that is, almost. She needed confirmation. But she was certain she was on the right track. After all, she had an exceptional visual memory.

The workers in the office, meanwhile, had all left, one at a time.

Some twenty minutes later, Piras arrived, all out of breath and with beads of sweat on his brow. He had the green folder with him.

"At last. Thanks. Let's have a look."

She took the folder from him and pulled out the photo of the Cappelletti family made by the town photographer. She then put the two pictures beside each other and began to compare them. She sighed.

"It's them, there's no doubt about it. It's them."

"Who's 'them,' Inspector?" asked a curious Piras.

Her first impulse was to call Giulio.

She dialed his cell phone number, and without waiting for him to say anything, she said all in one breath:

"Did you know that Margherita was killed—that is, she died from gunshot wounds in 1945? The autopsy report doesn't specify how, but I think she was killed. She and her sister, Maria, were living at Villa Regina during the German occupation period."

There was silence for a moment at the other end.

"You don't say," Giulio commented.

Swept away by enthusiasm for her recent discovery, Stefania paid no mind to Giulio's tone of voice.

"I do say, actually. And Paolo Montalti, the son of the former owner of Villa Regina, has a clear memory of Maria, the older sister, and remembers seeing her in the mountains with her father on the night they escaped."

"Incredible."

"And I've become convinced, though I have yet to prove it, that Maria was also the girl that Uncle Heinrich noticed during the following escape as well."

"Ah, Uncle Heinrich, of course."

"Giulio! This is important information! It's a major turn of events!"

"I don't doubt it. As long as you tell me who the hell Margherita and Paolo Montalti are. That might help me to understand a little better, don't you think? And who, while we're at it, is Uncle Heinrich?"

"But, Giulio, Margherita is the center of the whole affair; everything revolves around her."

"Well, I guess I missed a few episodes of the plot. I think I remember that the main character—or better yet, the only character—was a young man. Am I wrong?"

"But the family, all those deaths, and Margherita, her presence in that house . . . It's as though everyone still felt her presence . . ."

"Ah, a ghost story, my favorite."

"Something terrible must have happened in that family, something nobody wants to talk about."

"The Montalti family?"

"The Cappelletti family, of course."

There was a silence, which meant that Giulio was putting his proverbial analytical powers in gear.

"I'm having trouble following you, Stefania. This is no longer a police investigation that you're running; it's a systematic delirium, and it makes no sense."

"You don't understand."

"Of course I don't understand, how could I? You spend your days ruminating over imaginary stories and spinning plots worthy of Agatha Christie. You shouldn't expect people to understand. And anyway, you're no good at explaining yourself; you take for granted names and details that only you know."

"If you could somehow manage not to make snide remarks for five minutes straight, maybe I could actually tell you a few things, seeing that you are, after all, an intelligent person."

"How kind of you. And so?"

"And so I was thinking that maybe we could have a panino together at the bar behind the station. Right now, even, if you haven't got anything better to do."

"What a romantic setting. But seeing that I haven't got anything better to do, let's have that panino. Since, with you, it's catch as catch can."

"See you in three minutes."

⌁

"Mayonnaise?"

"No, thanks."

"Pink sauce?"

"No need to read me the entire menu. Just tell me what you think."

"Didn't you just say I should keep my mouth shut for at least five minutes? I've been listening to you for a good half hour now, and in the meantime I've eaten two panini while you've eaten nothing at all, cappuccino aside. I was just trying to be nice."

"And you are. But what do you think?"

Giulio looked at her through the beer foam still in his glass. Officers weren't allowed to consume alcohol while on duty. Apparently civilian police officials were.

"You said it yourself. It's fine, it's interesting, it's intriguing, whatever you like: but it has nothing to do with the investigation. That's the real problem. There's nothing connecting the different elements. At this rate you'll keep wasting time and you'll lose the case. Arisi's coming back next week, don't forget."

"Is that all?"

"What else do you want me to say?"

"Don't you have any ideas? Any advice to give me?"

"I think you have enough ideas of your own for both of us."

Stefania remained silent, staring at the little spoon in the cup of her cold cappuccino. She watched the people walking by outside the bar.

"Don't start playing the victim now," said Giulio. "You already knew from our first meeting how I felt about this whole affair."

"I thought that with all these new facts in the case you might change your opinion."

"What new facts? Let's try to recapitulate. The facts are that we happened purely by chance to discover a dead body dating from the war years. We know that he was young, male, blond or red-haired, tall, wore glasses, had broken a leg sometime before his death, and he had two holes in his head, as if he'd been shot. We found other lesions on the vertebrae and ribs, of less obvious origin. He had with him a cigarette case bearing the initials K.D. and a partial piece of feminine jewelry, and he was wearing clothes with metal buttons on them. Are we in agreement on all that?"

"Fine, go on."

"The corpse was found among the ruins of a mountain cottage, in a sort of underground burrow or inside that thing that you call a *nevera*. Based on a number of details concerning the form and orientation of the ruins, we hypothesized that the cottage was originally entirely aboveground and that later the embankment collapsed on top of it. We also thought that this might mean that someone had perhaps hidden or placed the body in the cottage, and then brought the house down or else had the embankment that was behind it come down on top of it.

What else? The cottage stood in a rather isolated area near the San Primo Pass, very close to the Swiss border but far from the customs office, and just a stone's throw away from the gorge of the torrent. The lake was visible from there, though far off. Have I left anything out?"

"No, that's a perfect summary."

"At that point you tried to get some information from the current owners of the cottage, to find out whether there was any foundation to the hypothesis of the willful destruction of the building, and whether, in short, they knew anything about the affair. The official answer was a firm *no* all down the line, correct?"

"Yes."

"That's it for the facts. Now begin the hypotheses. You started investigating the Cappelletti Durand family—without authorization into the bargain—by piecing together some information obtained from, let's say, confidential sources. You found some old photographs, death certificates, testimonies of various kinds—of a very 'informal' nature, if I may say so. Little scraps of events that occurred many years ago. Then you gathered some information on Villa Regina, talked to the former owners, and established the relationship between the two families. At this rate, if all goes well, you will have reconstructed a bit of local history. But investigations, my dear, are something else entirely."

"Listening to you talk, it sounds like I haven't done anything for weeks."

"I've said nothing of the sort. You've done some excellent research; you've found out many things about that family. Which would be perfect if the Cappellettis were the target of your investigation. It's too bad they're not. Why don't you realize this? The Cappellettis exit the stage the moment they tell you they're unable to give you the only information that you can ask of them—that is, information about that cottage. And the matter ends there. If you're unable to prove they're lying about the cottage, or that they're somehow involved in the young man's death, you haven't the right to pull them back into the game. That's just it, and it's exactly what Arisi will tell you, especially if you mention the Cappellettis without giving him a convincing answer as to why you're so interested in them. And one minute later he'll shelve the case, since that's what he's been wanting to do from the start."

Stefania pushed her cup into a corner and sighed.

"So what should I do, in your opinion?"

"If I were you, I would propose closing the case myself. That way you'll deprive Arisi of the satisfaction of doing so himself. And I wouldn't say anything to him about the Cappellettis."

⌒

She suddenly felt very tired when climbing the stairs of the forensics offices. Nobody'd come back from lunch yet, even though Selvini had said they were just going out for a sandwich.

She sat down in front of the big window in the hallway, looking outside distractedly. It was past one thirty, and Camilla, who got out of school early that day of the week, must have already been home. She dialed the number.

"Hi, Cami, how are you?"

"Why are you calling me, Mommy?"

"Just to know how you are. Is Martina all right?"

"She's in the kitchen warming up the food for lunch. She said we're eating Mexican today, because something Mexican just opened up around here and they even brought us Mexican presents with the food."

"Real Mexicans? Wow! Anything for me?"

"You don't like beans, and so . . ."

"So, no beans, no present? I get it. Well, enjoy your lunch. I'll be home early today, so maybe tonight we'll go out for pizza."

"Can we go to Spizzico?[7] They're giving away kites."

"Okay, we'll eat at Spizzico."

She sent her a silent kiss.

Selvini, in the meantime, had returned.

"Sorry I'm late, Inspector, but the line at the bar was really long. Have you found anything interesting?"

"I need a further enlargement of this part of the picture: the people sitting and the people standing in front of the staircase. Both rows."

"We can try, but I can't say how legible it will be."

"I would also like confirmation that these two"—and she pointed to Margherita and Maria in the family portrait—"are the same people as in this photo," and she indicated the candy striper and the nurse.

"We can see right away. We'll scan them and then compare them. It'll only take a few minutes."

A few minutes later the two photos appeared on the monitor, one beside the other. Selvini started manipulating buttons and keyboards, breaking up the images into pixels and selecting the areas of interest. He enlarged the desired details and put the images up on the same screen.

"Here we are. You can work this yourself, it's very easy. Click on the area you want to enlarge, then reduce it or move it as you wish. You can even print something if you like. I loaded some paper in the printer, so you can get some clear pictures. But just a few details, if possible, because it costs an arm and a leg, and the funds are always late arriving from Rome. At any rate, we'll be in the office next door if you need anything."

"Thanks. Don't worry, I should be able to manage by myself."

She began to study the images. The women in the two photos not only looked like each other, they were identical. Maria and Margherita. It was them. There was no doubt about it. Some time had passed between the two photos, and Margherita's facial features had sharpened. In the second photo she looked more mature, more conscious, and no longer wore her hair in braids, but had it carefully done up. A young lady, in short, though the smile and the sparkle in the eyes were the same as in the first snapshot. And she really was very beautiful, just as Germaine Durand had said. Maria, too, was exactly the same as she'd been described: tall, imposing, even more so with her starched Red Cross bonnet. Aquiline nose, cape, head rising above the rest. And then the expression. A proud, self-confident gaze directed straight at the camera. A decisive, defiant-looking person.

Power, control: these were the things the image called to mind.

She ran the cursor over one face, then the other, exploring the details slowly, centimeter by centimeter. On Margherita's neck there was a sort of gray shadow. She tried to center it, but as she tried to enlarge it, the outlines blurred.

"How can I get a further enlargement of this detail?" she asked Selvini after knocking at the door of the next office. "The object might be a pendant or just a shadow, I can't really tell."

"Further enlargement might make it difficult to maintain a legible level of definition. But let's try. Just one second."

Selvini sat back down in front of the screen and started moving the image around in a series of zooms. Fascinated, Stefania behind him followed the cursor's comings and goings. Actually the mechanism was quite simple: the part of the photograph being explored became smaller and smaller while the pixels got bigger and bigger but also more and more incomprehensible, especially when each detail was seen on its own. It became therefore necessary to refer continually back to the overall picture to understand what one was seeing, or what part of what one was seeing, with each new manipulation.

"Here, Inspector, have a look at the areas of interest to you. Is that better now?"

"Well, I can see, but I can't make out very well what I'm seeing."

Selvini did a couple of zoom-outs.

"I've selected the columns marking the limits of the image you're interested in. You can see the upper body of the woman over the head of the blond man sitting down. All this black here is the cape of the Red Cross nurse to the side. This is the man's face. Now I'll enlarge his shoulders. See the hand resting there? The white in the background, on the other hand, is the bib of the other nurse's uniform."

"There's a hand?"

"It looks like a hand to me. Here, see for yourself, just lightly resting on the soldier's shoulder. You can see just four fingers, but I'd say there isn't any doubt."

"Freeze the image for a second, please. No, there's no doubt that's a hand. Does it belong to the nurse or to the candy striper beside her, in your opinion?"

"I don't think it belongs to the candy striper. I think it's the hand of the nurse above the soldier, because the one on the left, from the position she's in, could never have reached that far."

"I think you're right, Selvini. Please print this image for me."

"As for that other detail, that, instead, is a band reflecting the light. It might be a necklace or a light chain, and this could in fact be a pendant."

"Isn't it possible to enlarge it a little more?"

"The problem then becomes bringing it into focus," said Selvini, fiddling with the keyboard. "I would say that this is the biggest we can get it. At least with this machine."

Stefania looked at the new enlargement, perplexed.

"I can't see much here."

"It seems pretty clear to me that it's a chain. See these little shapes in sequence? They're not spherical, so I would rule out that they're beads in a necklace. They might be rings, or else links in a metal chain, also because they're reflecting the light, and since the object is worn around the neck . . ."

"It can only be a chain necklace. And what can you tell me about the pendant?"

"It's oval in shape, also metal, with smooth edges. And rather thick, I'd say."

"In what sense?"

"It's not slender like a normal pendant. It's fairly wide, to the point that you can just glimpse a wedge of shadow on the side. It must also be relatively heavy, since it seems to be pulling the chain downwards."

"Okay, print these up for me, too, as well as the previous group shot, the one with the nurse, the blond man, and the candy striper to the side. I'll send someone to pick them up tomorrow. Meanwhile, could you send me advance electronic copies by e-mail? Thanks for everything, Selvini."

"Just doing my job."

She needed a little walk. She rang the office. Piras answered, which rarely happened.

"Everything quiet there?"

"Routine stuff, Inspector. Two evictions, a drunken hobo at the San Giovanni station throwing empty bottles at patrolmen, charges filed against the priest of the parish of Santa Eufemia."

"What did the priest do?"

"He rang the church bells. Three families in the neighborhood filed a complaint about the chimes at night. On the hour, half hour, and quarter hour."

"Vespers and funerals?"

"Did you read the complaint?"

"No, but I can imagine it. And what did you do about the hobo?"

"We took him to the emergency room. Once the booze wore off they gave him some hot tea and threw him out."

"Well, they couldn't very well give him free room and board. Okay, then, everything seems under control. I'll be there in less than an hour."

She quickly crossed the center of town, heading towards Piazza Cavour and the lake. It was starting to warm up, and summer didn't seem far away. A number of bars on the lakeshore had already set up their tables outside, and the days were getting longer.

She fished her cell phone out of her purse and dialed Valli's number.

"Hi, it's Stefania."

"Hi. How are you?"

"I'm here by the lake. I decided to take a break of about an hour. Feel like some coffee and a little chat?"

"Right now?"

"If you're not already back at work, that is."

"I'm struggling with some cadastral surveys. Just give me time to get my motorbike and I'll be there. Where are you, exactly?"

"In the little square next to the cable cars."

"Give me fifteen minutes."

Stefania smiled to herself and went up to the railing, leaning out to look at the water, which sparkled in the sunlight. She closed her eyes and listened to the lapping of the waves against the gravel, with the sounds of the city in the background. A few minutes later she heard the rumbling of a motorcycle. She smiled.

"Feel like going for a walk? I'd like to go as far as the fountain in Viale Geno," said Valli, smiling.

"What if it starts to get late?"

"In that case I'll give you a ride back to your office on my motorcycle, as long as you're not afraid."

"Me, afraid? Who do you think I am?"

They walked along the lakefront chatting and laughing. A cigarette by the fountain of the villa that marked their destination, and an American coffee at the little bar in the square, and it was time to go. As they were about to leave—with Stefania still sitting, and Valli standing behind her—he called to her attention a detail at the top of Monte Croce, and in doing so he'd momentarily laid a hand on her shoulder.

It was only a moment, but it hadn't escaped her attention. Nor had the faint scent of aftershave mixed with that of his leather jacket when he drove her back to the station on his motorbike. She'd felt weightless just then, with the wind in her hair, which she'd brushed back with a gesture she thought she'd forgotten forever. As she climbed down from the seat, Valli joked:

"I'd better leave you here. You never know, a police inspector going around on a motorbike without a helmet . . ."

She laughed and shook his hand.

Till next time, Luca.

⌒

Waiting for her on the landing was Piras, looking worried.

"Inspector, we tried calling you on your cell phone a short while ago, but it was turned off."

"What's going on, Piras?"

"This envelope came for you from forensics. Dr. Selvini said that if you still need him, he'll be there till six this evening. And Don Carlo's in the waiting room."

"Don Carlo?"

"The parish priest of Santa Eufemia. Carboni said you have to handle that case. He's already been here for almost an hour."

"Ah, the bells. What can I possibly do about it? Are we going to silence the bells and risk triggering a religious war?"

Piras looked at her in horror. He rarely understood irony.

It took her almost two hours to convince the priest that the complaint might be withdrawn if perhaps he agreed to have the bells ring only on the hour, leaving out the half and quarter hours. Don Carlo promised to shorten the chimes a little for the first Mass, at seven in the morning.

Afterwards, she opened the envelope from Selvini.

Top-notch work, as always.

He'd succeeded in getting a tight frame of Margherita, with Maria to the right and the blond soldier sitting in front. She fixed her attention on the details she'd requested: Margherita's hand on the soldier's shoulder and the pendant hanging from the chain.

What did it all mean?

Nothing, Giulio would have said. The fact that Margherita wore a pendant around her neck was neither here nor there, likewise her resting her hand on the soldier's shoulder as they posed for the group photo. It might be merely a gesture of sympathy or protection. Or maybe affection. Or understanding. And so? What did that change in the overall dynamics of her investigation?

Nothing.

She could ask Madame Durand for a copy of the photo of Margherita with the pendant around her neck. But what for?

She felt momentarily discomfited and set the photos back in the green folder with the others. She tried to busy herself with other things, but couldn't stop thinking about that photograph.

Maria, Margherita, the German soldier. The hand, the military overcoat, the leg in a cast, the glasses. The pendant.

"Feel like a coffee, Piras?"

"Sure, Inspector."

"How's your wife doing?"

As she distractedly listened to Piras tell her about his wife and how bad the poor girl felt, omitting no details as to the vomiting and all the rest, at a certain point she stopped pretending and stared at the frame resting on the desk.

"The glasses, the leg—the right leg! How could I not have thought of this sooner?"

"What glasses?"

"I'm sorry, Piras, it's nothing—I was just talking to myself. I have to run now."

"What about the coffee?"

"Get one for me, too," she said, leaving a two-euro piece on the desk.

12

⌣

"The most important detail is the earpiece of the glasses, and then maybe the metal buttons, if they're not too small, and then of course the little chain and the cover of the locket we found with the corpse."

Selvini had the pensive look of someone who no longer knew which way to turn.

"It might be better to shoot those exhibits again from different angles."

"If you really think so, I'll have them brought to you at once."

"It'll take a few days."

"You couldn't do it tomorrow?"

"The week is about to end, and we're behind on last month's work: reports to turn in, photos to catalog. A lot of stuff, really."

"Please, Selvini, I beg you. I'm asking as a personal favor. The case is about to be shelved, if I don't come up with any new, decisive elements in the next few days . . ."

"All right, Inspector, I'll do what I can."

Stefania returned to her office and checked her e-mail box

to see if the photos she'd requested were there. They were much crisper on-screen than in their printed versions. She felt excited and even a little anxious, like someone waiting for news who jumps up every time the phone rings or there's a knock at the door. She felt ready to spring into action.

She turned her attention back to Uncle Heinrich.

"Lucchesi! Piras! Isn't there anyone here?"

Lucchesi appeared in the doorway, already in civvies and looking like someone about to go home.

"Are we already done for today?"

"Inspector, it's past six, and I've been on call since yesterday morning."

"All right, then, when you pass the switchboard, tell them to call this number and put the call through to me."

While she waited she did a quick calculation: the colonel, being a relatively high-ranking officer during the war, must have been at least forty years old.

Now he would be around ninety and more, she thought dejectedly. But in the final analysis she had an advantage: she had nothing to lose.

"Inspector Valenti?"

"Yes, Signor Montalti, good evening, I'm sorry to bother you again. Do you mind if I keep you on the phone for a few minutes? It involves something very important."

"More doubts about Villa Regina?"

"No, this time I'm asking you for help: I'm trying identify by any means available a person about whom we've opened an investigation."

That wasn't exactly the case, but it was a perfectly fine way to break the ice just the same.

"I'm glad to help, provided I can."

His tone was one of great surprise, despite the customary politeness.

"The last time, you mentioned something to me about your uncle Heinrich and how he fled from Italy during the war in the company of his attendant, and how the escape probably came to a tragic end for the young soldier."

"That's right."

"I have reason to believe that a soldier who appears in a photo in my possession from just before the end of the war was in fact your uncle's attendant. What I'm asking of you, in essence, is simply to confirm this identification, as long as your uncle or father . . ."

The words hadn't come out quite right, but Montalti came to her aid rather naturally.

"Inspector, my uncle Heinrich has been dead for more than twenty years, and my father died shortly after him. Only my aunt is still alive, though she is very old. I don't know if we can be of any help to you."

The man was hesitating. After a few moments of silence, he resumed speaking.

"So you have news of this soldier? At the moment I can't remember his name. He was little more than a lad at the time of the escape, and my uncle had grown as fond of him as of a son. I know that when the war was over he tried to get in touch with the young man's parents, to see if they had any news of him, but I don't think they did. It distressed him terribly."

"It's not good news, unfortunately. If our suspicions are correct, we may have found his remains in a mountain area that was probably the same one where the events you told me about took place."

"I'm sorry."

"If you give me an e-mail address I can send you a copy of this photograph, for an initial, informal identification."

"Of course."

They exchanged e-mail addresses.

"May I call you again in a couple of days?" asked Stefania.

"Absolutely, Inspector. Until then."

She sat there at her desk, thinking. Now all she could do was wait.

She put the green folder into a drawer, turned off the light, and went out.

～

"Come on, it won't be long now till school's out. Then you can sleep as late as you like."

That way, maybe I, too, can get some sleep, thought Stefania.

Camilla answered with a sort of grunt. She was in crisis, as always happened as the end of the school year approached. Martina was also in crisis, because she had to pass two exams before the end of the month. Afternoons they would spend in Camilla's room studying: Camilla on one side, Martina behind her. Ron would oversee the situation, purring on the bed. Nutella jars were disappearing faster and faster.

That morning the alarm hadn't gone off, perhaps because Stefania had forgotten to set her cell phone. They flew down the stairs and then headed off to school, through the eight A.M. chaos of the city.

When she got to headquarters, half an hour late, she collapsed in front of a cappuccino. The fresh brioches, as usual, were already gone. She sat there fingering the customary sticky pastry with a fake cherry on top.

"Hey, princess, what's the matter, didn't you sleep last night?"

It was Giulio, dressed to the nines, close shaven and well scented, with briefcase in hand and newspaper under his arm. Upon seeing him, Stefania felt only hatred. She'd barely had time to grab the first pair of slacks and the first blouse within reach and put them on. The colors probably clashed, and she wasn't sure whether she'd brushed her hair properly.

"Storm signals, I see. Better steer clear. Any news?"

"No."

"All right, then, I'm going upstairs to talk to your boss."

"Best of luck," said Stefania, smiling.

She returned to her office, sat down, and turned on the computer. The icon announcing "new messages" was flashing. She opened her e-mail with a mix of trepidation and impatience. There were two messages from Montalti, sent around eight o'clock that morning.

Dear Inspector Valenti, yesterday evening after dinner, my cousins and aunt and I examined the photo you sent to me. Unfortunately none of them had ever seen my uncle's attendant in person. They did have this photo of the young man, however, together with other fellow soldiers, which I'm sending you here. He's the one holding the bridle of Uncle Heinrich's horse. To us there seems to be a strong resemblance, but you can judge for yourself. The boy's name is or was Karl Dressler, and he was from Leipzig. My cousin has kept some letters my uncle wrote to the boy's family between 1950 and 1962. All were returned to sender, opened by the censors and stamped "unknown." Years later my uncle said he'd also contacted some Leipzig city govern-

ment officials but always got the same answer: "Person un-
known at the indicated address." That's all we know, but
you can imagine how difficult it was, at that time, to reach
someone on the other side of the Iron Curtain, in a city half
destroyed by Allied bombs. My uncle did not have the good
fortune to see the Wall come down. And he never did suc-
ceed in getting any information about his soldier, despite
the fact that he had stipulated in his will that his officer's
sword should go to Karl.

We are ready to honor his last wishes, and if what you
told me yesterday turns out, unfortunately, to be true, we
would like to undertake the procedures necessary for the
repatriation of Karl Dressler's mortal remains.

I ask you please to keep us informed of any further de-
velopments in this matter.
        P.M.

The second e-mail contained the photo mentioned in the
prior message.

Four soldiers posing and, behind them, a magnificent, dark
stallion. Holding the bridle was a blond young man, tall and
slender, with glasses. A gentle face. Stefania filed the photo in
her computer and then opened the other photo, the one prepared
by Selvini.

Montalti was right. The resemblance was striking. In the
photo taken at Villa Regina the soldier was thinner and more
gaunt faced. The smile was more melancholic, but there was no
question that it was the same person.

Stefania stared at the two images.

Karl Dressler.

K.D.

Is that really you, young man?

She shook off these thoughts and called Selvini.

"I'm about to e-mail you another photograph."

"Another?"

Stefania ignored Selvini's tone of resignation.

"I think it may involve the same soldier portrayed in the photo from the other day. The one whom the nurse is touching on the shoulder with her hand."

"Yes, I figured that, but today we . . ."

"Did you get the exhibits I sent you?"

"Yes, but . . ."

"Well, now it's your turn. You have all the pieces of the puzzle. But be advised: I'll be in my office all morning and afternoon. I'll be waiting to hear from you."

"Yes, but Inspector—"

"Oh, I forgot something. If the chief inspector should happen to call . . . Naturally I've already reassured him that your lab is doing everything in its power to give us an answer as quickly as possible, perhaps by the end of today, but you know what Carboni's like. He's taken a great interest in this case, as has Arisi."

"Okay, I get the point, Inspector, that's quite enough. I'll get right to work."

She'd lied shamelessly, but bluffing, given the situation, had become a necessity. Time was pressing. And then, all things considered, it was true that Carboni and Arisi were interested in the case, just not in the same way as Stefania and, above all, not for the same reasons.

She spent the rest of the morning on documents and reports. Noon arrived, then one o'clock.

At that hour the forensics staff must surely be on their lunch break.

She took a short break herself and dropped in at the Noseda bookshop, near Porta Torre, just to have a look at the used-book shelves at the back. There was a very good bookseller who worked there, always available and polite. Stefania loved chatting with the girl.

The afternoon passed quickly. At half past three she had to pass by the clerk of the court's office to pick up some files.

At four o'clock, still no news.

Impatient, she picked up the phone. Busy. She tried again. Still busy. She took the time to smoke a cigarette before trying again.

Just as she was sticking her hands in her purse to look for the lighter, the phone rang.

⌒

Stefania spent all of Saturday morning working on her report for Carboni. At eleven she rang him but got no answer. She went to see him directly in his office, after having carefully formulated a strategy.

"Come in, Valenti. So we've solved the case. Congratulations. Please leave me the report. I'll read it right away and on Monday we'll send it on to Dr. Arisi the moment he gets back to his office."

Carboni was acting exactly like someone who had just removed a great weight from his shoulders.

"So his name was Karl Dressler. Excellent. Identified from some photographs of the period, and from the object specimens found with his remains. Flawless work, Valenti. That's the power of the new technologies. In my day, all we had was a magnifying glass and our intuition."

"Actually, sir, the identification concerns only the person portrayed at the villa when it was being used as a hospital. But we're quite certain that the seated soldier with his leg in a cast is the same person as in the other photograph, for which we have the testimony of firsthand witnesses."

"I see, however, that the specimens were identified as belonging to the person, and therefore there can no longer be any doubt."

"To tell you the truth, I specified in the report that the identification of the human remains as Karl Dressler's on the basis of the evidence we found is only a matter of probability. That is, it is highly probable that those remains do belong to Karl Dressler. The shape of the glasses is consistent, the type of uniform buttons is the same, and so is the kind of military fabric. Not to mention the circumstantial data: the time period and the poorly healed leg, formerly in a cast."

Carboni looked annoyed.

"There seems to me to be plenty of evidence."

"Yes, but it was you yourself who taught me that plenty of evidence doesn't always amount to proof."

"What other explanation could there be?"

"They might all just be coincidences, however suggestive. But I'm convinced there's much more that needs to be explained in this matter."

"Such as?"

"The light chain necklace found beside the remains, and the locket, look a lot like the same articles normally worn by Margherita Cappelletti. Why did Dressler have them? And the real problem is that we still have no idea who killed him and why. A probable identification is only a starting point, in my opinion."

"But do you think this Margherita Cappelletti was in some way involved in the homicide?"

"That's hard to say. I'm led to believe that Margherita is another victim in this unfortunate story. It's a fact, however, that there was some kind of bond between the two. We don't know the nature of that bond, but the indications are that it was strong."

"But didn't this Margherita Cappelletti die, like much of her family?"

"And what does that add to our investigation?"

"Nothing, that's the point. Listen, Valenti, leave me the report. On Monday I'll talk to Arisi about it, and he'll give us his recommendations, which we'll have to follow. That's all for now. You can go."

Whenever Carboni played tough, it meant he wasn't sure of his own position. Stefania knew him well. She may even have succeeded in shaking one or two of his certainties. All she could do now was wait. It would have been pointless to insist just then.

She went into her office to check that everything was in its proper place, listlessly put her desk in order, and then sat there looking at the reconstruction of the map of the area around the Alpine cottage.

She decided to ring Giulio Allevi.

"Are you in your office?" she asked.

"For a little while yet."

"Are you in front of your computer?"

"For a little while yet."

"I'm sending you the report I just turned in to Carboni. He'll be passing it on to Arisi on Monday."

"A report? You mean there are some decisive new developments?"

"There are some new developments, yes, but not decisive ones, as I just tried to explain to Carboni about ten minutes ago."

"And what'd he say?"

"He said he'll let Arisi decide."

"Very wise of him."

"And you'll take their side, I'd bet on it."

"Give me time to read the report at least. Then I'll call you back and tell you what I think. Okay?"

"I'm leaving now to go to the hairdresser's and then to the lake with Camilla. We're going on a little excursion today, and I'll definitely be leaving my phone at home."

"Then I'll send you a message."

⌒

"I don't see any reason to keep the investigation still open, Inspector. We've managed to identify the subject with considerable certainty. The circumstances of the time period and the manner of death are perfectly in keeping with the climate of political and social disorder that characterized the end of the war. It all fits to a T. Everything is coherent and clear."

After having stressed the word "disorder," Arisi closed the folder decisively and then pushed it to one side of his desk.

"But, sir, we still don't know who killed the young man. If it was a crime, it remains unpunished."

"Do you have any idea how many crimes from that period have remained unpunished, Inspector? There was a genuine settling of accounts. Hundreds of deaths in the province of Como alone. Let me remind you that there was an amnesty. With great farsightedness, the legislator chose to put an end to that time of torment, thus paving the way for the nation to a future of pacification and reconstruction. How many people from that time are still alive now, more than fifty years later? *Cui prodest?* And now, Inspector, if you'll excuse me . . ."

As she was descending the stairs, Stefania thought about the text message she'd just received from Giulio.

I read it. My compliments to the entire team. A superb job. But Arisi will close the case. Count on it. And you do the same. Let the matter end. Let the dead bury their dead. Giulio.

She went back into her office and laid the green folder down on her desk. She went and stood at the window and lit a cigarette.

It doesn't end here, young man.

I won't abandon you.

13

～

"Piras? Lucchesi?" The two appeared in the doorway almost simultaneously.

"Piras, I want you either to go up to Lanzo or to get in touch with Marshal Bordoli. I want to know everything there is to know about Maria Cappelletti. If she's still alive, where she lives, and so on. Whatever you can find."

Then, turning to Lucchesi:

"I want you instead to get in touch with the caretaker of Villa Regina, a certain Armando, ask him if Signora Durand is still in Italy, and send an official summons through the local Carabinieri station. But let it be understood that in view of the lady's age and health, we could arrange a meeting at her home. After you've done this, go to the photo department and have Selvini give you back the envelope with the exhibits of our man K.D. Everything clear?"

When both were gone, Stefania started thinking. Maria, Madame Durand, Karl Dressler . . .

Who can tell us something about you, young man?

Maybe Raffaella Moretto would know where to start.

She was thinking of asking her friend for advice when the cell phone rang in the inside pocket of her jacket.

"It's Luca, Luca Valli. Hi."

"And this is Stefania, Stefania Valenti. Hello."

They both laughed.

"There's nothing going on in this town, not even an art exhibition or a concert."

"What a shame."

"Yeah. But wouldn't you rather just walk around? I'll be up by the lake on Saturday and Sunday."

"Me, too—again by chance, mind you. Both Saturday and Sunday."

It was true. Camilla would be spending the weekend with her father, and Stefania had planned to go to the lake.

"Do you know the church of San Martino, the one atop Monte Calbiga, outside Menaggio?" Valli suggested.

Stefania suddenly had an idea.

"No, let's go somewhere else. You'll like it, you'll see. Trust me."

"Shall we meet at the Pasticceria Manzoni at nine?"

"Yes, and if it's raining, we'll console ourselves with *maritozzi* or *pan Matalocc*."

"See you Sunday, then."

"See you Sunday."

⌒

Hearing the alarm go off, Stefania thought how nice it would be, every once in a while, to be able to sleep late.

She had nothing personal against school, even though for her it meant getting up an hour earlier than necessary every blessed morning. But this had been going on since Camilla started elementary school. She and Guido had split up a few years after the girl was born, and ever since then her ex-husband took care of Camilla every third weekend.

Again that morning there awaited the customary ritual of breakfast, morning snack, satchel, car, traffic, red lights. She would make it all go well just the same, and anyway, there was no alternative.

Camilla was all worked up. She would be spending her morning snack time with her friends. Before long, school would be out, and in a few weeks, a month and a half in all, her life would assume more tolerable rhythms.

Once school was out, Camilla would go and spend a few weeks on the lake with her mother before leaving with her father for a vacation at the beach. Every time the school year was about to end, Stefania was surprised at how quickly it had passed. One day at a time, they passed—the school years, Camilla's childhood years, Stefania's years.

The years go by, life goes on, and I'm still here, thought Stefania.

She stopped at the bar behind police headquarters and ordered her usual cappuccino. That morning there were even fresh *cornetti* with jam inside. Before going back to her office she went outside into the already hot sun to smoke a cigarette. She exchanged some banter with Marino. The world could wait another five minutes.

When she got to her office it was almost half past eight.

She quickly dealt with a case concerning a guy who was caught by customs agents at Ponte Chiasso with hashish stuffed in his tires. Then she organized things a little in her computer, answered a few phone calls, and started to read the file of the new case Carboni had assigned to her, a nasty affair involving a series of likely arsonous fires at a well-known chain of clothing stores. The suspicion was that the protection racket was behind it.

As she was trying to concentrate on the testimonies of the owners and salespersons, there was a knock at the door. It was Lucchesi, back from the photo department, delivering the envelope with the new enlargement as well as the box with the exhibits.

After a moment of hesitation, Stefania put the box in a cabinet, which she then locked. She would have to take everything to the archive and warehouse, where she would sign a receipt and write on the identification card that they were exhibits pertaining to a case now closed.

She figured she would go to the archive later.

She sat there staring at the yellow envelope containing the photos, without opening it. She knew its contents by heart. At that moment there was probably another box, she thought, the one with Karl Dressler's remains, traveling across Europe on its way to Geneva. The authorization for the expatriation had been signed directly by Assistant Prosecutor Arisi. The soldier's mortal remains would rest, after a brief funeral oration, with those of the colonel. She liked to think that the colonel's sword would be laid down beside the young man's body. Provided, of course, that someone didn't suddenly appear to claim the soldier's corpse.

She shut the folder and dialed an internal number.

"Lucchesi? Piras? Are you there?"

"I'm here, Inspector. Lucchesi's out on patrol."

"Did you do what I asked you to do?"

"Yes, Inspector."

"And?"

"This Maria Cappelletti left Lanzo in 1947. She was still alive at the time."

"Well, that's certainly news. Do we know anything else, such as where she moved to?"

"To Bergamo province. I wrote the name of the place down—at any rate, the Lanzo station is supposed to send us a fax."

"Yes, but did you check at the city hall of the town she moved to whether they know if she's still alive and, if so, where she lives?"

"We sent the request through the Carabinieri station there."

"Good. When the fax arrives please bring it up to me. I'll wait for you in my office."

Piras arrived a few minutes later.

"The place is called Seprio al Monte, Via delle Gere, number seven, in Bergamo province."

"What else?"

"For everything else we'll have to wait."

Stefania shrugged and moved the mouse. She remembered a Web site containing information on every town hall in Italy.

Seprio al Monte, province of Bergamo. An image of a lovely mountain valley appeared on-screen: green meadows, cottages, woods. Snow-capped peaks in the background.

"What a beautiful place!" Piras said behind her.

"Less than half an hour by car from Bergamo. *A charming summer holiday destination since the early twentieth century. Local cheese production, woodworking, headquarters of the Istituto Santa Maria della Pietà.*'"

She clicked on the image of the institute. An austere white building, square and surrounded by a large pinewood. Small windows all the same.

"It looks like a boarding school," said Piras.

"Or a summer vacation colony. Actually it's a kind of hospital. An accredited psychiatric institution. Treatment, rehabilitation, and long-term hospitalization. Operational psychogeriatric unit."

"Kind of a loony bin," her colleague commented.

Stefania kept staring at the image of the building, trying to recall where she had earlier heard that name mentioned.

Santa Maria della Pietà, near Bergamo.

"Battista!" she exclaimed. That's where she'd heard it.

"Battista?"

"Yes, the very same Battista Cappelletti, twenty-seven years old, handicapped. You yourself brought me the paper with all those names on it."

Piras remained silent.

Stefania reopened the green folder and looked at the latest documents.

"Here it is," she said, pointing to a few lines with her forefinger. "Battista was interned at that institute in 1947. It's a clinic for the mentally ill."

She moved the mouse again and did a double click.

"Perfect: Via delle Gere, number seven. When Maria Cappelletti left Lanzo, this is where she came to stay."

"Was she crazy, too?"

"Let's hope not," Stefania said, smiling.

It took the rest of her morning to talk to the owner, manager, two supervisors, and four salesgirls from the clothing store. Naturally nobody had seen or noticed anything unusual. The fires were set at night.

A waste of time, thought Stefania. She was distracted and in a bad mood, and above all was waiting impatiently for news from Lanzo. She prayed that Maria was still alive.

It seemed strange to her that the big strong girl from the

photos could end up in a psychiatric institute like her brother. She must be a good eighty-five years old by now, she thought.

In the early afternoon she dashed over to the prosecutors' offices. By three she was back at her desk. While discussing the morning's interrogations with Carboni, her cell phone rang.

"Inspector, we have a call from the Carabinieri station at Seprio al Monte."

Stefania immediately noticed Carboni's inquisitive expression.

"Piras, I'm busy with the chief. We can talk later."

"But, Inspector, you said it was urgent, and so I put a rush on it."

Stefania quickly hung up before Piras could say anything else. Then, with a nonchalant air, she turned to Carboni.

"So, as I was saying," she said, "in my opinion we should check the bank accounts of the company with which the stores are affiliated and possibly look into phone taps and bugs in some of the rooms."

"Is there a problem, Valenti?" Carboni asked, raising an eyebrow.

Stefania put on an innocent face and pretended not to understand the question.

"Well, yes, of course there's a problem. I didn't expect them to cooperate so readily. It's clear they fear even worse developments. They're afraid that people might find out they talked to us. But by checking the accounts we might be able to tell straight off whether it's a case of the racket or loan sharking."

Carboni still looked at her inquisitively. Stefania decided to cut things short.

"You should evaluate the situation with the prosecutor and let me know what actions I should take. I'll be in my office."

"Yes, but you keep me informed. Constantly. On everything. Got that, Valenti?"

"Constantly informed, sir, you can count on it."

She said good-bye and dashed out before Carboni could reply. As soon as she was outside in the hallway, she heaved a sigh of relief. If Piras had pronounced the name Cappelletti there would have been hell to pay for everyone. Carboni, who had a world of experience and was well familiar with her stubbornness, seemed suspicious. She rushed upstairs and went straight to Piras. In the meantime Lucchesi had returned, and the two were chatting animatedly.

"Okay, tell me everything," she said to Piras.

"We got the information we wanted. Maria Cappelletti is still alive and indeed lives at Via delle Gere, number seven, in that place we saw earlier on your computer."

"And?"

"They told me over the phone that Maria Cappelletti is a nun. Everybody knows her there. She's a kind of mother superior or something like that. And apparently, despite her age, she's still very much with it and runs a tight ship."

"I'm not surprised. That's how she was when she was young, and she was only some kind of nurse."

"Why, do you know her?"

"Hell, yes, I was a nurse back then, too!"

Lucchesi elbowed him, but Piras remained unruffled.

"Very well," Stefania continued, "now get me the phone number of that institute. And you, Lucchesi, how did you make out with Signora Durand?"

"That guy Armando came out, nice guy, actually, and he said that the signora had already spoken to you and that she'd already given you all the information she had on the case. He added that in any event, from now on, if we want anything from her, we should contact her lawyer in Milan."

"Message received. We'll start by hearing out Sister Maria and we'll deal with Madame later. I may very well take tomorrow afternoon off and go to Bergamo, if everything's calm here. Or maybe Saturday morning. I should still have some vacation days left over from last year. Okay, guys, I'll be in my office. Keep me posted."

She'd just sat down at her desk with the idea of lighting a Muratti when there was a knock at the door. It was Lucchesi.

"Inspector, I wrote down the number of the institute for you here."

"Thanks. I'll try to call now."

She dialed the number and listened to the recorded message, which told her to wait so as not to lose her place in line. Lucchesi was still standing in front of her desk.

"Thanks, Lucchesi, you can go now."

The young man seemed undecided and kept fumbling with the piece of paper in his hands.

"Is there a problem, Inspector?"

Stefania looked at him in surprise for a moment, then smiled. He was a smart kid.

"No, Antonio. But this phase of the investigation has to be kept under wraps, so to speak. No uniforms or squad cars, and use only the utmost discretion, at least until things become a little clearer. Do you understand?"

"I think so. But if you need me for anything—I mean, if you need us for anything—me or Piras, that is—we're here. We've already talked about it, and we're in agreement."

Stefania kept looking at him.

"Thanks. And please thank Piras for me. I know I can count

on you, and I know you're good kids, but, believe me, for the moment it's better if I handle this alone. I can't get the two of you involved in a case that's been officially closed. Mum's the word with Carboni, I mean it."

She couldn't quite find the right words.

"In cases like this, I answer only to my conscience, first and foremost. But I can't ask you guys to take any risks. Thanks, anyway, both of you."

"As you prefer. At any rate, just remember we're always here, at all times. We've also got some vacation time left over."

"I'll remember that. Thank you both."

She watched him go out and close the door behind him.

They were good kids.

⌒

The neutral voice of the institute's switchboard operator interrupted her thoughts.

"Santa Maria Institute, good morning. How can I help you?"

"Good morning. This is Dr. Valenti, and I'm calling from Como.[8] I'd like to speak with Sister Maria Cappelletti, please."

"I'll put you through to her secretary. Please stay on the line."

She stayed on the line.

"I'm sorry, who did you say you were?"

"Dr. Valenti."

"Do you have an appointment?"

"No, I'm calling for the first time."

"All right, please wait just a minute."

She waited several minutes.

"Doctor, our relations with physicians are conducted directly through our health manager. Let me put you through to management."

"I'm not a medical doctor. I'm a police inspector. And I would like to speak directly with Sister Maria Cappelletti."

"I'm sorry, Inspector, I misunderstood."

Stefania was starting to lose her patience.

"Hello, Inspector, I'm Sister Carla. The mother superior is busy at the moment, could I take a message?"

"No, I'm sorry. It's a strictly personal matter. Please tell your mother superior that I need to ask her some questions about her sister Margherita Cappelletti. It would be preferable if we could meet in person."

"I'll let her know. Just another moment, please."

This time the pause was very brief.

"Would Monday at two thirty P.M. be all right?"

⌒

"Are you ready to trek?" asked Stefania.

"Ready as ever. The day's off to a pretty good start, I think."

"Between the cappuccino and the tart, we've got a full tank of calories. We're ready for the expedition."

"It was worth it, wasn't it? That apple tart just out of the oven was a pure delight, to say nothing of the *barchette* with whipped cream."

"I didn't know you were such a glutton, Luca. Though it's true, it's impossible to resist the pastries of the Pasticceria Manzoni."

"So where are we going?"

"At the moment, we're going to the lakeshore, to smoke a cigarette."

"Excellent idea. And then what?"

"A stroll back in time, by the lake."

"When you put it that way, it sounds a little lugubrious."

Valli laughed, then they both laughed.

Stefania felt in a good mood, as light as a feather. Valli had that sort of effect on her. Rather like when, as a little girl, on a summer morning when it was still cool outside, she was about to go out on an excursion or a hike in the mountains. She had always loved to walk, to run ahead of everyone else, in shorts and gym shoes and a backpack on her back.

After getting into Stefania's car, they took the Regina road towards Tremezzo, leaving the village of Menaggio behind. Out the car window, Bellagio looked within reach, with Punta Sparti-vento drawing the center line of the lake. Stefania could make out the silhouette of Villa Melzi and headed straight towards La Tramezzina. The riverboat *Milano*, packed with tourists, was going in the same direction as them.

She drove past Griante and the pink turret rising above the lake; the Hotel Bellevue and the banners of the Grand Hotel Tramezzo were where they'd always been, besieged, like every summer, by British tourists. The old Anglican church and Villa Carlotta, which at that time were looking their best with their azaleas in bloom, were among the favorite destinations of the English. But Stefania greatly preferred the mysterious Villa Sola in Bolvedro, with its imposing gate and sumptuous façade of an ivory, almost unreal white, guaranteed to stir wonder in anyone who saw it for the first time.

Before long they arrived in Mezzagra. Here, fifty years ago, the course of history was decided. They stopped in front of the Bonzanigo Villa, in which Mussolini had spent his last night in the arms of Clara Petacci.

"Are you going to take me to the gate of Villa Belmonte now?"

"Did you know that every year, on April 28, hundreds of nostalgics come here to pay homage?"

"Yes, I saw them once. I feel sorry for them—but I also find them sort of endearing."

"They make *me* feel angry. Not because I agree with them, mind you. But because I just can't understand what they're doing there, in front of that villa, when everyone knows that Mussolini was killed in Bonzanigo and not in Giulino."

"Don't tell me that you, too, believe in the theory of the double execution? You have a marked soft spot for conspiratorial hypotheses."

"No, the simple fact is that all you need is to be a little familiar with these places and with the people who still remember to know what actually happened at the time. And just to put an end to the discussion, he wasn't killed at four o'clock in the afternoon together with La Petacci, but in the morning, in the courtyard of the De Maria house."

"And Claretta?"

"Claretta was bumped off shortly afterwards, right where we are now, with a burst of machine-gun fire in the back, as the Duce's corpse was being carried away."

They got back in the car and went as far as Lenno, where they left it in a parking lot and headed off on foot. They crossed the national road, passing under a stone bridge.

"Okay, see? We're already on the Regina road. There are a number of stretches in this area that still follow the original routes. The road passes near the lake, through the inhabited areas or sometimes below them. It passes by villas and churches, and looks out on the lakeshore. When I was little I used to come here often in summertime. It was always shady, and along the first stretch there were a lot of hazelnut bushes."

"Like these?"

"Yes, but the nuts aren't ripe yet. By August they'll turn large and round. We used to crack them with stones and eat them."

They walked in silence. As they advanced, the sounds of the road became increasingly faint. Whenever Stefania traveled that road she felt as if she were entering another dimension and going back in time.

"What a smell!" said Valli. "And what a wall!"

"Look up," Stefania replied. "Those are extremely tall laurel hedges, and a bit farther down are some huge larches and magnolias, and whole expanses of ferns. What you're smelling is a scent of laurel and resin, and underwood. This wall here in front of us is the enclosure wall of Villa Monastero, which has the same name as the more famous one on the opposite shore. Take a good look at it. It has always reminded me of life passing and changing, and of the past returning."

"A simple wall has that effect on you?"

"Look at these stones at the base, how big they are. Two meters of massive wall, and yet down there you can see smaller rocks differently arranged. There must have been a door here, or a gate, since we can still see the squared stones. It must have been an entrance that at some point was closed up; if you think about it, at one time there must have been a lot of people coming and going here. Can you picture it? People going to the monastery, carts, animals, fishermen coming up from the lake with their baskets of fish."

"Are we already so close to the lake?"

"If you listen carefully you can hear the waves, the lake waters lapping and splashing. Back here there even used to be a water fountain—the water was very cool and used to pour right out into the mossy surroundings through the head of a mythological animal. When we were kids we always used to stop here and drink. Now it's dried up. Almost all the fountains have disappeared. In a minute we'll be at the villa's main gate. You can even see inside a little. You come to a point where the garden's wall and the walls of the house are so close that you can touch them both at the same time. There's a kind of dark, narrow, very high fissure. We found it sort of scary."

"Stefania!"

She shook herself out of it and smiled.

"You're right. Maybe all this talk of walls and stones bores you. You want to stop for a minute? Right here, down below, there's a little strip of shore with sand. There's not much in the way of beaches around here. It's all so small, you know, like being inside a miniature painting."

"Made to the measure of man."

"The men who used to go boating on the lake even when the *breva* was blowing cultivated the little bit of land that was there. Others went into the monastery, still others went up into the mountains with their animals. Whoever had any, that is. Owning animals in those days meant being well-off. Who knows how many children have run through this way? Imagine all the cats sleeping on these warm stones in summertime. Do you smell that scent? That's algae. A lot of people say it bothers them, they say it smells bad. Actually it's only lake water, lying stagnant. It's probably been that way for millennia."

"Stefania!"

"Okay, okay. I'll shut up now, for ten minutes at least. Let's go down to the lake. Here, be careful, it's a bit slippery. This way. Give me your hand."

"But there's not enough room for two people to sit down."

"That's only because we didn't make a reservation. Otherwise there would be tables and chairs ready for the occasion."

"Well, if need be, I can suffer and hold you in my arms."

"Gallant as ever."

They laughed and sat down side by side with their backs against the low wall, letting the sun caress their faces. Before them the lake waters sparkled and glistened like silver.

"It's beautiful here," said Valli.

"Isn't it?"

Stefania opened her eyes for a moment and caught Valli looking at her face. She didn't mind. It didn't bother her the way it did with all other men.

"When you want to move on, just give me a whistle."

"There's no hurry. There are so many things to see here, and anyway, I like to go slowly, when possible. Time passes so quickly, as a rule, and here it seems to slow down a little. Let's hold on to it for ourselves."

"I accept."

Valli lit a cigarette, and Stefania, too, reached out for her backpack.

"Want one?"

She opened her eyes in surprise. He was offering her a cigarette. She hesitated for a moment, then took one, closed her eyes again, and brought it to her mouth. For the time it took to smoke a cigarette, she listened to her heartbeat.

It was a pleasant sensation, one she was no longer accustomed to.

After the cigarette, they went up and down trails and pebbled footpaths, coming out sometimes on the lake side, sometimes on the mountain side. They crossed the national road a few times, but only for brief stretches. After Lenno, they came to Ossuccio. They passed through the Romanesque Oratorio of Santa Maria Maddalena, entering through the great portal, then walked parallel to the lakeshore opposite the *isola*.

"See how small this branch of the lake is here? The *isola* is so close you can even swim to it. And you can see all the details from here: the staircase leading up to the church, the footpath circling around everything. The sparse little wood up on top."

"Is there time to go onto the *isola*? That would be nice. I've never seen it before from so close."

"Maybe after lunch. Provided we can find someone willing to ferry us over in their boat."

"Lunch? Did you really say 'lunch'?"

"I just meant this afternoon."

"Too bad. It wasn't a bad idea."

"Don't tell me you're already hungry, Luca."

"Then I won't, if you care so much."

He smiled.

"All right, now we're going to travel down another part of the Regina road in this sort of tunnel, after which we'll go down to the church of San Giacomo, and then, if you behave, we'll have lunch at La Tirlindana."

"I wonder how old this passage under the house is."

"Smell that? These shadows smell of cellars and mildew. There used to be chicken coops and rabbit hutches here, and you could hardly breathe. Now there are tavern doors and garden gates. But the charm has remained. And there's one last thing I have to show you before we go home. We'll go down this way and walk along the torrent, and that'll take us right there."

"You mean Beccaria's tomb, which you mentioned earlier?"

"No, that's between Ossuccio and Sala Comacina. What I'm going to show you is instead a kind of common denominator in the stories of many people who lived at different times and in different circumstances."

"You stopped smiling the moment you started talking about it."

"Here we are. This is Villa Regina."

Valli stood there looking at the broad façade, the long lane, and the great gate.

"So this is *the* Villa Regina?"

"The one and only. We're looking at the rear, the part with the servants' and caretaker's quarters. Seen from the front, it's even more magnificent, but you can see that side only from a boat, or from the shore when the water is low. Or if you circle round that bit of wall down there, like we used to do when I was a kid."

"It's probably not advisable now. But you were right. It's very beautiful."

Stefania pressed her face up against the gate and looked at the large white water lilies in the fountain.

"There are other villas just as beautiful and more along this part of the lake. But this one has a history. Many people have lived here. Margherita, in the final years of her very short life, and her father, Remo. And Maria, the sister, whom I'll be meeting on Monday. . . . In short, the Cappellettis who came before the ones who live there now, a family of bankers, lawyers, and senators, half Swiss, half American. Not to mention the war, the Germans, the fleeing Jews. Did I tell you I came here to meet the current owner, Madame Durand?"

Valli looked at her and smiled with forbearance. Apparently he wasn't that keen to resume the discussion about Villa Regina.

"It's an ancient villa," he said. "Over its five hundred years of history it was bound to have a few owners with storybook lives, and who knows how many adventures. You, without knowing, have entered their lives, and so they all seem like extraordinary characters to you. But who knows how many similar stories one can find in places like this?"

"I don't doubt it. But it's not, you see, because they're people out of the ordinary. And anyway, I've never felt any fascination for the wealthy or powerful. The point is, something happened here that I haven't yet been able to understand. It's right there before my eyes, but I can't decipher it. A few pieces of the puzzle are missing."

"Not for long, Monsieur Poirot. But for now, shall we leave Villa Regina to its glories and mysteries and go eat some fresh fish?"

"Only if you promise me some boat-shaped pastries afterwards."

La Tirlindana was one of the best-known restaurants in the Tramezzina.

It was in Sala Comacina, right in the middle of the bay, opposite the Isola Comacina. Small in size, it was well ensconced in the old part of town, a cluster of houses all huddled together. One got to it after wending one's way through a labyrinth of little cobblestoned streets, or else directly from the lake. The small square in front of the restaurant, used as a terrace for customers' tables, was equipped with a landing dock. It was a quiet spot, with a subdued atmosphere, that served as the setting for a sumptuous menu of lake fish that changed daily.

That day, Mario, the owner as well as chef of the restaurant, had prepared some of his specialties.

Stefania and Luca sat outside and ordered sparkling Chiarella water and a carafe of white wine.

The menu called for antipasto alla Comasina, with Toc[9] and *missoltini, cipolle borettane,* and *alborelle in carpione.* As a first dish, chestnut ravioli with plums and sausage.

Valli ordered a gratin of whitefish with golden pancetta and a sampler platter of local cheeses.

Stefania kept to things she knew best.

When it was time to accompany Valli back to his car, Stefania felt a little sad.

"Well, here we are," she said, smiling, "back at the starting point. I hope it wasn't too boring for you wandering around the lake."

"It was fantastic, seeing all those places and the lake through your eyes."

"I enjoyed being with you, too."

She immediately regretted the statement and the tone in which she'd said it.

"If you want," she continued, "now that summer's on the way, we can go on other walks. There are so many things to see in these places, if you know what to look for."

"If you don't have anything better to do these days—that is, even tomorrow—a cup of coffee and a chat in town would do me just fine, as long as you don't have other engagements."

"It's certainly a nice idea. Tomorrow afternoon I'll be in Bergamo, and I don't know what time I'll be back. But I'll be free on Tuesday."

"Then I'll call you Tuesday morning."

"Okay. Good-bye, Luca."

"Bye, Stefania."

～

Stefania turned and crossed the street to head home. But when she reached the corner, she instinctively turned around. Valli was still sitting motionless in his car and looking in her direction. She waved and then turned back around, and at that moment, out of the corner of her eye, she saw him touch his lips and blow her a kiss.

14

Back at the office after a visit to the courthouse for a deposition, Stefania found an e-mail from Montalti waiting for her. It was from a few evenings before.

Dear Inspector,

The mortal remains of Karl Dressler have safely reached their destination. They are now resting in our family vault, as our uncle Heinrich would have wanted. We thank you again, and who knows whether we may not meet sooner or later. Deep down, we miss Italy, and I must admit that before I die would like to see Villa Regina again, assuming that's still what it's called.

I'm writing to you to let you know that we have officially informed the municipal government of Leipzig of the decease of Karl Dressler and his present burial place. We have provided them with all the documentation that was sent to us by the Italian courts. I don't expect much to come from this act, but our legal counsel tells us that this official statement on our part may finally lead to a serious search being conducted to find the Dressler family. And the results could be more satisfying than was the case in the 1950s, at the height of the Cold War. Should any important information emerge, I will not fail to let you know.

Cordially yours,

P.M.

Stefania thought for a moment about Montalti, his sensitivity, his sense of honor and commitment, which she seldom encountered in the circles closest to her. She certainly wasn't expecting anything concrete to come out of this, but the mere fact that someone so far away could become interested in this case put her in a good mood. She promised herself to write him back to thank him in turn.

Her thoughts then turned to the conversation she would have that afternoon, face-to-face, with Maria Cappelletti. She felt as if she were about to play her last card, and she knew she couldn't afford to waste the opportunity.

It wasn't quite eleven yet, but she already felt like heading out. She put the box with the pertinent exhibits in her purse, slipped furtively out the service exit, went to Via Italia Libera, where her car was parked, got in, and headed off towards the Bergamasca, on her way to national route 342. As soon as she was out of town she started to relax. She felt like a thief making off with the loot.

In the end it was rather like a holiday. Why all the fuss?

Clearly Carboni and especially Arisi would not have approved of her going to Bergamo and bringing along the material evidence to a case already closed. The fact was that for her superiors that evidence should already have been locked away in a file and labeled, buried in some cabinet and already gathering dust. In a way they had all, in their minds, already closed the case. Everyone except her. And since nobody else would lift another finger to seek justice for Dressler, she might as well try.

She would put everything back in its proper place before evening, and nobody would be any the wiser. That, at least, was how she saw it, and the idea that something might go wrong hadn't even crossed her mind.

She drove on serenely, passing through first the Como province and then the villages of the Brianza Lecchese. She reached her destination in less than an hour and a half. It was still early.

She stopped in the town's central square and went into a small bar full of old men to ask for information as to the best road for getting to the institute. She was the only female customer in the establishment and felt the others jovially eyeing her, but she got all the information she needed in just a few minutes.

She learned that the institute housed almost fifty chronic psychiatric patients of all ages. The youngest often came into town accompanied by orderlies to have coffee, ice cream, or to buy cigarettes. The lady running the bar told her this last detail after seeing Stefania light one up, adding that the patients were treated very well but that the nuns' rules were ironclad: long walks, no alcohol, gym classes, every sort of physical activity, early to bed every night and up at seven.

"The nuns run the show in there, even though there are only ten of them and they're not so young anymore," she said. "But they run a tight ship."

"Only ten?"

"Well, aside from a dozen orderlies, four psychiatrists who come and go, a social worker, and the service staff. But it's the nuns that manage the place."

"Do you also know the mother superior?"

"Sure. Every Monday she comes into town with her driver to go to the post office and back, or to Bergamo for business concerning the institute. She's a smart lady."

"Is she nice?"

"I find her a little intimidating, but everyone has only good things to say about her. Do you know her?"

"Not personally, but I've heard about her. I have an appointment with her today."

Stefania realized that she'd moved several steps up in the woman's esteem. She paid and went out after casting an amused glance at the main table, where a lively game of *scopa d'assi* was reaching its conclusion.

She got to the institute in just a few minutes. It was just like in the photograph: a massive white building amid the pine trees. She parked the car and headed up the main allée. Everything was very well maintained, from the perfectly mowed lawn to the orderly roses in the flower beds, to say nothing of the great windows in the lobby, shaded by white-and-blue-striped curtains. There was everywhere a scent of lavender mixed with the smell of disinfectant.

A corpulent attendant from the reception area came and accompanied her to the management offices, taking care that the new arrival had no opportunity to stop and look around along the way. The building must have had a series of internal courtyards with trees and gardens. A broad corridor around the perimeter gave onto the outside and led to rooms with linoleum floors and small sitting rooms furnished with sofas and chairs. It was all very tidy and orderly. Stefania didn't see a living soul in any of the rooms, which probably meant that people were resting. Visiting hours for relatives, as the sign posted at the start of the corridor said, were from four to five thirty P.M. They went through a door of colored glass and entered a different, apparently older area, the rooms used for management offices and the nuns' apartments. Great walnut armoires and red leather armchairs alternated with monumental plants in shiny brass pots. Fresh flowers were arranged outside the chapel intended for private prayer. A strong scent of pine wafted in through the windows, which at that moment were wide open. When the attendant knocked at the door of the mother superior's office, it was half past two.

The room was large and bright, with the same dark furniture Stefania had noticed in the waiting room. The only pleasantly different note was a bouquet of roses in a vase placed in front of a wooden crucifix hanging over a pric-dieu.

Sister Maria was sitting at the desk. There were a number of large open registers in front of her. When Stefania entered, she raised her head and leaned back gently in her chair. Then she put on a pair of glasses and started calmly observing her. Stefania put up with her stare.

"This is Inspector Valenti," the attendant announced.

"Thank you, Pinuccia, you can go now. Good afternoon, Inspector Valenti."

"Good afternoon, Mother."

"Please sit down."

The mother superior gestured towards one of the chairs in front of the desk.

"I won't hide the fact that your phone call the other day caught me entirely by surprise. How can I help you?"

Stefania looked up. The black coif and robe with a silver crucifix framed a gaunt, dour face, which contrasted sharply with the woman's lively, dark eyes, which were surprisingly still quite mobile. Her bearing was proud, and Sister Maria certainly looked younger than her eighty-five years. She kept her hands folded and immobile, waiting.

"I've come here to speak with you about events and circumstances from a long time ago, things that are related in part to your sister, or so I believe, based on what has emerged so far in our investigation."

"An investigation involving my sister?" the nun asked, showing no obvious emotion.

"That's right. The investigation I'm referring to got started when some human remains were found inside a ruined cottage near the San Primo Pass. You must certainly know the area. It's right where a new tunnel is going to be built through the pass."

"Yes, I've read about it in the papers."

"We have reason to believe that the human remains belonged to a German soldier who came into northern Italy during the Nazi occupation period."

At this point Stefania paused and looked straight into Sister Maria's eyes.

"His name was Karl Dressler. Did you know him?"

The mother superior's eyes flashed, but her tone of voice remained neutral.

"Yes," she said.

"Can you tell me in what circumstances?"

"He was interned for a few months at Villa Regina, during the period when the villa was requisitioned and turned into a military hospital for German soldiers injured in battle."

"Were you also at Villa Regina at the time?"

"Yes, I was a nurse before taking the veil. I worked there until the medical center was closed shortly before the end of the war."

"But didn't Villa Regina belong, and doesn't it still belong, to your family?"

"It became theirs afterwards."

"Some of your relatives still live there, is that correct?"

"If you're referring to my brother's widow and her children, then I suppose that's correct."

"Have you not seen them for a long time?"

"The last time I saw my brother Giovanni and his wife was the day of my father's funeral. I left Villa Regina that same day to enter a convent. And I've never gone back, not even when my brother died. That's why I said I 'supposed' that my sister-in-law still lived there with her children. I know she's still alive."

Stefania didn't reply, but remained silent for a few moments, pretending to look for something in her purse.

It was Sister Maria who resumed the thread of the discussion.

"What makes you think that the person you found was Karl Dressler?"

"A number of circumstantial details and objects that were found beside the corpse."

Stefania started rummaging in her purse again, trying to prolong the wait. Sister Maria's voice then betrayed a barely perceptible note of anxiety.

"Objects?"

"I was thinking you might be able to identify some of them. That's the real reason for my visit. These, for example."

Stefania set down on the desk the fragment of the eyeglasses' earpiece and the silver cigarette case, which was turned over so that the side with the initials was hidden.

"Do you recognize any of these things? Do you remember whether Karl Dressler smoked?"

Sister Maria eyed the objects without touching them.

"All the soldiers smoked and drank. And he smoked, too."

"And did he drink?"

"No, I don't think so."

"But this is a rather fancy object for a simple soldier, don't you think? Did he come from a wealthy family?"

"Not at all, as far as I can recall. On the other hand, for a while there was also a colonel at Villa Regina whom the soldier had served as an auxiliary. He was from a noble family, and it's possible he gave Dressler the cigarette case. It wasn't hard to get your hands on precious objects at the time, especially if you had money and connections. There were many such things in circulation, which had been confiscated and then resold cheaply on the black market, or things that had belonged to people who'd been . . ."

"Eliminated or deported, for example?"

"Yes, that too."

A silent pause ensued. Stefania decided to press on with her questions.

"Do you recognize these glasses? Could they have belonged to Karl Dressler?"

"Yes, they could. But what does all this have to do with my sister?"

"Margherita died more or less at that same time, as the war was ending. And the circumstances of her death have never been clarified."

Sister Maria looked up. Stefania thought she perceived a chink in the nun's self-assurance. She felt uneasy.

After all, the woman in front of her was nothing more than an elderly nun. She was forcing her to remember things, to reawaken a family sorrow that perhaps had never fully faded with the years.

Involuntarily her tone became softer.

"I realize I'm awakening painful memories for you, Mother, but I have to ask you these questions. It's imperative. You can help us to discover the truth. We must all do our utmost on behalf of that young man who was killed. We owe him justice, insofar as this is within the power of earthly justice."

Sister Maria said nothing, but continued to stare at the cigarette case.

Stefania resumed speaking.

"You see, Mother, we know that Karl Dressler and your sister, Margherita, knew each other."

"Yes."

"There's a photo that shows them together in a group of other people. Margherita was also at Villa Regina at that time, wasn't she?"

"Yes, she helped take care of the patients."

"Exactly what sort of relationship did your sister have with Karl Dressler?"

Sister Maria hesitated for a moment, as though trying to find the most appropriate words.

"That young man, who at the time, I think, could not have been more than twenty-five years old, was very nice and spoke English and French rather well. Margherita hadn't yet turned twenty-one, but she also spoke French well, thanks to my sister-in-law. In short, they could understand each other. He played the piano, and she used to listen to him, spellbound, in the main salon of Villa Regina. She didn't know much about music, but she felt it emotionally, so to speak. She felt beauty wherever she found it."

"Yes, I was already told that."

"By whom?"

"By your sister-in-law, Madame Durand."

"The two girls got along well because they were almost the same age. But Miss Durand was very different. Different from everyone, truth be told. All the same, she loved Margherita, in her own way."

"Go on, please."

"There isn't much else to add. Margherita never told me anything, but I realized that something had developed between her and that soldier. I watched her. She would push his wheelchair along the terrace every evening. She helped him in his rehabilitation, taught him to get around on crutches. Or she would support one arm as he walked with a cane."

"Had he been wounded?"

"Yes, in his right leg. It was a nasty wound that wouldn't heal properly. In the end the leg came out much shorter than his left one."

Sister Maria paused and looked far into the distance out the window. Then she resumed her account, speaking more softly.

"There were things—details, mostly—that an older sister couldn't help but notice. He was very attentive to Margherita. He would follow her everywhere with his eyes, turn around at the sound of her voice. The moment Margherita would walk into the great room with the other nurses, he would give a start. They spent a lot of time walking in the garden together. At a certain point, very early each morning large bouquets of fresh flowers began appearing outside our room. And I assure you they weren't for me."

Stefania made no comment.

"And what happened next?"

"Everyone could see what was happening, and after a while I thought it was my duty, as an older sister, to demand an explanation. She told me quite simply that she had fallen in love with him. She added that as soon as the war was over they were going to get married and she would follow him to Germany. Those were her intentions. It was a big blow to the family. My sister-in-law was scandalized, and my father hit the ceiling when he found out. Margherita was his favorite daughter."

"So what did your father do?"

"He decided to take her away from Villa Regina at once. Monsieur Durand offered to put Margherita up at his house in Switzerland. He said she could complete her education there. In reality, however, that last detail was simply what people in town were told, to silence the gossips. Margherita became desperate. She cried and cried and begged my father to change his mind, but he was unshakable. In the meantime he forbade her to go back to the villa. Margherita went and stayed in our old house up the mountain, with my mother and our brother Battista."

"And what did Karl say about all this?"

"My father confronted him, in a harsh way. I never did find out what was said. My father never wanted to tell me about it."

Sister Maria leaned back in her chair. She looked exhausted. Their talk seemed to have suddenly aged her. Stefania waited without saying anything, and the nun resumed speaking.

"Then everything happened very quickly. Less than a week later the hospital's military commander received the order to evacuate. In a single night, the wounded and convalescent were loaded onto trucks and smaller vehicles. We were woken up in the middle of the night and ordered to move the most seriously wounded on stretchers. I clearly remember the orders being given in German, the sound of the engines rumbling, the cries of the wounded. We didn't have time to change all their dressings. Shortly before dawn, when the column was ready to leave, the colonel and his young ward were nowhere to be found. They looked everywhere for them, smashing in doors and searching the attic, the closets, the cellars. But they were in a big hurry to leave. And in the end they did, amid a tremendous uproar. We nurses were left alone in the abandoned villa. Some who had relatives in the area left that same night. Others did the same the next day. The great house fell silent."

"And what did you do? And what about your sister-in-law?"

"I stayed at the villa with two servants who didn't have anywhere to go. We closed everything up, barred the doors and windows, covered the furniture with white sheets, as at the end of the summer holidays. It was madness, thinking back on it now."

"Why do you say 'madness'?"

"Yes, madness, quite so. And vanity. Our concern was for the furniture, the paintings, the carpets, when people outside were fighting and dying. The Germans had taken away the most valuable things, which none of us was in a position to prevent. In the end we locked the great gate and left. It was evening."

"And your sister-in-law, Madame Durand?"

"As pandemonium was raging around Villa Regina, she had shut herself up in her rooms together with her personal chambermaid. She came out only when I pointed out to her that if she didn't, she would be left completely alone in the abandoned villa. After much insistence on my part, she was finally persuaded. She came away with me and set herself up in an apartment not far from the villa. She didn't want to join us at our house in the mountains. She probably thought such an arrangement unworthy of her social standing. She would wait there, in the apartment, for her father to send her a car to take her back to Switzerland."

"Was Margherita with you?"

"No, she'd already gone up to the house in the mountains a few days earlier. My father had arranged with Durand that the two girls would leave together as soon as it was possible. Everything seemed taken care of."

"And instead?"

"The car arrived the following day, late in the evening. I was informed by a trusted person. I was given the task of accompanying my sister-in-law and Margherita. But Margherita had disappeared. I looked for her everywhere, I called her name, but to no avail. And I never saw her again after that. I never saw her alive again."

Stefania could hear the ticking of the clock on the wall. Sister Maria sat with her head bent forwards and her hands folded, as though praying.

"And what about your sister-in-law? Didn't she know where Margherita was, or why she'd run away?"

"My sister-in-law certainly knew more than she has ever wanted to admit—also because the two girls shared confidences; they had the sort of intimacy that young women have only with girls their own age. At any rate, she didn't seem very surprised, nor very worried. And she didn't wait very long for her. She left in the middle of the night that same evening, with that silly chambermaid of hers and the driver."

"And what did you do at that point?"

"I let her leave. In reality it meant having one less disturbance around. I went back up the mountainside, where we had a hut where I knew my father and brother were. I wanted to let them know that Margherita had disappeared, but they were out that night, and I had to wait until dawn the following day. When they finally came back, they had Karl Dressler and the colonel with them."

"Were you surprised to see them?"

"Yes, and seeing the German boy at that moment seemed like a kind of miracle to me. I was hoping he would have news of Margherita. I said this several times to my father, and as I was telling him what had happened I begged him to go and look for her, or to allow me to look for her. I knew those mountains well, at least as well as they did. But my father was inflexible. He ordered me to return home at once and said nothing else. My brother Giovanni even offered to come with me. But my father wasn't the kind of person you could argue with, especially at moments like that. Two days later, Margherita was brought home dead."

Stefania said nothing. Sister Maria closed her eyes, overwhelmed by the burden of these memories, and then heaved a long sigh.

"Forgive me for insisting, Mother, but didn't it seem strange to you to see Karl Dressler, of all people, up in the mountain with your father and your brother?"

"No, not really. Let's speak clearly, Inspector. I was perfectly aware of my father's activities—aware, that is, that he was helping whoever needed to leave the country to cross the border clandestinely. On top of that I also knew that Karl Dressler and the colonel had disappeared from Villa Regina the day of the evacuation. I merely put two and two together. In other words, it didn't seem the least bit strange to me that they wanted to escape. It's better than being shot as deserters, don't you think?"

"No doubt. But that's not the point. I'm thinking about the coincidences. First your father talks to Karl Dressler, and from what I have gathered I don't think it was a very friendly conversation, given the circumstances. Then, in the confusion of the evacuation, two German soldiers disappear from the villa, alone and in uniform, certainly not the best way to pass unnoticed. You remain alone in the villa the Germans have abandoned, practically defenseless, together with your sister-in-law, a chambermaid, and two servants, but, despite the obvious danger, and despite the fact that it wasn't your house yet—based on what you just told me— you actually stay there for a whole day to close up and put things in order. Amid this general confusion, if I've understood correctly, Margherita also disappears, at the very moment when she's supposed to leave for Switzerland with her future sister-in-law—that same Miss Durand who, again based on your story, doesn't seem terribly surprised by Margherita's disappearance, and who doesn't have any great qualms about leaving without any further delay. Finally, you, Sister Maria, go up the mountain to inform your father and brother that Margherita has disappeared and you see them appear in the company of Karl Dressler and the colonel. Two days later, Margherita's lifeless body is found. Don't you think there are too many coincidences in all this?"

"I won't deny it. But everything happened just as I said, Inspector. I, too, often think back on it and have trouble making any logical sense of it. At any rate, it often happened that before crossing the border, people would have to wait a while, sometimes even a few days, hiding out in the area while waiting for the right moment to cross. My father never took any more risks than was necessary, neither with his men's lives nor with his clients'. And he was an honest man, in his way, though you may find that hard to believe."

Stefania noticed that the nun was stiffening uncomfortably, and so she changed subject.

"Of course, Mother, that's not in question here, I didn't mean to imply anything to the contrary. But what seemed strange to me was that your father was helping to lead to safety the very man who wanted to take away his daughter. Doesn't that seem odd to you?"

"My father never turned down a good deal. And anyway, with such a move, he was getting the German out of his hair forever."

"I don't doubt it; but, all the same, it's a rather strange approach."

Sister Maria remained unruffled.

"Whatever the case, I have a final question, Mother. Do you remember whether Karl Dressler, when you saw him up the mountain, was wearing his uniform?"

"Yes, he was wearing the same one as the last time I saw him at Villa Regina."

"And what kind of buttons did that uniform have, as you remember?" Stefania asked, taking the exhibits out of her purse.

The nun looked at the buttons for a moment.

"I don't know anything about military uniforms, and I can't really say whether these belonged to his. But this is the kind of button they had."

Her tone was still resentful, even a little impatient. By this point the conversation had gone on too long, even for Stefania. But she had no choice. There was one more important question that needed to be asked, and she wanted to get to the bottom of it.

"Is this—or was this, I should say—your cottage, that is, the one where you last saw Karl Dressler?"

She laid out on the table the photographs taken of the outside of the cottage from different angles.

This time the nun studied them long and hard, one by one.

She moved them around and turned them various ways, tracing invisible lines on the desktop with her finger.

"I would say yes. That is, it's quite likely." From her tone and expression, she seemed sincerely perplexed.

"Do you have doubts about something?"

"Too many years have passed, and I've never been back there since that day. My memory may be deceiving me. However, if this is the front of the cottage—since you can see the lake in the distance—and this is the side, since the pinewood gave onto the torrent, then this must necessarily be the back."

Stefania, knowing every last detail of those photos by heart, was holding her breath as she followed the nun's train of thought.

"There's also the fact that this"—and Sister Maria pointed to a precise point on the photograph—"looks to me like the squared stone that we took from an old, collapsed chapel dedicated to the Virgin Mary—as one used to do back then, to bless the cottage and the animals. Except for the fact that in that case the mountainside shouldn't be right behind it like this, with all these plants. . . . But . . ."

"But?" asked Stefania.

"In that spot there was a small patch of meadow, between the cottage and the side of the mountain. It had been leveled and raised a little, made into a sort of small embankment that was then dug out underneath, to create a sort of loose stone foundation to allow the walls to breathe and make a sort of . . . How can I explain it? Do you know what a *nevera* is, Inspector?"

15

~~

"You must be totally out of your mind," said Giulio, in a fit of anger quite unusual for him.

Stefania shrugged and got ready to endure her colleague's tantrum.

"What on earth were you thinking? You practically stole exhibits from the warehouse without authorization and subjected someone to an out-and-out interrogation even though the case had already been closed. And you weren't even on duty when you did all this. I really don't know what to think about you and this whole affair anymore."

"Actually, Giulio, that nun revealed things to me that I never would have managed to find out otherwise. I thought about them the whole way back, and I would like to discuss them with you, but if you're going to put it in those terms, I just won't bother."

"Well, it's too bad that you had to violate the basic rules of professional ethics to extort all this information, since you won't be able to use one scrap of it. Any lawyer would contest it without any problem, assuming that in the meantime you weren't already kicked out of the police force."

"The fact remains that now I've got that information, and the pieces of the puzzle are starting to fall into place. Sooner or later I'll be in a position to reconstruct the whole picture."

"Provided they haven't reassigned you to direct traffic in Lipari in the meanwhile."

"I came here to get your thoughts on an idea I had about the whole affair, but if you're going to carry on like this, I'll talk about it with Carboni."

"Just the right man! And how are you going to explain to your boss your little escapade of this afternoon? Why not just go directly to Arisi?"

"The way I see it, after what happened, Remo Cappelletti wanted to be rid of Karl Dressler, to get him out of his hair so he couldn't tempt his daughter anymore. So the first thing he does is send his daughter far away from the villa, with the idea of actually banishing her to Switzerland. With the whole thing being done in a flurry and under the direction of the future daughter-in-law, who seems like the person best fit to make the girl forget her little soldier boy. In the meantime, however, things fall apart, the hospital is evacuated, and all those soldiers who have already cheated death once are faced again with the very real possibility of returning to the front lines. The wounded have no choice. The healthy patients and those on the mend have no desire to risk their necks again for a regime already headed for total defeat."

"That's likely."

"So whoever can, tries to cut and run before it's too late."

"Which is easy to understand in such a situation, despite

the ironclad unwritten laws of the German military code of honor."

"But it's not as simple as it seems. To run away alone, into the brush in a land crawling with resistance fighters and irregulars, is tantamount to suicide. At that point you're better off being shot as a deserter by a firing squad of your own countrymen."

"Quite a quandary, in effect."

"But Remo Cappelletti doesn't really care a great deal about how Karl Dressler ends up once he's separated from his daughter. And this is where Uncle Heinrich comes in."

"The classic X factor triggering a sudden turn of events."

Stefania smiled in spite of herself.

"This uncle is a big cheese—he's got money and connections. He knows Durand, who in all likelihood had already pulled strings to bring him to the safety of the Villa Regina field hospital. Their escape had probably been planned sometime before—perhaps ever since the man was able to walk again unaided. But the right moment for crossing the border came earlier than expected, and this is where Cappelletti comes onto the scene. He's got men and means and even has a base camp near the border. The colonel, however, is fond of his young assistant and wants to bring him with him. He probably even pays to have the kid taken across. At that point Remo Cappelletti, who's a businessman above all, must have thought: Kill two birds with one stone. He had a chance, in one fell swoop, to get his daughter's sweetheart out of the picture and at the same time pocket a tidy sum."

"Elementary, my dear Watson."

"But something goes wrong at the last minute."

"Namely?"

"First, Margherita disappears mere seconds before the arrival of the car that's supposed to take her to Switzerland with her future sister-in-law—who, I should add, doesn't seem the least bit surprised and in any case doesn't wait a minute more than necessary before leaving the scene. What do you think Madame Durand's behavior means?"

"It means she didn't wait for her because she knew she wasn't coming back. Or else she wasn't sure if she'd be coming back and so, in her uncertainty, she didn't want to take the risk of being left behind in Italy herself."

"Exactly. Her fondness for Margherita wasn't enough to make her want to risk compromising her own escape. And, in fact, by leaving, she abandoned her to her fate."

"That's only your surmise, however plausible. You have no proof to support it. The girl didn't tear her hair out, it's true, but not everyone is as sentimental as you are."

"Fact number two: Dressler, the colonel, the other fugitives, and the smugglers head towards the border, but instead of moving briskly along as the urgency of the situation would dictate, they are slowed down by the colonel and Dressler. The first doesn't see well and is no longer a young man, and the second keeps stumbling and falling, mostly due to the improperly healed injury to his right leg. In the end the group decides to leave them behind, in the famous hut, or cottage, promising to come back and get them the following day."

"I'd like to see what you would do in that situation. Walking through the woods at night, not knowing where to step, and with a gimpy leg to boot. But they came back to get them, didn't they?"

"Of course, but they came back only because they couldn't allow themselves to abandon the colonel. Durand would never have forgiven them. If Dressler had been alone in that situation, things would have turned out differently."

"That may even be so, but we'll never know. There were a lot of people running around in our mountains on those nights, apparently. Those who wanted to escape were willing to take every sort of risk imaginable. For some it went well, for others, not so well."

"So you, too, think there was somebody else running around in the mountains that night. And I don't mean partisan fighters or secret service agents looking for high-ranking representatives of the Reich. I'm thinking of Margherita, for example."

"I meant in general."

"Well, where, in your opinion, was Margherita that night?"

"How should I know?"

"Just think for a minute. It seems like so many things happened, but if you calculate the time frame carefully, you'll see that essentially everything took place over the course of a single night."

"Well, you're the expert on this affair."

"And where do you think a girl of twenty-one could have gone, alone, that night?"

"Given the circumstances, I would rule out that she went dancing. But she might have been anywhere, since she knew the area so well."

"That's the point. Let's suppose that Margherita, after leaving the villa, remained in some way in contact with Dressler, or that she later learned that he and the colonel were about to cross the border. Let us also suppose that in the meantime her father had already informed her of his intention to send her to Switzerland for an indeterminate amount of time."

"Okay, let's suppose that. What then?"

"The evacuation of the villa then forcibly speeds up the course of events. As of that moment, here's what happens: the group of escapees heads for the border. The car with the driver sent from Switzerland comes to pick up Miss Durand. The ever efficient Maria has already established the meeting point after trying to save what could be saved inside the villa. Margherita and Germaine, in the meantime, have had a chance to meet and talk."

"I don't think there were many other ways to pass the time in that place."

"Therefore Mademoiselle Durand knew that Margherita wouldn't be coming with her to Switzerland. She knew that she would be leaving the villa that same evening and she even knew why. In spite of this, she said nothing, at least not to Maria, and then left very quickly herself. Why, in your opinion?"

"That's what the nun told you, but there's no guarantee that it's true or even partly true. Just to take one example: Miss Durand would have had a chance to talk to some other people as well at that time. Let's take Giovanni, Cappelletti's son, for instance. Wasn't he her fiancé? It would have been normal for them to talk about things concerning the rest of the family. And he, in turn, could have talked about it with his father, perhaps when they were in the mountains together. There can be a lot of variables in a case like this. You can't afford to rule out any possibility. And you absolutely must not fall into the trap of giving greater weight to those that support your initial hypothesis."

"Okay, but just listen to the rest. So the young guy—Dressler, that is—was waiting for someone. Maybe this someone was late in coming, and Dressler had no choice but to put on that whole song and dance to delay for as long as possible his flight across the border."

"Risking his own life and that of the colonel, who among other things had vouched for him and even paid for him? That's a laughable hypothesis, in my opinion."

"You mustn't think only of money. There are other things that people are willing to risk their lives for."

"Their own lives, however—not other people's. The colonel had no reason whatsoever to want to delay their escape. On the other side of the fence he had his family waiting for him, plus freedom, and no more war."

"But the young man was waiting for Margherita, who was his life!"

"And what makes you so sure about that?"

"It's just a hypothesis, but what else, when you come right down to it, could have been worth such a risk?"

"You're not going to tell me now that you think it possible that Dressler created all that hullaballoo just so he could say good-bye one last time to his beloved! Who, among other things, if she'd turned up in the area, risked getting slapped around by her father, if I've understood the situation correctly."

"But why not? Every person gives importance to whatever he or she believes in. And for Margherita, Karl at that moment was everything. And vice versa."

Stefania sat down and stared out the window, looking discouraged.

"Come on, don't be upset. Want some coffee?"

"No, thanks."

"An ice cream?"

"I don't like ice cream."

"Caviar and champagne?"

"Go to hell, Giulio!"

"Only after you, my dear."

⌒

"So, are you ready, Mommy? You said we'd be leaving in the afternoon and it's already four o'clock. When are you coming home?"

"I'm leaving the office now. But are you ready yourself?"

Stefania, in fact, was still putting her desk in order and hoping that Camilla hadn't yet finished getting her things ready. She also wanted to send one last e-mail to Montalti.

"I'm as ready as I'll ever be. I've already packed four bags and a backpack. I put them in the stall next to the bike and the skateboard. That way, when you get here we only need to load them into the car."

"Bike, skateboard, four bags, and a backpack? Where on earth are we going to put all this stuff?"

"In the car. In back, naturally. The bike and skateboard underneath, and the bags on top, otherwise they'll get crushed. What's the problem?"

"There's no problem," Stefania replied. Camilla had an infallible sense of logic for the things that interested her. "I'll be home soon," said Stefania.

"Soon, right. Seeing how when you usually say 'I'll be home right away' . . ."

The long May 1 weekend had come at the right moment. Stefania was happy that Camilla could spend some time by the lake with her grandmother. It would free her up to go back and forth to Como without having to race the clock every minute of the day. The fact that she would have a little time to herself was an encouraging thought. She might even have the time to see someone, and it wouldn't be just anyone.

She wrote quickly to Montalti.

Dear Mr. Montalti,

Thank you for your e-mail and interest. I have no significant new information for you and, to be honest, I should tell you that the prosecutor's office has decided to shelve the investigation. But I'm not ready to throw in the towel. Villa Regina is still called Villa Regina. It's probably changed a little since the last time you saw it, but it is still magnificent. Should you decide to come to Italy, I would like to meet you.

Warmly,

Stefania Valenti

She wondered whether it was appropriate to tell Montalti she was carrying on the investigation on her own. She decided to avoid direct mention, so he wouldn't get the wrong idea about her and her professionalism.

If he or anyone else had news that might help to reopen the case, she would of course be pleased to accept any and all advice.

She turned off her computer and headed for the door. As she was going out her cell phone rang.

"Hi," said Valli.

She felt a rumble in her stomach, something like a slight shudder.

"Hi, Luca."

"It's nice to hear your voice, Stefania."

There was a moment of silence at the other end, then a little chuckle. Stefania smiled.

"Would you like to go for a walk along the lake on Sunday afternoon? We could start out from Santa Maria del Tiglio, at Gravedona."

She hesitated, remaining in limbo for a moment, then gave up trying to resist.

"Of course, I'd love to see you again, Luca. Shall we say four o'clock?"

She'd laid the stress of her intonation on his name.

"Four o'clock would be fine. See you then."

She smiled as she hung up, certain that he was also smiling.

~

Back in her office the following Monday, she was determined to get back in touch with Madame Durand. Whatever the cost.

She'd thought about it the whole weekend, from the time she passed by Villa Regina and continued on along the lake road, curve after curve. She'd told herself she had to try. She owed it to Karl, after all. She needed only to find a pretext, a plausible excuse for going back and speaking tête-à-tête with Madame Durand. If she could get that far, steering the conversation in the right direction would be child's play.

When she got to Como she decided she would have a coffee in peace. It wasn't yet seven thirty and she felt like taking a walk. She avoided the usual bar by the station and took advantage of the opportunity to go into the walled city, stopping at one of the town's most elegant cafés, the Arte Lyceum.

On her way back she ran into Lucchesi at the hot-drink dispenser in the station's lobby, leaning against the counter, rubbing his eyes with one hand and stirring his coffee with the other. She remembered that he was the last person to have any contact with the Cappelletti family. She wanted confirmation.

"Yes, Inspector, I called them up and talked to that guy Armando."

"And it ended up with them requesting that we stop bothering them, correct?"

"Exactly."

So Lucchesi wasn't going to want to call them back, even if tortured. Unless . . .

"Great, then take it easy and finish your coffee, but don't fall asleep over it. Then you can do me the favor of calling that guy back. You can tell him that Inspector Valenti has instructed you to tell him that she would like to meet again with Madame Durand to discuss some new developments in the case. Did you get that?"

She stopped a moment to observe her colleague's reaction.

"More specifically, you can tell him the inspector would rather meet with her confidentially, because she wants to talk to her about some very personal things involving some old family belongings. Then get back to me immediately with his answer. Okay?"

Lucchesi nodded and set off for his office with his head down.

Stefania went upstairs thinking over the whole affair. Since she wasn't technically certain that the partial locket belonged to Margherita, she couldn't say definitively that it was a "family belonging."

But at this point she had to risk forcing the issue. How else was she going to get Madame Durand's attention? There was no other way to get an audience with her without having to go through her lawyer. So she might as well try. It was a calculated risk. The matriarch presided over the destinies of the living and the memories of the dead, keeping a close watch over both. This seemed to Stefania reason enough to give it a try.

Then there was that other aspect of the case that kept nagging her.

Madame couldn't *not* know. She was there during those crucial days, and no doubt was privy to Margherita's secrets. Perhaps she'd even had occasion to exchange a few words with Maria, even though the two didn't seem terribly fond of each other. She was, after all, Giovanni's future wife. She could well have learned a great many things from him and guarded them jealously all these years.

The minutes ticked by. Stefania read her mail, organized some open files on her desk, put a few shelves in order. She envied the clear, tidy desks of Giulio and some of her colleagues. Her own always looked like a battlefield.

But I never lose anything, she thought.

By now almost an hour had gone by. She lost patience.

"So, Lucchesi?"

She heard a sigh at the other end of the line.

"Well, Inspector, I called and I explained things the way you said."

"And so?"

"He said they would let us know."

"I see. Okay, thanks."

She was irritated. She'd betrayed the promise she'd made to herself to leave her boys out of this investigation. Maybe she was just deluded. She was merely wasting time waiting for something to happen. Maybe Giulio was right. How could she think that something would happen? On her desk the file concerning the arson cases was clamoring for her attention. She had to discuss them with Carboni at nine thirty—that is, in twenty minutes.

She snatched up the file and headed down the hall.

"Lucchesi? Piras? I have to go see Carboni shortly. Did you take care of those interrogations? Do I have to think of everything around here?"

"Look, everything's already in the file. I put it on your desk last Friday," said Piras.

"Yes, but we should have talked about it sooner. Are we a team or not?"

She went out without waiting for an answer. She was in the wrong and didn't want to admit it.

She went upstairs to Carboni's office. When she was outside his door the bells of the nearby church rang half past nine. The chief inspector was sitting at his desk talking on the phone to someone who seemed to be giving orders at the other end. She couldn't hear the words, but she could sense the authoritarian tone. Carboni looked tired, with his one-day stubble and dark circles under his eyes. As he spoke he ran his hand through the gray and now thinning hair on his forehead.

"Yes, Your Excellency, I understand perfectly. And I share your concern, but I can guarantee you that, though we don't have unlimited resources . . ."

A pause. The voice at the other end seemed to impart orders with the same peremptory tone as a few moments earlier.

"Our investigation is casting a wide net," Carboni was anxious to say, "and I can guarantee you that there is no underestimation of the problem whatsoever on our part. Law enforcement in this town is as dear to our hearts as it is to yours, Your Excellency."

Stefania, who'd remained waiting in the doorway, turned as if to leave, but Carboni gestured to her to close the door and sit down. The phone call came to an end. Stefania felt bad that she'd been an unwilling witness to that dressing down from the higher spheres. She said nothing. Carboni recovered from that heated conversation after drinking a glass of water.

"So, Valenti? Where are we in the investigation of those fires in that chain of stores? Are there any new developments?"

"Inspector, I have here the transcriptions and depositions of witnesses ranging from sales clerks to the owner. To say there's nothing useful is an understatement. If you want you can see for yourself. I'm still sticking to the idea I had right from the start."

"Which is?"

"To check the store's accounts' books, the owner's private accounts, and maybe even set up some wiretapping, of both the owner and his personnel. And then I would see what the insurance company has to say and find out the exact monetary value of the damages."

"Why?"

"Because based on what I've seen, the actual damage is almost laughable."

"And so? Explain what you mean, Valenti. I don't feel like playing guessing games today."

"Mr. Carboni, all that went up in flames in the end were a few large boxes, which just happened to be empty, because the clothes they'd contained had already been stored elsewhere. All that smoke merely blackened the walls. There is no structural damage, apart from a few stools and curtains, because, again purely by chance, the fire was set on the side of the store where there are only the bathrooms and staff's dressing rooms. Let's be clear about this: with a little scrubbing and a whitewash it'll all be as good as new again. In my opinion, it's some sort of initial warning, some signal to soften someone up."

"So you think there's some sort of blackmail or protection racket behind this, as some of the papers have written?"

"Maybe, or maybe gambling debts on the owner's part, that sort of thing. Didn't you see the expression on his face? He has no record, of course, but the whole thing smells fishy. Maybe he set something up with one of his employees and they set the fire to collect on the insurance."

Carboni looked thoughtful.

"The authorizations may come sooner than you expect, Valenti."

Stefania looked at him inquisitively.

"And when we've got them we'll have to close the case, do you understand? *We will have to*, and quickly, even. *That* case, at least, Valenti. I already have other problems to resolve."

"Why, what will happen otherwise? Will we be sent out to direct traffic?"

The quip wasn't her own, but sounded like it was. Carboni made a hint of a smile and gestured that she could go.

Descending the stairs, Stefania heaved a sigh of relief. Despite the sympathetic attitude she'd assumed in front of Carboni, she had no interest in that case or in His Excellency's concern for law enforcement. She prayed that the authorizations would wait until the following week to arrive.

What she really wished at that moment was to know whether Madame Durand would see her. When she ran into Lucchesi on the staircase, her colleague shook his head no.

The whole day went by, then the following morning, before something happened. But it wasn't what she'd expected. When Stefania returned to her office after lunch, she saw a long, elegant paper envelope on her desk, ivory in color, with no stamp on it. Curious, she opened it and found only two lines written in a cursive hand, slanted and stylish, if a bit retro: *I'll expect you at*

ten o'clock on Saturday morning. Coffee with milk and no sugar, if I
remember correctly. G.D.

She summoned the guard to find out who'd delivered the
letter, which had no return address, but all he could tell her was
that a tall, somewhat taciturn man had appeared, saying he had a
personal letter for Inspector Valenti, and that after giving it to the
guard, he'd turned on his heels and left without another word.

It was only a few days till Saturday.

16

She got to her appointment a few minutes early.

At the front door she was greeted by the same butler as the first time, who on this occasion led her through the garden along the western side of the villa. The lake in the distance sparkled in the morning sun, beyond the balcony that gave onto the dock. The air smelled of freshly cut grass. The rose espaliers along the path were bursting with color and scent. The butler gestured to her to go and sit down on an open-air veranda furnished with small white wicker armchairs. The patio faced the garden.

"The signora will be with you presently," the man said and then left.

Left alone, Stefania began contemplating the lake and the roses blooming everywhere along that side of the park. One branch extended towards the pane of glass, full of magnificent, sweet-smelling reddish-purple blossoms. It dawned on her how rare the scent of roses had become, and how the ones she would buy from the florists in town smelled mostly of plants and refrigeration. Instinctively she reached out to touch one and pricked her finger.

As Stefania stood there with her forefinger between her lips and frantically searching for a handkerchief in her purse with her other hand, Madame Durand made her entry. She looked at her with surprise and then amusement.

Stefania smiled likewise.

"Your roses are magnificent."

"Yes, but they sometimes have too many thorns."

"Thorns and essence of rose. We're no longer accustomed to either these days."

Madame nodded, gesturing to Stefania to sit down.

"All right, then, my dear, what was it you wanted so urgently to talk to me about?"

"I wanted to show you some objects, one in particular, and to ask you a few questions."

Stefania would never have imagined it would be so easy to broach the subject.

She opened her purse and took out the bag in which she'd placed some of the exhibits. She put it on the table, taking care not to open it before she needed to.

"The last time we met, we were trying, in our investigation, to identify the man to whom the remains found in your ruined cottage near the mountain pass belonged."

"I remember perfectly well."

"We've succeeded in identifying him with certainty," said Stefania. "His name was Karl Dressler, a German soldier stationed in this area shortly before the end of the war. We know that he lived here for a few months before he died, during the period when the villa served as a military hospital. Do you remember?"

"Do I remember the military hospital or Herr Dressler?"

"Both."

"I remember the soldiers, the wounded, the doctors and nurses. Like my sister-in-law, Maria, for example. They took up a whole wing of the villa: the guest apartments and the stables."

"And what about Mr. Dressler?"

"Him I remember much less. I think I saw him perhaps two or three times, and I never actually talked to him directly. We did sometimes happen to dine or take tea with some of those guests, but only the officers, to tell you the truth."

Stefania took out the photo of Dressler among his fellow soldiers, and showed it to Madame Durand. She looked at it for a few seconds, then pointed with her middle finger.

"I think he's this one. But when he was here he was different—thinner, and he looked older than this."

"Do you think these might be his glasses?"

Germaine carefully studied the fragment of an eyeglass frame that Stefania had set before her.

"Yes, perhaps. It may be the same kind of frame, but too much time has passed and I could be wrong."

Germaine Durand fell silent and turned her blue eyes on Stefania.

"Just now you said you'd identified those remains as belonging with certainty to Dressler, and so I'm wondering why you're asking me these questions, Inspector."

"I'll get to the point, Madame. You see, we know that man was Dressler. We also know that he disappeared from the villa right before the sudden decampment of the entire German column. We know he was up in these mountains, in the area of your cottage, but we don't know how or why he died, and how he ended up in that building—or rather, under that building."

She said it all in one breath. A few moments passed before Madame Durand resumed speaking.

"I see. And you think I might somehow be useful in helping you solve this enigma?"

This time it was Stefania who looked Germaine Durand straight in the eye.

"I think you probably know a lot of things that could help us to understand what happened."

"Such as?"

Stefania didn't answer, but extracted from the envelope the photograph showing Margherita and Maria together with Karl Dressler and the other soldiers in the villa's garden.

"Have a look at this photograph."

Madame studied the image and almost instinctively extended her fingers as if to caress Margherita's face, but then withdrew them at once. Then, in a subdued tone, she said:

"This is Margherita and Maria in their nurse's uniforms, with Dressler and other German soldiers. This one with the bandage over his eye is Colonel von Kesselbach. Dressler was his attendant. They were wounded together in a military operation. The colonel said that Dressler saved his life. He was very fond of him, to the point that he insisted that Dressler be interned at Villa Regina and given the same treatment as was usually reserved for officers."

"Heinrich von Kesselbach, by any chance?"

"Yes, my father knew him well."

So we now have a surname for Uncle Heinrich, thought Stefania.

"You see, Madame, in a way this photo contains the beginning and the end of our story. It shows all the characters of the tragedy that would unfold shortly after it was taken."

Germaine Durand leaned back in her armchair. She took off her glasses and ran her fingers dramatically over her eyes.

"So you think it was a family tragedy?"

"Yes."

"And what do you think happened?"

"I can tell you my impressions, the idea I've formed about this whole affair. Dressler and Margherita apparently met at the hospital, fell in love, and the matter came soon enough to the attention of her older sister, Maria. Let's assume for a minute that Margherita confided to her sister not only that she was in love with Dressler but that she intended to marry him as soon as the war was over. At that point the sister, driven by a sense of family loyalty, felt duty bound to tell her father. Let us imagine, on the other hand, that Margherita, not yet twenty-two years old, told her secret as well to a girl her own age, a friend. A kind of relative, let's say, the person she confided in most: her brother's fiancée. Girls like to talk about love, after all."

Madame Durand said nothing.

"Let's continue. The girl's father flies into a rage upon hearing this news from his elder daughter, perhaps because he had ambitious plans for the young one's future. Let us hypothesize that the father tried to solve the problem by immediately sending the girl away from the villa and directly confronting the German soldier to persuade him to desist. Then, as sometimes happens, circumstances altered the course of events, so to speak. At the moment of the villa's evacuation, the love-struck soldier finds himself having to choose between returning to battle or trying to flee the country. The colonel was probably thinking along the same lines. He found himself in the same situation, and let's not forget that he was a dyed-in-the-wool military man with a precise code of honor and had never been a fanatical Nazi.

So let us assume that, at that moment, the colonel did everything in his power to make an escape possible. But then the hand of fate enters our story. In an ironic coincidence, it is none other than the girl's father who is called upon to organize the two Germans' flight through the mountains, something he did quite routinely and with excellent results.

"That left the question of the girl to be dealt with, and what better solution than to entrust her to her young friend and future sister-in-law and her father, which would meanwhile also solidify Cappelletti's bond with his best business partner? But something, at this point, must have escaped his control. Right when she is supposed to leave with her future sister-in-law, Margherita disappears. Everyone looks for her but no one can find her, nobody knows where she's gone off to. Nobody except one person."

"Is that a hypothesis or a question?"

"Both, Madame."

All right—Stefania thought—the moment has come, the game is beginning. And, just as she'd hoped, Germaine Durand made the first move.

"Then who, in your opinion, Inspector, could have known where Margherita was?"

"You, Madame, naturally. And maybe your husband, or maybe both of you."

"It's an interesting hypothesis, but you've no proof to support it. Some coffee, my dear?"

A maid arrived with the coffee tray. The conversation was interrupted for a few moments that to Stefania seemed to last an eternity.

"Thank you, Luisa. You can just leave everything here. We'll take care of it."

The maid nodded and left as quietly as she'd come.

"Would you like some pastry?"

Stefania was surprised to see a platter of apple *sfogliatine*, the kind she loved, though these were in a format unfamiliar to her, smaller and in different shapes: some shaped like swans, others like flowers with open petals.

"Those are my favorites. I always get them at the Pasticceria Manzoni. They're delicious, though they make them bigger there, and in simpler shapes like stuffed *fagottini*."

Madame smiled.

"These are made specially for us, whenever we come to stay by the lake. It's sort of a family tradition. The first time was many years ago, when they brought us pastries like this for a birthday party, and the birthday girl, who adored the swans on the lake, just loved them. Ever since then we order them in this shape, and luckily there's still someone there who knows how to make them. They told me it's not easy to work such fine, stuffed dough in that way. Do you know what a pastry like that is called? A Margherita."

"Did she like the swans on the lake?"

"Yes, whenever they would pass this part of the villa she would sit there spellbound, watching them, until they disappeared from view."

Instinctively, Madame Durand turned her eyes to the lake, gazing into the distance. It was only for a moment, but when she turned back around she realized that Stefania was observing her. She sat there for a moment in silence, as though waiting for something. Then she nodded.

"I knew that Margherita wouldn't be coming with me to Switzerland. I also knew why and I knew where she intended to go when she disappeared from the house. Just as her sister knew all these things."

"Sister Maria? Are you sure?"

"Try asking the good woman again, perhaps her memory will have improved. Of course she knew. I told her myself. I told her everything.

"After we left the villa I found Margherita in the house where Maria had set me up while I waited for the car sent by my father to arrive. We were in an apartment left uninhabited for years, in a very old, uncomfortable stone house. The building still exists, just a few hundred yards from here. Do you know the Peverelli café in Lenno? That's the building, though it's been completely restructured over the years. So we spent some time together in a freezing little room looking out over the meadows and woods, chatting and making plans for the future. Nobody knew that Margherita was coming to see me. She would come down from the house in the mountain in the afternoon and we would talk. Then before nightfall she would go back up the mountain to avoid arousing suspicion. For those two days I never once saw my father-in-law or my husband. I was told they were away, even though I was certain they were busy up in the mountains with their business of clandestine expatriations. They were staying in some Alpine huts that belonged to them. I can't tell you where they were exactly, though it was some-where in the wooded area near the San Primo Pass. Even my sister-in-law, Maria, had got rid of her nurse's uniform and put on some boots, a heavy woolen sweater, and wore a rifle strapped across her shoulder. She was always coming and going with one of their men. To look at them, they seemed like simple peasants or farmers. But in fact they were going around armed to the teeth.

"I happened to see them a few times, on those rare occa-sions when I went to that area. They would appear and then leave. They would eat and then sleep on benches, fully dressed. My mother-in-law would cook for everyone and look after that poor boy she always had by her side.

"Nobody paid us any mind, except for the person Maria had assigned the task of bringing us two meals a day. I never left the place during those days, whereas Margherita would come and go, wander about town, exchanging a few words with the local men at the bar and attracting nasty stares from other women, who said that wasn't any place for girls.

"When we were alone, Margherita would tell me about Dressler and fantasize about things she'd never seen and knew nothing about, such as Germany, wooden houses, her Karl playing the piano and the church organ, having all these little blond children, and so on.

"I told her she was mad, that she could have the best things in life: comfort, friends, peace and quiet, and men all falling at her feet in a country that wasn't at war, whereas all of Europe was going up in flames. She wouldn't even listen to me, lost as she was in thoughts of her dream. She would take out her locket, kiss the two locks of hair intertwined inside it, one blond, the other dark brown, and then sigh and smile."

"I'm sorry, but are you sure Margherita had the locket with her when you were in that house?"

"Of course, she always wore it around her neck. Why do you ask?"

"Just a detail, I'm sorry, you can continue."

"Margherita had been in an anxious state ever since her father had sent her away from the villa. But then she'd managed to get news of Karl—don't ask me how, because I don't know. And she therefore knew about his escape plans, and for days she felt torn between the relief of knowing he would soon be safe and the fear that she wouldn't see him again for a long time.

"When she learned that we'd left the villa, she took an interest in us, in the hope that we had news for her. As soon as we were alone, she came secretly to see us and anxiously questioned us. I hadn't seen either Dressler or Colonel von Kesselbach and had no news of them. For the past few days we'd been thinking only of the life awaiting us in Switzerland—also because Cosette, my maid, was hardly any more than a little girl: she didn't speak a word of Italian, and wasn't even able to make her way around the area.

"Then Margherita tried to find out more from Maria, after joining up with her in the mountains. But Maria was very hard on her and told her Karl had left and that she must stop looking for him. She should forget him as quickly as possible, just as he had forgotten her.

"This was a blatant lie, of course, because at that moment Karl and the colonel were still in Italy and hiding not very far from there, waiting for calm to return after the German troops garrisoned at the villa had left. At that point Margherita started fearing the worst for herself and her beloved. She cried and cried. Then, driven by despair, she pulled herself together and, as soon as she could do so without being seen, she went back out in search of information and to try to talk to some of the people who were coming and going between the town and the mountain. That was how she ran into Giovanni, who was coming down into town on some errands."

There was a long pause.

Stefania made a great effort to remain silent, to ask no questions but merely let the woman resume the thread of her account on her own.

Germaine Durand had lost a good deal of her natural aplomb. She kept stirring the coffee in her cup without ever bringing it to her lips. Moments later, she resumed speaking, her tone of voice even more subdued than before.

"Sometimes the worst things that befall us are caused by the people we love most. Isn't that terrible?"

"I'm not sure I understand, Madame Durand."

"The people who love us, and whom we love, sometimes don't have the courage to say no to us, precisely because of the bond that unites us. They are unable to deny us what we demand most insistently, even if it is harmful to us. And in this way they often become, unwittingly, the cause of our downfall. You see, Inspector, Giovanni adored Margherita, he would never have done anything to harm her, he would have sacrificed his own life to defend and protect her. But that one time he gave in to her. He told her where Karl was and said he was about to go over the border. That admission, which came from an excess of love for his sister, was the beginning of the end.

"After talking to her brother, Margherita came back to the house where I was staying. I remember those moments very clearly. She hugged me tightly and then told me what her brother had said. She was agitated and could barely stand still. She kept going over to the window, looking outside, and coming back, saying all the while that she'd always known and had never doubted him, and that Karl could never have forgotten her. He was there, nearby, just a few kilometers away.

"After her initial excitement, she seemed to calm down a little. She barely touched the food that the woman had brought us. Then she lay down on the bed beside me. She was probably unable to fall asleep, but I did. And to this day it gives me no rest, though more than fifty years have passed. Later—I don't know how much later, but it was already dark outside—I was woken up by the feeling of somebody touching my face. It was Margherita, dressed all in dark clothes with a dark scarf tied around her head and a small backpack on her shoulders.

"'I'm going,' she said to me. 'I can't sit still here any longer. I'm going to Karl. He's crossing the border, maybe tonight, and if I don't see him now I don't know if or when I'll ever see him again.'

"'Where are you going? Are you mad? Can't you see it's dark outside?' I replied, still half asleep. 'How are you going to go out without being noticed? Do you know that if somebody sees you it'll be more trouble for your father? And what's the point, anyway? If he goes to Switzerland, and you come, too, sooner or later you can meet up with him there.'

"I tried to persuade her, speaking softly for fear of waking up Cosette, but it was no use. She'd made up her mind. She embraced me one last time, whispering in my ear: 'I may return before dawn. But if morning comes and you don't see me, don't worry. It will all go well, and one day, very soon I hope, we'll see each other again.'

"Those were her last words. And she headed for the stairs in silence. The last I saw of her was her slender figure blowing a kiss from her fingertips at the window. All around there was only the moon's pale glow.

"I was left alone in the dark, silent room. Cosette, who'd set up a cot in a corner of the next room, hadn't heard a thing. She was sleeping peacefully. I pulled the blankets back up over me. I was worried, of course, but mostly incredulous. I just couldn't understand how anyone could risk everything, even life, for . . ."

"For love?"

"Yes."

Madame Durand finally set her coffee cup down on the table and leaned back in her armchair.

"It all happened very quickly. When I was finally able to fall asleep again, it was already daylight. I spent the morning and afternoon in a kind of trance. From where I was it wasn't possible to communicate with Giovanni or the other Cappellettis. Towards evening there was a knock at the door. Moments later somebody came inside. They had a heavy step. I could hear it from the stairway. It was Maria, who'd come in with a sack of food.

"'It's time, let's go. Germaine, your father's man is here. You have to leave. Hurry, the car's waiting. Margherita, wake up. And hurry.'"

"She was still talking when she realized her sister wasn't there. She fell silent for a few moments, as if bewildered.

"'Where's Margherita?' she asked.

"'She's gone,' I said.

"'Gone? What do you mean, gone? Where'd she go?'

"'She went to be with Karl. Where, I don't know.'

"'And how did she know he was still around?'

"'Your brother told her. Yesterday afternoon.'

"She stood in the doorway without moving. Then she shook herself. 'The imbecile!' she said angrily, meaning her brother, then added, 'And you two, hurry up. They're waiting for you downstairs.' And she turned on her heels without another word and raced outside.

"When we got downstairs Maria was already gone. Waiting for us were two men, who then led us through orchards and fields and then up a deserted trail. At last we came to the car that was waiting for us. Its lights were off and it was hidden behind a row of trees outside of town. We immediately headed in the direction of the border crossing. We passed through without a hitch. Nobody stopped us, and a few hours later, at dawn, we were drinking our first coffee in Lugano, on the other side of the border.

"What happened next I didn't find out until many months later, after the war was over and I saw my husband again in Italy. In the meantime my father had been visited by Colonel von Kesselbach, who had arrived safely in Switzerland. Reunited with his wife and children after a long stay at a famous ophthalmological clinic, he had moved into a house not too far from us, at Vevey, which belonged to some relatives of his wife."

"The Montaltis?"

Madame looked at her in astonishment.

"Yes, but how did you know? Do you know them?"

"In a way. But that's of no importance. Please, continue."

"The colonel had come to see my father. He wanted to thank him for the assistance he'd provided him and his family in the difficult circumstances of their escape from Italy."

With a little help from Remo Cappelletti, thought Stefania, deciding that it was best not to interrupt Madame with the addition of that detail. Neither did she mention the sale of Villa Regina to the Cappellettis, made possible, at least in part, by the money Durand had paid out to the Montaltis. There would be other occasions for covering that aspect of things. What mattered right now was that Madame continue her story.

"In fact the colonel asked for news of Dressler, whom he hadn't seen since the night of his escape, in the hope that my father might reassure him that the young man had managed in one way or another to escape to safety.

"My father was vague. He knew nothing about the young soldier or what had happened to him, and all he could do was promise to put the question to all those who had materially participated in his escape. I wasn't present for that exchange, but I did manage to catch a few snippets of the conversation when I walked past my father's study.

"I remember feeling a stabbing pain in my heart, a kind of dire premonition. I'm not superstitious, I assure you, and never have been. At that moment, however, for the first time, I felt sure about something—that is, that young Kessler had not made it, and neither had Margherita.

"And it was terrible, I can tell you. I felt responsible for the fate of both. There had been moments where I'd thought this before, but I'd always refused to consider it a concrete possibility. Haven't you ever thought that those we love, those we love differently from others, could never die?"

"Of course I have, Madame, I've thought that many times. About my father, for example."

The lady nodded in understanding, then leaned back in her armchair again and closed her eyes, as if wanting to rest. A deep silence fell over the little open-air sitting room, despite the constant chatter of birds in the garden. The lapping of the lake waters and the hum of a lawnmower in the distance barely disturbed the calm.

After a few minutes of this Stefania began to feel a little awkward. She didn't quite know what to do. She felt as if she'd become transparent. She certainly couldn't stay there forever, she thought. And so she did the first thing that came to mind. She coughed politely. Madame seemed to rouse herself and smiled at her good-naturedly.

"Forgive me, my dear. Where were we?"

Stefania figured it was best to carry on.

"At the moment of your return to Italy after the end of the war."

"Well, it was very simple. Giovanni took me to the cemetery to see Margherita's grave."

"And that's all? He didn't tell you anything about how she died?"

"Of course he did. He said she was shot in the mountains, killed by gunfire. They never did find out who shot her—whether it was the Germans, the Fascists, or the partisans, or whether she was caught in the crossfire of a gunfight between warring factions."

"Do you think your husband actually knew more than that?"

"I don't think so. If he'd known more he would have told me, I'm sure of it. The one who might know more is Maria, but that may also be just a hunch of mine. I won't hide from you that there has never been much common ground between the two of us. Still, one day we ran into each other at Margherita's grave, in the cemetery of Croce, above Menaggio, a place Margherita used to love. I tried asking her for more information. All she said to me was: 'Don't you already know enough?'"

"What about her father? Or the other members of the family?"

"The father was simply unrecognizable, compared to the determined, almost fierce man I'd known before. He became as thin as a ghost, his clothes would hang on his body as on a coat hanger. Hollow cheeked, unkempt beard, wild eyes. He looked like a madman. Everyone at the villa kept an eye on him. He was always running away. He would go up the mountain on foot, even in the middle of winter, in the rain or in the snow, in shirtsleeves and without covering his head. He died not long afterwards. He fell into a ravine. Margherita's mother never came down from her house up the mountain. I saw her only once, on the day of her husband's funeral, the same day that Maria announced to her family that she'd decided to become a nun. She left the villa that same evening. The poor widow died less than three years later, after which the family put the handicapped son in a home for the mentally ill."

"What a tragedy."

"It was a very difficult situation. The villa itself, in those days, had become unrecognizable—deserted, ghostly. The grass had grown as tall as hay up to the front entrance. I went back to Switzerland almost immediately, according to my father's wishes. He didn't think it was advisable to stay in a house and a situation so fraught with problems, and so for a while even relations with Giovanni became a bit complicated. Then things changed. He was left basically alone and he came back to get me. We were together again, and we got married. And little by little, for us and our children, this place became what it is now. But none of us has ever forgotten."

When she had finished speaking, the woman closed her eyes, as if in need of rest and silence. Stefania, too, remained silent, reflecting on everything she'd just heard. Now she needed to think it all over calmly. That was the way she was. Her brain needed to rethink things, to compare and contrast and put all the elements together again one by one. She stood up.

"I think I have taken advantage of your patience, Madame. I thank you very much. You've been extremely helpful."

Madame Durand made a vague gesture with her hand. Stefania took it as a gesture of dismissal. Without saying anything else, she turned and headed for the door. She hadn't yet reached the end of the allée when she heard herself being called.

"Inspector?"

She turned around in surprise.

"Madame?"

"You said you had something to show me. Didn't you?"

Stefania realized what Madame meant. She walked back, put her purse down on the table, and opened it, taking the partial locket out of its bag and handing it to her. Germaine studied it for a long time, holding it in the palm of her hand and then delicately grazing it with her fingers, as in a gentle caress.

"You found this, too, among Dressler's things?"

"Yes."

"So they died together?"

17

Contrary to custom, Giulio didn't say a word when Stefania finished telling him over the phone the details of her conversation with Germaine Durand. No ironic quips, no comments. Just silence. For a few minutes it seemed as if the call had been cut off.

"Well?"

"Well what?"

"What are your thoughts about all this? I've been talking for the past half hour and you haven't said a thing."

"I was listening. You always complain that I don't listen, and so this time I didn't breathe a word, didn't you notice?"

"Yes, thanks. And so?"

"And so I don't know. I'm not convinced. Everyone tells the same story, apparently, but each one adds or subtracts a detail here or there, and in the end the story's not the same. Do you know what I mean?"

"More or less."

"Take, for example, the night of the escape. If we listen to

Montalti, who has no personal interest in the matter and recounts simply what he's been told by his uncle, the colonel and Dressler head out towards the border with the whole group, but along the way they have problems, or so he says. They walk too slowly, time passes, it gets late—better yet, dawn is on the horizon. At that point they're brought back and left in the cottage. Next, in his account, there's the woman who comes and apparently talks to Cappelletti. This is certainly Maria, and it's the first night of the escape. Dressler and the colonel spend a whole day hiding out in the cottage, waiting to leave the following night. They have the same problems as before, and we know what happens next. In the end they take the colonel across, but the simple soldier is left behind, after which point we know nothing more about him. A short while thereafter, when it's already light outside, the colonel hears some faraway gunshots, followed by an explosion. Final tally: two nights, two days, the gunshots at the start of the second day, and the final explosion."

"It would all seem to make sense, so far."

"No, because the nun says she went up to the hut to look for her brother and father so she could tell them that Margherita had run away. But she says she found nobody there, and so she decided to wait, until she saw them return with Dressler and the colonel. Therefore, in this second version, given by the nun, we are at the end of the first night of Dressler's escape, with Margherita already vanished and Germaine who has already blithely slipped off to Switzerland with her chambermaid. This last part of the nun's account, moreover, tallies perfectly with Madame Durand's story, with just one difference. Going by what Germaine Durand says, it would seem that the nun lied to you when she said she didn't know where Margherita was or why she ran away."

"Well, it may only have been a partial lie to say she didn't know why Margherita had run away. As for not being aware of where she had run off to, she was probably telling the truth. How could she have known?"

"So she only half lied. Okay. But why did she do it? If she did indeed, as she says, go all the way to the hut to look for her father and brother, she can only have done so in the certainty that Dressler and the colonel had already crossed the border the night before, as had been planned. In other words, her father and brother should only have returned to the cottage once they'd finished their work, before dawn. And, of course, if she didn't go to the cottage but joined back up with them on their way to the border on the first night, well, that would change things."

"Why? What does it matter whether she was at the cottage or somewhere between the cottage and the border? How does that change anything? At any rate, she did succeed in finding her father and informing him that Margherita had run away, which was what she was most anxious to do at that moment."

"I wouldn't be so sure of that. And in any event it does change things, and a lot. Whatever the case, when she found her father still with Dressler, she probably felt quite relieved, but not, in my opinion, because she was hoping he would have news of her sister, or know where she was, but because she imagined that as long as Dressler was still around, Margherita couldn't be very far away. Whereas if the meeting with her father took place, as Montalti says, as the group was laboriously making their way towards the mountain pass, there may even be a connection between her arrival and the father's decision to take the colonel and Dressler back to the cottage, postponing their escape until the following day."

"In what sense?"

"Do you remember that map you showed me? The one with all the huts and the border line? Could you go and get it?"

"Of course not. It's Saturday morning and I'm at the lake. But why are you so interested in it?"

"Do you remember the position of the ruined cottage with respect to the border line and the old customs police barracks?"

"Of course."

"Do you remember the aerial distance between the cottage and the border? It was a very short distance, almost nothing, as the crow flies, maybe five hundred meters or so. We can even say a kilometer if we had to calculate the path traveled on foot through the woods. Agreed?"

"A kilometer through a dense wood, or even just five hundred meters, at night, on a bum leg that hurts, can seem very long."

"Fine, whatever you like, but we're not talking about tropical rain forests here. You're not going to trip on lianas. We're talking about one of our familiar mountain thickets at the very start of spring, with still rather sparse foliage. And they, moreover, were already past the cottage, they'd almost reached their destination."

"And so?"

"And so, in my opinion, Cappelletti intentionally had them turn back. There is no other explanation."

"And what about Maria and the others?"

"He had his men accompany the other refugees to the border, while he went back to the cottage before dawn with his son and Maria, who was with them—just as Montalti said—and not waiting for them, as the nun claimed. Whatever the case, from that moment on, there are no other witnesses outside the family to what happened, except for the colonel."

"And so what do you think happened afterwards?"

"First of all, they'd already brought home one result: they'd gained time. They had a whole day to think about what to do."

"That doesn't seem like such a great result to me. A night of wasted effort, having to do the same thing all over again the next night. More effort, more risks. The colonel still to be taken care of, the young guy only a hindrance, not being able to walk or, as you say, not wanting to walk. Since the colonel absolutely had to be taken to safety, given his relation to the Durands, all they'd done was waste time."

"That the colonel had to cross the border at all costs is clear. Durand would never have forgiven Cappelletti otherwise. But Dressler was another matter altogether. He was a nobody, a kid, and the only reason he was still around was because the colonel had grown so fond of him that he didn't want to be separated from him, even at the cost of compromising the success of their escape. He risked a great deal, did the colonel, just so as not to abandon the young man. And this definitely complicated things for Cappelletti."

"Both of them had to be escorted out, therefore, even though one was worth a lot less than the other, so there was no need to think things over for a whole day to reach this conclusion. And in my opinion there was another good reason to get things done quickly: Margherita. Let's not forget that she'd run away with a precise goal in mind: to try to meet up with Dressler. So the sooner they got the soldier off their hands, the better. In fact, from this perspective I really don't see why they delayed things for a day, given the risk that Margherita might succeed in finding them and create further problems."

"Right."

There was another long pause. Giulio seemed not to have

anything more to say. He distractedly said good-bye and hung up. Stefania sat there thinking, turning her cell phone over and over in her hand.

Every time she seemed to be on the verge of understanding, of sorting out the tangled skein, she suddenly had to start over. Some detail would undermine her reconstruction and she had to resume the hunt. A tabby cat lay lazily in the sun atop a high wall, grooming itself beyond the view of the other cats. It seemed to be looking at her haughtily when her cell phone rang again.

Ready to lay into whoever it was daring to violate the intimacy of her Saturday morning, Stefania answered, surprised to see the name GIUILO on the display.

"How could I not have thought of it sooner? It's so obvious."

"I'm sorry?"

"The trap. It's so clear."

"What trap? For whom?"

"For Margherita, of course. Listen, it's all very simple. Maria is aware that Margherita has run away. The older sister, however, is only a few hours ahead of her, probably only a few kilometers. Maria knows perfectly well that Margherita will do everything within her power to join Karl, but doesn't know whether the two have already made plans and have decided to meet on the other side of the border. She's also well aware that if Margherita wants to cross the border by herself she is capable of doing so, since she knows those places and those woods at least as well as she and her father do. And if that's the case, there's nothing Maria can do about it. But if the two lovers do not have a plan, and Margherita is merely trying to reach Karl in desperation, then Maria knows what road they'll have to take to cross the border. She thinks about this and realizes that if Margherita is still on this side of the border, she cannot in any case approach Karl as long as he is in the middle of a group, together with her father and the other men. She will wait for the right moment to try. Maria fears that her sister might try to do in fact the most logical thing, which would be to follow the group, while remaining unseen, from a short distance away, and then cross the border herself at a point close by, so that she can join up with Dressler on the other side."

"That could have been very dangerous."

"Of course, but Margherita had already chosen her destiny the moment she ran away, and she cannot go back, in every sense of the phrase. Maria at that point decides to do the only thing that can still prevent her sister's escape, wherever she might be: to stop Karl Dressler and watch his every movement. And so she rushes up the mountain, reaches the group, talks to her father, and succeeds in persuading him to stop the young man's escape. It probably was she herself who gave her father the idea to break up the group, have the others go on to the border, and bring the colonel and Dressler back to the cottage. Her gambit is clear: if Margherita is nearby, she will realize what is happening and she will stop. And with a bit of luck, she might even come out into the open. If Margherita is not in the area, she won't notice anything, and will continue on her way. And so everyone goes back to the hut, and from that moment on, they alone will manage things."

"Aside from the colonel . . ."

"Right. He, in a sense, intervenes. And since he's a big cheese, a friend of Durand's, they don't dare cross him, at least not beyond a certain point. And so they backtrack and all remain in the area of the hut, to wait until the following night. Twenty-four hours to resolve three problems: Margherita, Dressler, and the colonel."

"And what happened next, in your opinion?"

"I wasn't there."

Giulio remained silent for a moment, then, in a tone unusually placid for him, he ended the discussion.

"Much as I would like to, I can't write or direct the final act of this drama. The stage is yours now, if you want it."

18

Stefania was puzzled.

The tone Giulio had used, and the fact that for once he was interested enough in a case of hers to seem almost caught up in it, got her thinking. She appreciated her colleague's analytical gifts, his ability to synthesize, his investigative acumen.

Giulio had been able to spot contradictions that had escaped her attention. And this bothered her in a way. Maybe he was right that she'd let herself get too emotionally involved in the case, to the point where she could no longer distinguish those who told her the truth from those who told only half-truths. Sister Maria, for one.

But now all the pieces of the puzzle were there. Many were already in the right places. What didn't fit in the overall picture were the details. Small details, though ultimately decisive.

She felt as if her hands were tied. After all that effort, she finally had the solution within reach, but now she had very little time left. As in a game of chess. An anomalous game, however, one in which only a limited number of moves were still available. She could no longer afford to make any mistakes. She would have to weigh the pros and cons of every decision. And she still had to bear in mind that the investigation had officially been shelved.

She decided to take a few days to study the situation.

Santa Maria del Tiglio was a twelfth-century Romanesque church not far from the old center of Gravedona.

When Stefania pulled up in front of the churchyard, she saw Valli's figure in the distance, busy taking photographs of the façade. As usual, he had arrived before her.

"Do you know the legend of this church?" he asked, smiling, after pointing his camera at her.

"I would guess it has something to do with Atlantis or the Templars," Stefania replied.

"Luckily, no. You should know, Stefania, that this church was built in the twelfth century on the remains of an ancient place of worship from the pre-Roman age. Built with local materials, such as white Musso marble and black stone from Olcio, it has an unusual central-plan structure more typical of baptisteries. Legend has it that in the late Middle Ages there was a huge fresco of the *Adoration of the Magi* on one of the interior walls. This detail is even cited in a text of the Carolingian epoch found in *The Annals of Fulda* in Germany. According to tradition, in the distant past a bizarre event occurred and gave rise to tales of miraculous cures: during a storm the fresco started to glow with its own light, emitting luminous beams without interruption for several days."

"Do you like legends, Luca?"

"No, to tell you the truth, I prefer miracles created by human beings," he replied. "Like this church, for example."

They approached the church, over which soared a splendid

belfry with an octagonal base. They entered in silence, admiring the three semicircular apses and a large wooden crucifix.

The church stood about twenty meters from the lake. When they went out, Stefania headed towards the back of the building, where a short walk along a path dotted with plane trees allowed for a better view of the rear of the church and the panorama of the Alto Lago, with the Olgiasca peninsula and Piona Abbey on the far shore directly opposite them.

She was the first to sit down on one of the benches. The sky was clear, the air pleasantly warm. Luca took a couple of snapshots and then joined her.

"Feel like an ice cream?"

"Is that all you ever think about, eating?"

They laughed. For the first time since they'd met, Stefania talked about herself. She recounted stories of her childhood related to her memory of her father. The high school years in Como, the endless hours spent on the bus very early in the morning and the adventures on the steamboat on the days when she happened to sleep in. Then university, graduation, the decision to go into law enforcement, and the death of her father after a long illness.

"Why did you get married? Were you in love?"

"Of course I was in love—or, more precisely, Guido was the person I cherished most in life. We'd spent our final years in college together. He was always at my side. It was natural we should get married. In a way he was a replacement for my father."

"And then what?"

"And then, after trying for a long time to have children, Camilla finally arrived when we no longer thought it was possible. I was almost thirty-five."

"And why did you break up, if I'm not being too indiscreet?"

"After Camilla was born, Guido started slowly to drift away from me. First it was our job demands—both mine and his, which took him far away. He ended up renting an apartment in Milan. Then, as Camilla got older, things between us changed, to the point that when we finally separated I realized we'd become strangers to each other."

Valli was about to say something when the phone rang. Stefania was momentarily tempted to let it ring, but then decided to check, since it might be her daughter.

An unknown number.

"Zero zero four one?" asked Stefania.

"It's a Swiss exchange," said Valli.

Stefania set aside all hesitation and answered with her heart beating wildly.

"Inspector Valenti, please forgive me for bothering you outside your working hours."

The voice belonged to Montalti. But it didn't have its usual placid elegance. In fact it seemed, on the contrary, to be trying, and not succeeding, to repress a rather perceptible joy.

"Actually, Inspector, I have some important news to impart to you. I've been thinking about it since yesterday, when the postman left this house. And I couldn't sleep last night because of it. But I don't feel like talking about it over the phone. You understand, I'm sure."

"Not even a hint?"

"I got a letter from Leipzig. That's all I can say for now. Could we make an appointment for tomorrow afternoon?"

"Shall we meet in my office, at police headquarters?"

"Actually I had the lake in mind. Do you know the bell tower of Ospedaletto?"

"Of course I do, Signor Montalti. Would two o'clock work for you?"

"That would be perfect. Good-bye, then, Inspector. Please don't forget."

Stefania kept clutching her phone for a few seconds after the call had ended.

Valli's smile brought her back to reality.

"Good news?"

"Unexpected news, rather," replied Stefania.

⌒

The following day Stefania woke up feeling agitated and nervous about her appointment with Montalti that afternoon.

She'd slept poorly. Montalti was right. It would have been better not to give her any hints at all. She'd spent the night thinking about the letter that had arrived from Leipzig, wondering who might have sent it and what new information it might contain. She used up a good part of the morning working out a logistical plan that would make her meeting with Montalti as untroubled as possible. The unexpected appointment would give her a chance to spend a few extra minutes with her mother. The years were passing for her, too, and she often had back pain. But it wasn't physical ailments that worried her. In recent times her mother was starting to have little lapses of memory. She'd once even gone down into town to go shopping only to find she didn't have her wallet with her. Other times she would forget the name of the person she'd called on the phone.

Luckily things went smoothly at the station. Carboni was out for a briefing with the commissioner. Lucchesi and Piras were talking about soccer.

At twelve thirty she went out of the office, got in her car, and headed for the lake.

It all seemed so strange as she drove down the road. As soon as she'd left the city behind, Stefania felt as if she were entering another life, where time passed more slowly, the panoramas were vast, and life in the village and among friends was peaceful. The rhythms more human, experience more intimate and contemplative.

When she got to Argegno, she stopped at the *piazzetta*, where there were already a good number of bicycles and motorbikes parked. Though it was Monday, it was already full of tourists, all huddled around tables for a snack or a fish-based lunch. She parked near the dock and went into the Caffè Motta.

Montalti wasn't very familiar with the roads around the lake. He rarely came down into Italy, and when he did, it was usually for work-related appointments. Milan, Brescia, Bologna, Genoa. For thirty years he'd dealt in important financial affairs for a Swiss consulting firm. He'd retired from the business years before, but his consultation services were still in demand.

He hadn't been to Como for a long time, or to any of the tourist destinations scattered along the shores of the lake. Even his driver had trouble negotiating the narrow streets of the "low road," the one Montalti had told him to take once they'd come to the roundabout outside Cernobbio.

The towns still looked pretty much the same as he remembered them from his childhood and adolescence. Small houses clustered together, some giving onto the lake, and others—most of them, really—taking a piece out of the mountain.

Near Pizzo di Cernobbio, he asked Hermann, his chauffeur, to slow down.

"If somebody hired a team of deep-water divers to search this part of the lake," he said, "they would find more human remains than in any cemetery in Italy."

"What do you mean?" the driver asked.

"I mean that at the end of the war, all those who, in one way or another, made the winners uncomfortable—Fascists, their supporters, former regime bigwigs, and even unorthodox partisans—ended up at the bottom of this end of the lake. A shot in the head and another in the belly, so that the body wouldn't float back up."

The car continued along the Regina road, which afforded a better view for admiring the lake's magnificent villas from up close. A bit farther on, a small crowd was gathered outside the gate of Villa Oleandra, home of George Clooney.

The road then went back uphill, to intersect with the new road, the "high" one, which went on to Argegno and from there towards the valleys and the Tramezzina.

⌇

After drinking her coffee, Stefania sat there for a few minutes taking in the show put on by all the tourists' cars and blue buses along the small pier of Argegno.

Taking her time, she headed for her car and traveled the next few kilometers through the old towns of Colonno, Sala Comacina, and Ossuccio. Just before one of the tight curves in the road, as often happened, a bus had been blocked by a truck coming in the opposite direction. It took several minutes for the knot to become untangled. When she got to the parking lot above the bell tower of Ospedaletto, Stefania was half an hour early. Time enough to smoke a cigarette and visit the gardens of the park below.

⁓

Montalti pointed out to his driver the bell tower in the distance. Moments later Hermann found a parking spot, got out of the car, walked around the vehicle, and, after opening the rear door, helped the elderly gentleman out.

The woman standing some ten yards away could only be Inspector Valenti. She was just as he'd imagined her: slender, slightly taller than average, light brown hair, with the shy demeanor of someone who always feels a little out of place.

"I imagine you wouldn't accept an offer to continue a bit farther down the road," said Stefania, referring to Villa Regina, which stood barely half a kilometer away, just past the bend outside the parking lot.

"There are certain pages, Inspector, that once they've been turned, are best not reread," said Montalti, leaning heavily on a cane.

Stefania offered him her right arm—after all, the man could easily have been her father—and together they slowly headed towards the sloping path that led to a small garden just opposite the Isola Comacina.

They sat down at a kiosk, under a broad umbrella. Montalti ordered a cool soft drink, while Stefania limited herself to her fourth coffee of the day.

Hermann had stayed behind in the car.

"As a boy I often used to go directly to the Isola from home," said Montalti, pointing to the island with his walking stick. "It was sort of a family tradition."

"Actually, it's probably only about two hundred yards away,"

Stefania added. "And at Villa Regina there used to be that beautiful pier."

"Yes, but we used to swim there," said Montalti, smiling, as he dug into the inside pocket of his jacket.

"So, this letter . . ." said Stefania, the curiosity eating her alive.

"You'll be surprised to learn that there are actually two letters, Inspector," the elderly gentleman said, setting down on the table two envelopes with numerous pages inside. "The first," he said, after taking a sip of his soft drink, "was sent to me a week ago by Katrine Dressler, Karl's sister. It was posted in Leipzig."

"And the second?" asked Stefania, feeling restless after eyeing the other envelope, which had yellowed and looked much older than the first.

"The second is a letter that Karl Dressler wrote to his parents in the days following his escape."

"So he was able to send it to Germany in spite of the war?"

"No. It's written in his hand, but it was never posted."

"So how did it find its way to his sister?" asked Stefania, who was seeing the few sure things she knew about the case begin to vanish.

"It was delivered by hand. The person who came to Leipzig and delivered it directly to his parents was my uncle."

"Colonel von Kesselbach?"

"I can see that certain details of the case haven't escaped your notice," Montalti commented with a smile.

19

... and the reason, dear mother, I am telling you these things only now is that at this moment, for the first time since this accursed war began, I fear for my life. Not so much for the fact itself that I might leave this earth—something many of the people I've had the good fortune to meet now have in common—but because of how this fact would affect the lives of other people. Such as you, first of all, Mother, and then your husband, and my sisters. But above all because of the person I have beside me, Margherita. You should see her, Mother. She is a wonderful girl, as sensible as she is necessary, and courageous. I have no doubt that if the Good Lord allows it, we shall marry once the war is over. Margherita would be delighted to come and live with us in Germany. And there's one last thing I must confess to you. Forgive me if these seem like the words of a luckless son. Margherita is expecting a baby. That's right, Mother. I'm about to become a father, and there is no way to express this feeling—which you must know quite well—other than in words of love and happiness.

Stefania, who had a good grasp of German, reread the last lines of the letter, incredulous.

The content more than surprised her. She was astonished to learn that Karl Dressler was well aware of the danger he was in during those last days of his life, and likewise that Margherita, the girl he loved, would be bearing his child a few months thereafter.

At that point, her worries, doubts, and questions got the upper hand. This was a decisive turning point in the case. She was sure of it, in this new light. But there were so many new elements of such unexpected importance that she could hardly believe her eyes in the face of the words contained in that letter of March 1945.

Montalti watched her in silence.

"Surprised, Inspector?"

"Confused, rather, Signor Montalti. I need to think about this."

"I understand. I had the same reaction after I first read the letter. In my case, however, there's a further complication, of a familial nature, let's say."

"And what would that be?" asked Stefania, not following his reasoning.

"Well, to begin with, the ambiguous attitude assumed by Uncle Heinrich for all these years. I'd been hearing the story of his escape and friendship with Karl Dressler, about the young man's mysterious disappearance and all the rest, ever since I was little more than a child. I'd been living all this time with the idea that Karl might turn up at any moment. It was sort of a family legend. In reality Uncle Heinrich had always known much more than he'd led us to believe. But my question is not why he'd decided, over the years, to let everyone think he was still waiting for Karl to return, or to give some sign of life, but why he'd insisted for so long on his being buried in the family vault."

"Do you think your uncle was in some way working for the Allies?"

"No, absolutely not. Of course it wouldn't seem at all strange to me if, at that time, he actually had chosen to be a double agent in the service of the Allies, even if his reputation as a dyed-in-the-wool military man would have come out a little tarnished because of it. The main question is: Why did he lie to us, of all people, his family relations, when he knew perfectly well that Karl was, in all probability, dead? It was he who'd told the young man's family about Karl's last moments. Why the whole song and dance, even in the will, about the burial, the sword, and all the rest?"

"Apparently your uncle needed to justify himself in the eyes of someone else."

"Do you see, Inspector, how in the end we always come to the same conclusions? Except for Durand, with whom my uncle maintained good relations till the end of his days, what other person could he have wanted to keep contented in this way?"

"This is all conjecture. What if there was another reason? Something still eluding us, so to speak? Something we still haven't taken into consideration? We shouldn't jump to any conclusions, Signor Montalti. In this investigation I've learned that nothing is what it appears to be."

At that moment a motorboat passed right in front of them, kicking up a wave of white foam. The garden around them had come to life. Families, youths, and small children passed cheerfully by. The hum of a hydroplane overhead made them look up.

"What I can't figure out," said Stefania, "is why Karl gave the letter to your uncle Heinrich."

"He was someone he trusted."

"But what need was there? After all, they'd been together the whole time, both at Villa Regina and during their escape. It's almost as if the young man, at some point in this unhappy story, had sensed that he was in danger, as he says, in fact, in the letter. Let's imagine the scene. The two have decided to escape together. They make a plan. We don't know exactly when, but at some point before setting out, or maybe even right in the middle of their escape, Karl decides to write those lines. He can't mail anything, because of the censors. And so he entrusts his last will, or at least the last expression of his feelings, to the person with whom he is escaping. A person he trusts. It's as if he knows that their fates are in some way linked, but that the old colonel has a better chance of making it."

"So far I follow. Please continue."

"So, as the moment of the escape approaches, Karl writes the letter. Maybe even on the day he spends inside the cottage after backtracking at the insistence of Remo Cappelletti. He reveals the most intimate details of his life to his mother. In a way, he is confessing. The man who represents an obstacle for him, Remo Cappelletti, is also the father of the woman he loves, who is pregnant with his child: Margherita. So he gives his confidential letter to the colonel as though knowing that his superior has a better chance of survival. We have to acknowledge that Karl already senses that something doesn't seem right. Otherwise he could just as easily have kept the letter himself."

"It was probably during that brief span of time that he noticed something strange in Cappelletti's behavior," Montalti suggested.

"Exactly."

She rummaged through her purse, took out a cigarette, and lit it.

"Then there's the question of the fate of the letter itself," she continued. "Did the colonel read it? How did he get it to Dressler's sister? What path did it travel?"

"That's an easier question to answer," said Montalti. "You need only read the other letter, the one written by Katrine Dressler," and he opened the second envelope. "The girl writes that my uncle came to Leipzig in 1946. He got in touch with the family and personally met with Karl's parents. Her memory is a bit hazy because she was practically still a little girl at the time. She does remember, however, the imposing figure of the colonel and his brief visit, with him sitting in their apartment's small kitchen as her mother wept in silence. Apparently Uncle Heinrich had to admit that as far as he knew, their son had got mixed up in some murky affair."

"And do you think he was telling the truth?"

"We have no reason to doubt it."

"And what happened next?"

"Then history with a capital *H* took its course. The Wall, the Cold War, the closing of the borders. Dressler's father, suspected of being pro-Western, was put in prison, where he ended his days in the mid-sixties. His mother followed him a few years later. Katrine was left alone in the former East Germany, but ended up leading a normal life: she married, had children, and worked in a factory that produced military uniforms."

"Didn't she ever look into what happened during the war, try to inform herself about her brother? Didn't she ever do any research?"

"You have to imagine what those years were like, Inspector. Even if she'd wanted to, she probably wouldn't have been allowed. First, because the situation made it practically impossible to have any news of the outside world. Second, even if there was news concerning Karl, it would never have reached his family on the other side of the Iron Curtain."

"For political reasons?"

"In a sense. It is quite unthinkable that a collaborationist, or even his memory, could ever, in those years, receive any kind of preferential treatment."

"Let's move forward, Signor Montalti. What will you do now? Will the mortal remains be repatriated to Leipzig?"

"His sister gave me to understand that she didn't want this. She also said she's willing to reimburse me for whatever expenses I've incurred. I, of course, declined. Money and logistics have nothing to do with it, for her. Nor embarrassment. I think she wants things to stay the way they are, to avoid stirring up old sorrows and creating confusion among her present family and children by digging up things from more than half a century ago."

"I don't blame her, though in the same position I would probably have acted differently. It's hard to accept that a person dear to us should lie far away. Our loved ones always remain tied to us in one way or another."

"And what will you do, Inspector? You said the case had been closed. The mystery of what happened that night will probably never be unveiled."

"You're right, Signor Montalti. But before closing the book on this story there's still one more person I have to talk to."

20

~~

She spent the rest of the day doing ordinary things.

Once back at the office, Stefania took care of a couple of administrative matters, gave some orders to Piras and Lucchesi, and tried to keep her mind occupied. After assuring herself that everything in the house by the lake was in order and that her mother and Camilla didn't need anything, she decided to hole up in Como for the night.

For dinner she granted herself the luxury of cooking only for herself. She liked to cook, but the dizzying pace of her days often allowed her little more than snacks on the run, frozen foods, and takeout.

On her way back from meeting with Montalti she'd stopped at one of the few fresh fish shops by the lake. She felt like eating *lavarello*, a kind of whitefish, in green sauce, a specialty of her mother's and a dish that reminded her of her childhood, the dinners with relatives, her father sitting in the living room.

The fish was perfectly fresh: four whitefish, one perch, and some *alborelle*, which she would fry up the following day. She liked the idea that they'd been caught by one of the few remaining fishermen on the lake, one of those who got up at three o'clock in the morning to go out on the water in a rowboat.

The first thing she did was turn her attention to the whitefish. After scaling and gutting them, she cut them into fillets, leaving the layer of skin on the outside. Then she made a fish broth with the heads and bones, adding a glass of water, some white wine, and a clove of garlic. She then finely chopped an assortment of parsley, sage, rosemary, and thyme, and added this to the broth.

She melted two pats of butter in a skillet and then sautéed some finely chopped onion in it. To this she added the whitefish fillets, after first coating them in a paste of flour, milk, and egg. Then she added a pinch of salt and a sprinkle of pepper.

She fried them for about ten minutes, turning them over several times, until they turned a light golden color. Once browned, she set them down on a serving platter covered with absorbent paper.

In the meantime she'd prepared the green sauce: two hard-boiled eggs, olive oil from the Tramezzina, parsley, bread soaked in vinegar, salt, and pepper. Working this up into a dense, creamy paste, she spread it in generous spoonfuls over the fillets. A sprinkle of parsley, and the dish was ready.

Cooking was something that helped her a great deal. She would relax, think of what she needed to do, and the tension of the preceding day would dissolve in minutes.

She thought of Valli and his local fame. For a moment she felt tempted to ring him, then decided against it.

The mission she had assigned herself awaited her the following day. She'd already given notice at the station that she wouldn't be coming in. "Family problems," she'd said. This was contrary to habit, a sort of violation of the code of ethics she had imposed on herself since her first day on the job.

After setting the table, she went out on the balcony. Now that the days were growing longer, her desire for a vacation increased. The lake in the distance looked mobbed with tourists, outdoor restaurant tables, families out for a stroll. On the horizon she noticed the steamboat *Milano* heading out on the water, with its white-and-black smokestack and its suggestive foghorn. At that moment, for the first time in many years, she no longer felt alone.

⌒

The choice to head out on the road to Bergamo early in the morning was dictated more by insomnia than by any real logistical consideration. She had no engagements that day, so she could take things easy. She would do what she'd planned to do and then return to the lake in leisurely fashion. At that hour her mother and Camilla were still sleeping. She thought again of Valli. She would have liked to talk to him. She decided she would do all these things after she had met with Sister Maria.

On the passenger's seat lay a folder containing copies of the letters Montalti had given her. They would be her secret weapon. The fact of showing up at the institute without prior warning could backfire. But she'd given it a lot of thought, and it was the only way available to her to catch the old nun by surprise.

After arriving in the province of Bergamo she stopped in a small town, spotted a café, and grabbed a spot at an outside table.

It was half past nine, and at that hour, there was only one person who could reassure her and perhaps even help her.

"Hi, Giulio, already at the office?"

"Actually I've been here for over an hour. But what about you? What's going on? You haven't called me at this hour since our days at the academy."

"I'm in Bergamo, Giulio. I'm on my way to talk to Sister Maria."

"Are there some new developments?"

"Do you remember Montalti, the former owner of Villa Regina? We met yesterday. He gave me some new materials. I'm getting close to solving the mystery."

"What do you mean? What have you discovered?"

"I can't tell you anything at the moment. I'll call you tomorrow and let you know. I just wanted to tell you that I was right to carry on the investigation."

"But why did you call me if you don't want to tell me anything?"

"To thank you for the help you've given me."

"So what should I expect?"

"Nothing, as usual. I just wanted to hear your voice."

Giulio tried to say something, but Stefania hung up at that exact moment, turning off her cell phone. It wasn't only to reassert her good faith in carrying on the investigation that she'd called him, and to show him that he'd been wrong to underestimate her. She really did want to thank him.

Now it was ten o'clock. She paid her bill and headed for her car, determined to go straight to the institute. At this point it was only five or six kilometers away.

⌒

Her entry into the main salon of the institute triggered a certain commotion among the maintenance staff still busy cleaning, and sent a number of little nuns running back and forth like wind-up dolls given a jolt of electricity.

As a third nun was asking her if she was "Inspector . . . ?" the figure of Sister Maria appeared through one of the side doors. At that moment the cleaning ladies resumed sweeping the floor, ending the buzz that Stefania's arrival had stirred up.

"Inspector! What a surprise," the nun exclaimed with a sardonic smile.

"I came by to say hello and inform you that the case has been closed," Stefania replied.

The nun led the way into one of the inner courtyards, then took a pair of garden shears and started trimming the branches of an enormous rosebush. After a few moments of silence she resumed speaking:

"And you want me to believe that you came all this way just to tell me that the case has been closed?"

Stefania was about to answer when the nun turned around unexpectedly:

"Will you have some coffee, Inspector?" she asked.

"With pleasure," replied Stefania, her eyes following the nun's hand gesture indicating the way to her office.

They'd just sat down in the office, which Stefania was already familiar with, when a younger nun, not more than fifty, came in with a tray, two cups, and an espresso pot.

"One teaspoon of sugar?" asked Sister Maria.

"No, thank you, Mother, I prefer it without."

The nun sipped her coffee, set the demitasse down on the saucer, and said:

"I'm listening."

Stefania took in the self-assured tone with which the nun was challenging her. For a moment she thought it might be better to drop the whole thing and feared she might never manage to open a breach in Sister Maria's defenses. She waited a few moments and then began talking, looking her interlocutor straight in the eye. She had to be able to withstand the nun's stare. She had to appear determined.

"As I said, the prosecutor's office decided to shelve the investigation. Karl Dressler's mortal remains were interred in Switzerland in the family vault of the Montaltis, the former owners of Villa Regina."

She fell silent for a moment, just to allow the nun to open up.

"Let the dead bury their dead," commented Sister Maria, who seemed reassured by Inspector Valenti's words. She'd used the same words as Giulio a few days earlier.

"In a way, I think the Gospel precept represents the moral of this story," said Stefania, "even though, to tell you the truth, Karl is not the only one among the dead not to have found peace."

"What do you mean?" snapped the nun in a tone that combined curiosity and apprehension.

"What I mean," said Stefania, "is that while Karl may have had his funeral, he has not had justice, and that while Margherita is resting in peace, there is another person, too, still awaiting much-deserved justice."

Upon finishing her statement she rummaged through her purse and laid Karl's letter on the desk.

"Read it for yourself, Mother. It's only a few lines."

$\backsim$

"The day Margherita disappeared, I rushed up the mountain to inform my father. It was evening, and the car sent by Durand had already arrived. You can imagine how upset and confused I was as I ran up the road from town towards the mountain, all the way to that cottage of ours. I was the eldest daughter, and I felt in a way responsible for my younger sister. After all, it was I who'd told my father about her relationship with Dressler. But you must believe me, Inspector, I did it only the way an older sister would, out of the fear and dismay that discovery had awakened in me. And I did it above all for her, for everything that might come of such a choice. Don't imagine for a moment that I've spent a single night over the past half century not turning those moments over and over again in my head. I'm the first one to admit that if I hadn't said anything to my father, Margherita would probably still be alive today, and my father would have lived out his life. And my own life would probably have been quite different, even though, over all these years, I've never once regretted or reproached myself for taking the veil."

Stefania observed her, trying not to get too drawn in by that display of sorrow and contrition. That was not her role. More pressing was the need to understand what happened on that night in the mountains so many years ago. She had skillfully managed to throw the nun off balance. Having her read Dressler's letter had achieved the desired effect. In learning that her sister was pregnant at the moment of death, the nun had lowered her defenses. In all likelihood, after all those years of silence, these new details had awakened new emotions in her—of anger, anguish, guilt. And that life—a life whose existence she'd never known about, and which cast her again in a guilty light—was now demanding to be seen, to have a place of its own. A place in a story, if not an outright confession.

"My father and brother were out. Only my mother and my brother Battista had stayed behind in the house up the mountain. The hut was empty, there was nobody there. When I tracked down one of our men, he told me they were working on an expedition. In those months the number of expeditions increased beyond all measure. A great many people were asking to be taken over the border, and my father would take on anyone who could pay. He'd managed to work out a tacit arrangement with the partisan fighters in the area. The people who came to my father were political prisoners, dissidents, former Fascist turncoats, and partisans. And, naturally, many Jews. I decided to go and find them up in the mountain, despite the obvious dangers. You can't imagine how surprised I was when I came upon a band of men that included Colonel von Kesselbach and Dressler. Surprised, but also heartened, because their presence there increased the chance of finding Margherita, even though there was still the possibility that she'd decided to cross the border on her own. She was very familiar with the terrain, and knew all the paths and escape routes through the net at least as well as my father did."

"So what happened, Mother?"

"I took my father aside and told him what had happened. First he went and discussed the matter with Giovanni. I don't know what was said, but to judge from his gestures and whatever I was able to intuit, my father was very hard on my brother for giving Margherita news of Dressler. They decided to go and look for her in the surrounding area. But in order to do this, they had to bring the two Germans back to the cottage. He ordered me to go back to my mother, and I obeyed. My father assigned two men to watch over the cottage from a distance after escorting Kesselbach and Dressler back there himself, using their slowness as an excuse. The expedition was carried on with the other men, who then came back. They broke up their search into the areas around the border and spent a good part of the night and the entire morning combing all the trails. But there was no trace of Margherita. Around midday my father and Giovanni went back to our mountain house for a quick meal. Giovanni kept insisting that in his opinion Margherita at that hour must have already crossed the border. But my father didn't agree. At that point he decided to settle the matter on his own. He told us to stay put and not to tell anyone about what had happened. He didn't return until much later, when it was already evening."

"Where did your father go?" asked Stefania, who sensed that Sister Maria, this time, was telling the truth.

"I never did find out with any certainty, but to judge from what happened that night, it's not hard to imagine. In short, when it got dark my father went out again, this time in the company of two of his most trusted henchmen. My brother had to stay behind at the house, despite his pleas. My father didn't want any arguments. I overheard their last conversation outside the kitchen door. After my father left I decided to follow him at a distance. I knew they would be going back to the cottage to get the two Germans, so I positioned myself outside and waited. They finally came out in the middle of the night, with one of my father's men leading the way, followed by Kesselbach and Dressler, with my father and another man behind with rifles at the ready."

The nun heaved a long sigh.

"As they were huddled a few hundred meters from the border, I heard my father's whistle, and then two screeches in reply, a bit like a buzzard's cries. This was the arranged signal. At that point the colonel crossed the short stretch of meadow and reached the other side."

Stefania was at the breaking point. The tension had been rising as the nun told her story. The solution to the mystery was finally within reach. The nun closed her eyes, trying to summon the courage to recount the final moments of that night so many years ago that had changed the course of her life and that of her entire family.

"For several minutes nothing else happened. I tried to get as close as possible without making any noise. I could see the silhouettes of the men lying on the ground. There was Dressler, my father, and his two men. At a certain point I heard a sound, a kind of hissing that came from the woods. It wasn't the same sound as a few minutes earlier. I saw my father's silhouette get up and crawl on hands and knees towards the wood. The rest of the small group stayed put. A few more endless minutes passed."

The nun clutched her Basque rosary between her fingers.

"At that point I heard the distinct sound of footsteps in the woods. They were clearly not my father's. It sounded like numerous people, and to judge from the racket they were making, they didn't care if they attracted attention. Then I suddenly saw some lights as well: one of them was carrying a lantern. I saw the silhouette of my father at the head, and beside him, four partisans with their weapons cocked."

"He'd decided to sell him to the partisans," Stefania interjected. A moment later she bit her tongue.

"I don't know what my father had decided. But I remember perfectly what immediately ensued. Everything happened very fast. The partisan fighters advanced towards the small group hiding in the grass. I heard Dressler's voice shout something in German. At that moment, from another part of the woods, another person appeared: Margherita. She'd been following the whole scene from a distance. She yelled some incoherent words at my father and then ran towards Dressler, who in the meantime had come out into the meadow, having slipped the grasp of my father's men. Then everything happened at once. My father shouted something at Margherita. My sister, after running to Karl and embracing him, had grabbed his arm. Karl pulled out a pistol hidden in his trousers and aimed it straight at my father. It was over in an instant. A burst of machine-gun fire came from the group of partisans. My sister shielded him with her body and fell to the ground, cut down by the shots. The young German was wounded. At that moment I, too, came out from my hiding place and ran to the spot of the shooting. Dressler, though bleeding, kept firing his pistol. Then a shot struck him from the side, and he fell beside Margherita's body. They had just enough time to look each other in the eyes, and that was when my sister took off her locket and put it in his hand."

The nun was visibly shaken. Stefania could only look at her, waiting for her to resume speaking.

"When I reached the middle of the meadow, and my father was shouting desperately and trying to stanch Margherita's wounds with his clothes, Karl Dressler was still alive, but Margherita was dead. Her dress was soaked with blood. The partisans were yelling and my father's men were silent. Dressler lay on the ground, wounded, blood oozing from his chest. In one hand he clutched the locket. He couldn't breathe. I'm not quite sure what happened next. My father had him carried away by his two men. He was in despair, and had threatened the group of partisans. 'I'm going to make you pay for this!' he yelled at them repeatedly."

"What happened next I can tell you myself, Mother," Stefania said softly. "Your father had Dressler taken back inside the cottage, more precisely to the *nevera* below. Minutes later someone finished him off with a shot to the base of the skull. The cottage was then loaded with explosives and blown up."

21

The drive back was like heading into the coming summer.

Sister Maria hadn't been able to hold back her tears as she remembered the terrible moments of her sister's death, her father's torment, and the misfortune that would plague the Cappelletti family from that moment on.

In the end the nun had been right when she'd said that it would be the dead who buried their dead. The protagonists of the story were almost all deceased. Margherita, Karl, the colonel. And her father, her mother, her brother Giovanni, and poor Battista. Reopening the case on the basis of these new elements would have only meant causing new pain and suffering to persons who had already suffered enough. But Stefania had found out what she'd been keenest to know—that is, what had happened that night on the mountain. Karl and Margherita could now rest in peace.

On her way home, while still at the wheel, she rang Camilla to make sure that she and her mother were okay. It was starting to get unbearably hot, and the feeling of the air coming through the open car window and the wind ruffling her hair made her think of her adolescent years, the festive atmosphere of going on field trips with her schoolmates, that sense of plenitude one feels only during times when everything is within reach.

She felt light.

For a moment she thought of calling Giulio and telling him everything. Then she decided that she would wait a day or two to do so. The story was over, after all.

She called the office to say hello to Piras and Lucchesi.

At the gates of Como she decided not to stop, and so headed straight for the road to the lake.

At Cernobbio she turned onto the low road.

Once past the Piccolo Imperialino at Moltrasio, she pulled up, parked the car, and went into to La Vecchina, the café just behind the dock.

She ordered a *panaché* and a slice of tart fresh from the oven.

She was in a good mood. A flyer posted just below the bar announced the feast of Saint John in the third week of June, an event that officially marked the start of the summer season by the lake.

She paid the bill and went out. After crossing the street, on the other side of which was a broad square of fine white gravel, she started walking along the lakeside promenade.

It was a gorgeous day. At that time of the afternoon, the lake, from her perspective, looked emerald green, as the sun's rays glanced off the gentle water and all the vegetation of the surrounding hills was mirrored off its surface. Near Carate Urio, the motley colors of the painted buildings in the old quarters shone bright, with their green shutters and an unbroken suite of azaleas and oleanders, bougainvillea and jasmine, peering out from the balconies.

Her thoughts turned to the festivals slated for the following month, and she remembered when, as a little girl, her father and mother would take her down into town to see all the preparations for the festivities.

She remembered the enchanted, fairy-tale atmosphere, and all the different kinds of boats, dozens and dozens, gathered behind the Lavedo promontory at Lenno, not far from the Isola Comacina, and all the men and women attentive to every detail so that the historical reconstruction to be unveiled that evening, before the fireworks, would ring true.

And then the delicate movements of the boats in the gulf of the Zoca de l'Oli, the extras mingling with the fishermen, the whole town working hard to make the event a success.

It was about a month away, maybe a little more.

All around, along the paths and cobbled streets and outside the front doors, there would be a buzz of tourists and curious onlookers. Some would be strolling with their families, while others would be seeking a last-minute reservation at one of the many local restaurants. The youngest would exchange furtive glances and promise each other eternal love behind the walls of abandoned houses.

Long successions of *lumaghitt*, little candles arranged along the streets and walls, on the balconies of houses and on windowsills, ready to be lit after sunset for that one time a year, would provide the ideal frame to the celebration.

Darkness would enfold the town in the absolute calm of the Tramezzina. Little by little the lake and the Isola Comacina would take on the colors of the feast. The boats would begin to move like hundreds of colorful dots across the mirrorlike surface of the lake outside the house. Amid the general silence the *isola* would begin to glow red, at first gradually, then in a dance of light, until it was completely aflame. The speaker would narrate the historic events that gave rise to the legend, with Barbarossa as protagonist.

At that moment the fires would begin to rise in the sky, lighting up the entire surrounding area as in daytime.

And from that day on, for the rest of the summer and well into October, the lakefront would become an unending succession of celebrations and festivals, solemn masses and evening dances, with the old folks listening to the music to the scent of sausages and grilled fish.

Stefania felt happy.

She wanted to leave behind the investigation, her daily routine, the customary workaday irritations. She could feel the summer on her skin.

Looking up at the lake, she dialed a number on her cell phone.

As Luca answered at the other end, she heard a noise behind her.

Turning around, she saw, as if by magic, a hydroplane fly through the sky before her, in an endless series of revolutions.

AUTHORS' NOTE

There is no actual Villa Regina, of course, on Lake Como, just as there is no Cappelletti Durand family.

The villa described in this book is, however, the fruit of ideas taken from a variety of historic villas in the area of the Tramezzina, an amalgam of elements borrowed from Villa Sola (in Bolvedro), Villa Balbiano (in Ossuccio), Villa Carlotta (in Tremezzo), Villa Balbianello (at Lenno), and Villa La Collina (in Griante).

This being a book of fiction, the authors have taken some narrative license as well. The main instances of this involve the following:

—the toponym San Primo, which in the book refers to a mountain pass near the Val d'Intelvi, in reality is the name of a mountain located on the opposite side of the lake, more precisely at the top of the peninsula that includes Bellagio;

—the real distance separating Villa Regina (in its imagined location) and Lanzo d'Intelvi (an actual place located at the level of the Val d'Intelvi and the Swiss border) is much greater than stated in the book;

—the restaurant La Tirlindana (in Sala Comacina), a well-known establishment appreciated the world over, is very much the way it is described in the book. The menu presented here, however, contains a few elements and dishes more broadly connected to the traditional cuisine of the Lake Como area;

—the church and parish of Santa Eufemia have no direct correlative in the actual urban area of Como.

NOTES

22   *sciuri:* Lombard dialect for *signori*—meaning, in this case, upper class.

27   *missoltini:* A shadlike fish from Lake Como.

72   *maritozzi:* Currant buns typical of the Lombard region.

104 *repubblichini:* The term *repubblichino* designates a supporter or functionary of the so-called Repubblica di Salò, the puppet government set up by the occupying Nazis in 1943. After the Italians had overthrown the Fascist regime and deposed Mussolini that same year, the Germans invaded and sprang the disgraced dictator from his prison in a spectacular raid, appointing him figurehead of the quisling government, which had its seat in the town of Salò in the Alpine lakes region of northern Italy.

126 **Black Brigades:** A Fascist paramilitary militia formed after the establishment of the Nazi puppet government in Italy in the second half of 1943.

133　**the eighth of September:** September 8, 1943, was the date of the official announcement of the so-called armistice—in reality an unconditional surrender—whereby the nation of Italy would cease all hostilities against Allied forces. The Germans, however, already controlled the northern half of the peninsula and sprang Mussolini, who had been deposed and arrested some six weeks before, from his mountain prison just four days later, on September 12, guaranteeing more than another year of Fascism and bloodshed for Italy.

176　**Spizzico:** Spizzico is an Italian fast-food restaurant chain.

205　**Dr. Valenti:** In Italy, anyone with a full university degree is considered a doctor, and Stefania Valenti's position as *commissario di pubblica sicurezza* requires a university degree.

215　**Toc, etc.:** Toc is a polenta preparation rich in butter and cheese. *Cipolle borettane* are Italian pearl onions, often served in a balsamic vinegar sauce. *Alborelle in carpione* are small freshwater fish fried and served with a sauce of olive oil, garlic, leek, celery, bay, carrots, onions, white wine, and white wine vinegar.